EMPTY THREAT

A NOVEL OF THE BLACK PAGES

D1316788

BY AUTHOR
DANNY BELL

Publisher's Note: This is a work of fiction. Names, characters, places, and incidents are a product of the author's imagination. Locales and public names are sometimes used for atmospheric purposes. Any resemblance to actual people, living or dead, or to businesses, companies, events, institutions, or locales is completely coincidental.

Ordering Information:
Quantity sales. Special discounts are available on quantity purchases by corporations, associations, and others. For details, contact the "Special Sales Department" at the email address above.

Empty Threat (A Novel of the Black Pages) / Danny Bell – 1st ed.
ISBN-13: 978-1545594827 | ISBN-10: 1545594821

For Whitton, the only person at the party.

For the really cool guy who took a ride with me,
took a chance on me, and had exquisite taste in Sci-Fi.
I'm glad we got to be friends.

But mostly for everyone I have ever known who didn't know their
own worth or who felt like they didn't quite belong or who felt
uncomfortable in their own skin or who felt like they would
always be alone. You were all wrong. You are all beautiful and
wonderful and you were always more than good enough.
A thousand of you inspired me.
You're all perfect weirdos and this book is for you.

I love you. All of you.

EMPTY THREAT

A NOVEL OF THE BLACK PAGES

Kate —
Thank you for
supporting me. I genuinely
hope you enjoy the
book, and good luck on
your first book!

Danny Bell

I was struck by the sudden idea of how absurd it would be if my life were a story somewhere and this is where it began. You never see the really boring beginnings of most literary characters. *Wuthering Heights* begins with Lockwood having a crap time with his new landlord, which—okay, might not be the best example to start with. I think most of us can relate to fighting with a landlord. All right then, pretty much any superhero. You get the essential small parts of their day-to-day lives before they get hit by lightning or find an artifact or get bitten by an insect and then yay! Super powers! But presumably, they lived an entire life before any of that happened. You don't see anyone stuck in traffic or eating alone in a food court while wondering if they should take up Swing lessons. Maybe I'll get bit by a magic spider!

I looked around. No spiders. I took a sip of my whiskey. This is terrible whiskey. Maybe it was magic whiskey, and I'd get alcohol related super powers! I took another sip, and…

... no, no powers. Unless a sore throat is a power? I became a little more aware of my surroundings then and felt just a twinge of claustrophobia.

"This was a mistake," I said out loud to myself, sincerely and entirely by accident. It was true but that didn't change the fact that I was hoping desperately that no one had heard me. I was usually much better at internalizing that sort of thing, so I could only assume I had truly meant it. I looked around, and if anyone had noticed, they didn't care. Or they cared, but just didn't want to show it. The most likely scenario was they were all too self-absorbed with whatever they had been talking about to notice me. Thi was preferable.

I've often had the problem of liking people whose idea of fun is vastly different from my own. The entire house seemed too small, and the air unnaturally humid. Vibrations came from a speaker on the other side of the living room; the sound was the lyric-less mess of incidental noise you heard at every party. I was convinced no one actually liked it but seemed to think that everyone else did. Except for this one guy who stood nearby. I'd never seen him before, but was sure of two things: he really liked this noise, and he'd hit on nearly every woman there. I feared I was next. I would have left if not for the fact that three more people I didn't know had created an impenetrable triad between my spot in the kitchen and the salvation of the exit. To me, interrupting a conversation is worse than drinking orange juice immediately after brushing my teeth.

I wanted more than anything to be on the other side of them, but I couldn't blame them for talking to each other. It was a party, after all, and it was my fault for being there in the first place. It's not that I don't like parties, it's just that—I don't know.

Yeah, I just don't like parties. Not even housewarming parties for good friends. I don't want to be the type of person who doesn't like parties, but that doesn't change anything. People are capable of amazing things, change being one of them, but I've yet to meet someone capable of explaining how change works. I wouldn't even know who to ask, so I guess that's a bit of a non-starter. I never know what to say, for one thing. In Los Angeles, it seems like at least half of the time, everyone wants to talk about entertainment. Which would be fantastic, except it's never about the worlds or the people or the stories or any of the other outstanding things that make entertainment ... well, entertaining. To most people here, it seems to be about video editing, being someone's assistant, or the post production. I'm going to level with you: I don't actually know what post production is, but I've heard people mention it enough times that I'm convinced it's a real thing.

Sometimes I just want to shout the truth about me and what I'm capable of at the world. It's not a good idea. I don't know why it's not a good idea, but I'm pretty sure it is. You know what? That's a lie. I know exactly why. It is because as much as everyone claims to love individuality, there's a limit and my life almost certainly dashes past that and wears it as a first place ribbon for weirdness, then takes a victory lap before car surfing a stolen food truck off a cliff and into—

"Elana Black! What up?"

What kind of obnoxious jerk announces someone's first and last—Wait. I forget this guy's name. Brett? Brad? Bard? Bard would be a pretty sweet name.

"Hey!" I replied immediately, with a smile. His name would come to me in a moment. I was spiraling anyway.

He hugged me, which I really wasn't happy about. I'm not against hugging in general, I just ... have a thing about it sometimes. He also seemed to disregard the fact that I was holding a drink, and preventing it from spilling became the full focus of my attention for the next two very precarious seconds. Like a pro, I quickly slipped into the small talk that he confused for genuine friendship. I could hear the answers coming out of me before I was able to stop and consider what I was actually saying. It wasn't that I disliked Jeff—

Jeff! I was way off.

It's not that I disliked him. There was nothing inherently offensive about him; he was just so uninteresting. He also stood too close, never quite smelled right, and never talked about anything other than himself. He would talk and talk, and yet never actually say anything.

You'd think with how often I'd seen him that I would have remembered his name. I suddenly felt very guilty for that. Even so, I almost didn't notice when he finally left.

I don't know why I feel the way that I do when I get into large social situations like this. I sincerely care about people; I guess just not as an audience. I came here to hang out with my friend Olivia, this was her party. But as is usual with Olivia, she was nowhere to be found. Neither was Logan, her boyfriend. I liked him too, which is strange because I typically don't get too attached to the partners of close friends, but he'd passed the test (the test being whatever arbitrary and secretive test that I thought of at the time and only made sense to me, that test). My other friends Ann, Jason, and Teague had all failed to show as well, so that accounted for the five people I could relate to and felt safe talking to at a party. From my hopefully secure location in the kitchen, I could count maybe twenty people and knew none of them to varying degrees. The range was anywhere from a complete stranger to I kind of recognize them from maybe the last time I saw them and didn't know them.

While gauging my level of intoxication, I identified trepidation at the notion of a stranger talking to me. So that meant the level was "Not Very." I further decided to get the hell out of here. I thought about hiding in Olivia's room, but it was locked. I made a mental note of that, what was that about? It's almost like she didn't want a house full of people to have access to her bedroom. Okay, mental note discarded, that actually makes perfect sense. But another room was open, and it had what I needed: Books. I walked right up to the flimsy wire frame shelving and was disappointed. I couldn't use any of these. Books on art history, an entire book about motorcycles, some apparently heavily used textbooks. There had to be something decent here.

I spun at the sound of the door opening up wider behind me. It only just now occurred to me that I was in someone else's room without their permission.

"See anything good?"

I didn't recognize this man, but his appearance struck me all the same, mainly how well he dressed. Put together. All of his clothes were immaculate like they'd been purchased earlier that day. He wore white slacks, white shoes designed for some sport which was irrelevant given they would never be used for their intended purpose, and a white vest over a white dress shirt. He completed the look with a white cap, like the kind you might see on a golfer. Not the kind with the fuzzy ball on top, the regular kind, I guess. You know what I mean.

It was in stark contrast to my disaster of an outfit. Canvas high tops that I'd painted nonsense on at some point, beige slacks I had slept in the night before, a bluish, purplish and somewhat wrinkled blouse, red suspenders, an oversized vintage brown coat I'd found at a yard sale off Miracle Mile and immediately had dry cleaned, a bright multi-colored scarf I found at a dollar store, and a white straw sun hat hanging off the back of my head, which barely hid my thick head of red hair. My hair was thick, not my head. Ok, maybe also my head. I was only just now becoming aware that I was still wearing the hat indoors and at night. My finishing ensemble piece was a too large, beige canvas book bag I had made myself on my first attempt, just to see if I could. I could have fit a small child or a medium sized dog in there, but I liked it. It was also devoid of books at the moment, a rarity for me.

My mind wanted to go to its default party speak mode, but it was too late for that. I'd been surprised, and was now present.

"Not really, honestly," I said. "I'm not sure I can exactly curl up with a glass of wine and *Honors Geometry*." I could already tell that was less charming than I'd intended.

He smiled and said, "You must be Ollie's friend."

She hated that name. Less charming than he'd intended.

"And what makes you say that?" I asked. That was dumb. I was in her home at her party.

"I'm her new roommate. I don't believe we've ever met, and you're standing in my room, so I'm hoping you're her friend and not a homeless woman who wandered in off the street." He was still smiling.

The homeless crack kind of stung, but I let it go. He was joking, but I already felt uneasy about my fashion sense compared to his. I like comfort over form, and I didn't want to apologize for it. Maybe he could swing past my home later and ask me if the neighborhood was safe, maybe come inside and point out things I should replace.

"You got me," I said, returning the smile, not letting him see anything else.

"They say you can tell a lot about a person by what they have on their bookshelf. So what can you tell about me?"

"Who says that?" I challenged him on instinct.

"English majors, probably," he offered. "Or maybe just people who are too proud of their bookshelves."

"Fair enough." I decided to go along (and that he didn't need to know about my English Lit degree). "You're not a big reader. I don't even think you can call this a bookshelf, I use something like it for cleaning supplies. Some of these seem like they might be for school, but I don't think you're a student anymore. The textbooks seem like things you never got around to throwing away. The rest is just a bizarre compilation of topics that don't make any sense together. It's almost like you just bought a box of random books from a thrift store and just sort of dumped them here. Why do you even have this?"

I held up a book that offered knowledge of how to develop psychic powers through a vegan diet.

"For research," he replied curtly, his smile fading. Catching himself, he offered an explanation. "I'm an actor."

Of course you are, I thought sarcastically. Maybe cynically? I felt awful for thinking like that. Or at least, for judging as quickly as I did.

"Oh! Here's a good one!" I exclaimed, reaching for another book, both due to genuine excitement and to distract from feeling like a jerk. Or was he being a jerk too? I read the title out loud. "*Crome Yellow!* An Aldous Huxley title that's not *Brave New World*. I'm impressed!"

"Well, thank you." His smile was returning but I had barely noticed.

"Have you read this? It's pretty awesome." I couldn't contain myself and kept going. It didn't even occur to me to wait for an answer. "The story itself is very obviously fiction, there's a man named Mr. Barbecue-Smith, and I mean, come on. But the house in it is actually based on this real place called Garsington Manor, and all these famous literary types of the day used to hang out there and just create. So Huxley writes this book about a party that was being thrown there, and it's honestly just the worst party ever. Everyone is pretentious and trying too hard, no one is happy by the end, and nothing really happens. I love it."

I was beaming. I could feel the tightness in my face coming from a smile growing that full.

"You, uh, you definitely know more about the book than me," he said, forcing the kind of small laugh that comes from being intimidated. "I didn't even know I had it. But that's cool though."

"Oh." I hadn't expected to be *this* disappointed.

"Tell you what though. You keep it. My gift to you. I need to get back to the party, but it was lovely meeting you, uh …" He did that thing where he wanted my name without asking for it.

"Elana," I answered without wanting to. He offered me a quick handshake, and I accepted out of instinct.

"Yeah, cool. My name is Jason. You take care!"

I didn't have the chance to tell him I knew another Jason who was supposed to be here. He left in a hurry. Weird that he just left me in his room like that. I guess his only qualifier for someone being alone in his room was if they were homeless or not. Maybe I just weirded him out and he wanted to get away. I could relate to that.

I considered the book in my hands. *Crome Yellow* would work. It wasn't like I had a lot of other options and now, more than ever, I wanted to get out of there. I took the book into the bathroom—sadly, not a new experience for me. I've spent more time pretending to go to the bathroom at parties than actually using it for its intended purpose. But I wasn't just hiding every time and definitely not this time; I was escaping. There was a huge difference; one made me anxious and shamed, the other was adrenaline inducing.

I opened the book and started to look for an entry point. I don't know how I know where they are, I just sort of find them.

"At least I won't have to attend the party over there," I muttered to myself. I locked the door and made myself as comfortable as I possibly could on a throne that was not a seat. I opened the book, careful of the glue of the paperback. This was not a book which had been handled with care. I started to read, and as always, my eyes cascaded over the words like water over a hill.

EMPTY THREAT

Along this particular stretch of line no express had ever passed. All the trains—the few that there were—stopped at all the stations. Denis knew the names of those stations by heart.

There it was. My way inside, much sooner than I'd expected. I wasn't complaining.

I sat on the toilet seat, reading furiously and long enough for my butt to start numbing. I didn't care. Not about the pins and needles in my leg, not about Jason or this party. It was happening. Words became colors. The colors danced and swirled, becoming more vivid than ever intended.

Oh, this is my favorite bit!

And that smell! Like daybreak, like clean water. The poorly lit bathroom was giving way to the luscious greens of an English Manor. Then the familiar sensation of falling, losing both the fight with, and fear of, physical gravity. The dull thuds of music against the thin door were replaced by birds and the background hum of the universe, in that order. The slight ceramic chill around me faded into the sharply refreshing feel of morning mist on my face. The very pages in my hands disintegrated into sunlight and wind.

Goodbye, Highland Park. Hello, Oxford.

You should never drink and make yourself fictional.

Understandably, that's not a PSA you're likely to see on the side of a bus. I really have no idea if anyone else can do what I do. It would make more sense for there to be someone else than not, but then again, the phrase "escape fantasy" was never meant to be taken literally. Wait, was it? Either way, I barely even had time to register my surprise when I found my face about an inch from the ground. I did, however, have enough awareness to register how it felt to face-plant onto cold, wet earth—something akin to running straight into a wall made of mud and grass in an attempt to aggressively kiss it. Not my favorite thing. But it wasn't incapacitating, and I only needed a moment to right myself.

"You know what would be fantastic? A door, that's what. If I could step from there to here; that would be just…" I realized that I was openly complaining about the nature of my reality breaking super powers after making the effort of using them in the first place. Like someone who complains about a text message taking three seconds to reach another phone instead of just one. Sometimes, when you actually stop to consider what you're upset about, it seems kind of silly.

I stood up to wipe away some of the dew from my face and clothes, and paused briefly to notice my nose now felt tender.

"At least I didn't land in a tree. Again," I mused to myself, taking in my surroundings.

Looking up I took in the sight of the world of *Crome Yellow*, far larger and more vivid that I had previously imagined it. Part of me was impressed, but mainly I just wondered why anyone needed this much house in the country. The pieces were all there, just as described: Three towers jutting out from behind dark, almost black trees. Warm, inviting brick glowing in the illumination of the fresh sunrise, but it felt more alive now that I was truly here. Like going to an amusement park after seeing pictures, it was both more than I could have ever expected and yet just another place. I'll never get used to this feeling though, the disbelief of being someplace that I was never supposed to visit.

Crome Yellow is a book which is meant to be funny, written by someone who is not funny. Huxley was a fantastic writer and story teller, but this novel is about nothing, telling a story where nothing happens. As a genre, it's hard to place. People didn't have access to Facebook in the 1920's, so Aldous Huxley seemed to have written about his most uneventful day and then changed the name. You might be tempted to call it satire, but artisanal trolling might be more on the nose. Nothing happens in the book, the exception being the party, and intellectually one-upping does not a plot make.

A thought occurred: the house wasn't empty. Based on the time of day, I was at the beginning of the story, before Denis arrives on his crazy bicycle, awestruck at the very concept of a house. Mr. and Mrs. Wimbush who lived here would be awake at some point. I really wanted to leave before Denis got there. For one thing, I don't think I'd enjoy the company of Denis Stone, a character utterly self-obsessed and lacking any self-awareness, oblivious to the fact that his friends take advantage of him, enthusiastic about things that don't matter. He makes you want to see him perform a card trick and then guess the other person's card wrong. Not to mention the fact that he's getting ready to attend a terrible party in this story.

I just *left* a terrible party.

That reason didn't matter though, not really, not that much. The more immediate reason, the one that already started me heading towards the road, is that I didn't actually want to become a part of the story. Not this story. I'm a lot of things, but I'm not stupid, at least as a rule.

Most of the time anyway.

I just sincerely didn't know what would happen if *my* story, for lack of better term, were to cross paths with the story of the characters from this book. Maybe their world would explode! Ok, probably not. I didn't know what would happen, but a world-ending explosion probably wasn't it. I just had the suspicion that whatever happened, it wouldn't be very good. I've watched events unfold from inside books before, as well inside stories from TV shows, movies, comic books; so I know that they actually happen, but I'd rather not run the risk of meddling in forces bigger than... well, I don't know that they're bigger than me. I don't even know if they're forces. There's a lot that I don't know. I don't know most things.

I do know how to distract myself though, and walking nearly always does the trick. The road took me through a series of rugged hills that my shoes did not agree with. Chucks make for terrible hiking shoes, and between the dips and the rocks littered in the road, I was certain I would roll an ankle at any time. I absently thought of the description from the book as I turned back from the top of a hill and looked down past the increasingly taller hills to the Crome home. Denis Stone would soon be riding a bicycle down this hill; arms, or maybe back, full with luggage. I remembered a line from the book.

The hill was becoming steeper and steeper; he was gaining speed in spite of his brakes. He loosed his grip of the levers, and in a moment was rushing headlong down.

I decided Denis Stone was an idiot. Then again, I just thought up the phrase, "Crome home," so maybe I shouldn't judge.

I tried to focus on the lush scenery instead. I know a lot of people in LA who are hiking types; I'm not one of them. I'm more of the "pretend to be sick so people don't bother me when I want to binge watch a show" type. But even I had to admit, scenery like this made for a compelling argument to get outside and move my body a bit more. Stunning colors from the rising sun came through the spotty clouds and reflected on a tranquil lake just below me as I reached the top of another hill. A pleasant heat gently penetrated my coat. Moving uphill though was starting to get to me. My calves were burning. I know some people use that expression when what they really meant to say was that they felt sore, but I really felt a burning sensation and I took it as a point of embarrassment and felt grateful that no one was around to tell me what a good job I'd just done or encourage me to keep it up.

I'd reached the top of maybe the tenth or eleventh hill, and it felt like as good a time as any to stop and enjoy the view. It was not at all because I thought I needed to catch my breath before I had a heart attack at a very premature age. I have had my power for just a couple of years, and I'd already seen more exotic locations than most people would ever see in their lifetimes and I didn't even have a passport. It was important to me not to waste my experiences, no matter why or how I'd been able to have them. I've seen hopeful futures and the distant past. Magical lands and technological wonders. And though I knew somewhere inside of me that, unfortunately, these places weren't real, when I stood in them they seemed as real as anything I'd ever see.

And what does reality mean anyway? If I can see new places and appreciate different cultures, why should it matter that they don't exist in a way that is real to other people? Maybe I do like some places more than others, but almost anywhere is worth traveling if you haven't been there before. Victorian England was fun, and also kind of gross, but thankfully I've had all my shots (though there's no immunization for Lycanthropy that I am aware of, so I'm glad I never met the werewolf that had everyone worried).

Oh, I've been in space! Wow, that's a sobering thought. I've been in space. Screw you, astronauts. Why dedicate your life to the space program when '80s sci-fi is a thing that you can watch right now and, with a special power, then experience for yourself? Plus, *my* version of space had a wisecracking robot. The closest thing Neil Armstrong got to that was Buzz Aldrin, and his jetpack sucked.

Maybe my favorite place to travel is New York in superhero comic books. I've seen people take flight! Oh, what's that? Someone just drove a school bus over a bridge? Yeah, let someone just fly over there and catch that for you, no big deal. Are you even for real right now with that? And now I'm alone in an English countryside enjoying a hill top view of a sunrise. How much better could my life get?

There was a sudden near-deafening buzzing in my ear. I jumped in brief panic as a small, prickly weight touched down on my head. Maybe it thought I was a giant flower? My uncoordinated head shaking scared the small bug, which left after a brief struggle with my hair, only to then return and land on my knee. I didn't flail any further now that I could see the offending creature: a small beetle of yellow and blue. The light on its body made its colors shimmer across the spectrum.

"Aw, hey. I haven't seen someone like you before," I cooed to it. It didn't seem particularly dangerous, or even curious about me. I just happened to be something else along its path. I sat in stillness for a moment, allowing it to explore the strange new land of my pant leg. After a bit, it became bored and buzzed away, both out of sight and mind to whatever business beetles get up to on their adventures. And yes, the view around me was lovely, but the beetle served as the perfect reminder that I had my own journey ahead of me to get back to. So, I continued on my way, which happened to be east, I think. I'm not particularly great with directions. We can just call it "that way."

I took off down the hill, my legs reasonably rested for the trip up the next one, the processes repeating as I got lost in thought. The hills continued up and down for so long that I almost hadn't noticed when a second house had come into view. It was considerably smaller than Crome, but still very nice. Two story cottage, nothing fancy. Maybe large enough for a family of four if everyone didn't mind being cozy. A horse and carriage out front. A barn, though this was clearly not a farm. Maybe that's just where he kept the DeLorean. A front porch with a very pensive-looking young man who looked like he had no idea what my deal was. I caught myself staring and tried my best to recover.

"Oh! Uh, hey. Man. Hi." Yup. Smooth.

"Where are you going?" He asked suspiciously, not getting up from his seat on the porch.

"Yeah, I was just going to, umm…" Quick! Think of a clever lie. If I was going somewhere specific, where would I be going? Come on; I had this one. Name of the stop in the book. It had a stupid name. Well, not a stupid name, just a British one. A stupid British one. "West Bowlby!"

"West Bowlby?" the young man asked, noticeably raising his eyebrows.

"Yeah, for breakfast," I doubled down.

"And you're walking there?" he continued, now nearly invasively trying to read me. Crap. That wasn't the right town. "Are you a medium?"

"The hell?" It was more of a reaction than a question. I don't see what my clothing size has anything to do with—

"My apologies," he said as he stood. "An American medium then. For Mrs. Wimbush?"

I face palmed at my own derp. "Yeah. Sorry, yeah." Might as well go with it. Why not? "How did you know?"

He slowly walked towards me. "Well, you're dressed like a nomad, the only thing between here and oblivion in the direction you've come is Crome, and you're drunk as a king at the Lord's hour!"

Oh, I had something for this! Smiling, I said, "Well, sir, it is only ten o'clock. What is your objection to the hour? I think the hour is an admirable hour!" Ha! AP English for the win.

He rolled his eyes. "A drunk quoting Oscar Wilde. Surely the world has never seen such a delight!"

"I'm not that drunk," I muttered. Maybe I was. Not important.

"Ignoring that I was able to smell the spirits downwind before I saw you, would you like to know how else I know that you're drunk?" He was clearly exasperated now and didn't give me the chance to respond. "You're trying to walk to West Bowlby, and you're headed the wrong bloody way!"

"Crap." I knew I had the wrong town. And yup, I smelled it then. I was sweating beer, cider, and whiskey. I regret that combination now.

"Do you remember your name at least?" he asked, now more amused than irritated.

"Yes!" I nearly shouted with pride. Then, almost as if to prove that I had the right answer, I added, "Elana!"

"George," he replied, moving around myself and the horse. "Come on, up you go. I'll give you a ride." He climbed into the front seat of the buggy and motioned for me to join him.

"Where we going?" I was already climbing into the carriage.

"Not West Bowlby, I can tell you that!" he exclaimed with a smile. "I'm buying you breakfast."

"Oh, and what is the reason for your generosity, George?" I asked.

"Well," he replied thoughtfully, "God takes care of fools and drunks, but I'm not sure where he's run off to."

I couldn't help but smile in return. "So, it's up to you then?"

He gave the horse a gentle nudge with riding straps as we slowly made our way down the road. "Quite! It's the Lord's work."

3

I came back to Olivia's bathroom and landed in the bathtub because of course I did. Where else would I land? As the epitome of suppleness and grace, I subconsciously felt that it was my duty to knock over every bottle within arm's reach. I don't have long arms, but it's not a large bathroom. Even with the music, someone must have heard that.

Wait, where was the music?

I panicked and yanked my phone out of my bag, needing to see exactly how bad it was. It was 3:27. Thankfully that was AM rather than PM, so I hadn't been gone a full day at least.

Olivia slammed open the door with a look of concern that morphed into a single bark of raucous laughter, spreading into a grin large enough to look like it might actually hurt.

"Seriously?" she asked me in mirthful disbelief.

"Seriously," I confirmed, trying to get to my feet. She relaxed a bit, letting the nervous energy of a potential intruder fade.

"Everyone thought you must have gone home, but no one saw you leave and your car was outside." She glanced past me to the scattered bottles in the tub. "This makes more sense."

Strange as it was, I began to relax as well. This could've been so much worse if her roommate had been using the bathroom when I came back. Instead, it was just one of my best friends, who was in her underwear and a wrinkled T-shirt, in her new home, without anyone else around to judge me. The makeup was off. No one had a drink in their hand. No need to keep up social appearances. There were just two friends who could see each other, and had seen each other, in their least graceful moments and didn't think anything of it. Let's be really honest here, this was a legitimate reason to get mad at someone or at the very least a reason to start hiding the contents of your medicine cabinet when they visited, but that wasn't a concern with Olivia. It would have definitely been a concern for Jason if he'd heard it, and how could he not? But I'm pretty sure we were never really going to get along great anyway.

"Yeah, I have no idea what happened." This wasn't a lie, at least not technically. I had intended to return to real life five minutes after I left the party, but my track record with precision was spotty at best. Although, who knows? Maybe I'm the most precise person who has ever done this. Given that I am one hundred percent of the people who I can verify have done this, I chose to take the optimistic option.

"You don't look so good," Olivia said, undoubtedly hit by the need for sleep. Sleep I ruined for her. "Do you want to crash on the couch?"

I probably looked like someone who passed out drunk in a bathtub wearing a large jacket and a hat. I didn't feel great, but that was probably more to do with the angry gauntlet of food and beverage I just experienced a hundred years ago and in another country.

"No," I said. "Really, I'm okay to drive. For real." The extent of that statement meant solely that I wasn't drunk, she didn't need to know about the other stuff. "Besides, I need to open up tomorrow, and you just moved to Narnia."

"Yeah. Traffic. Forgot." She was rubbing her eyes now. Geez, I must have really woken her up.

"I'm going to get going," I said. "Sorry about, you know, me." She gave me the kind of hug with a warmth that only comes when you're ready to melt into someone because you straddle that enviable, tingly place between consciousness and unconsciousness. I immediately returned it.

"Get home safe," she said with a tiny yawn. "Text me."

I offered her hurried promises about texting that I wouldn't keep and left as quickly and quietly as I could. I love Olivia, and I know she loves me, but I felt horrible waking her up like that, even though I knew she thought nothing of it. If not for the fact she was likely already asleep again, I'd have expected a Facebook post about it to hit my phone any minute now.

My phone hadn't buzzed by the time I made it to my ride home. I'd named her Big Sister. A 1984 Chevy Cavalier station wagon, yellow. Pale yellow, in fact. The tires were okay, actually, but that was only out of pure necessity given recent events. I'd run over those wrong way teeth, the evil teeth that usually accompany a sign saying something along the lines of "Dear Lord, please do not drive this way! We could not possibly warn you any more clearly! I promise that you will regret this!" I'm paraphrasing. I didn't listen, needed four new tires as a result, and had to seriously consider abandoning the car when weighing the price of four new tires against another ancient station wagon. But Big Sister is family to me, so I patched her up. Now the tires stuck out in contrast to the rest of the machine. It was perhaps the worst car ever made. Perhaps the worst, and maybe most dangerous, but definitely mine. I'd never abandon her. Despite its namesake, there was nothing cavalier about my car. It handled like a tugboat, and the engine reminded me of a sewing machine, but at least it had a sweet tape deck. And complaining aside, it was so simple to repair that I didn't understand fully how it managed to run. I really felt like a proper car needed to have more parts. Given everything else in my life, I wouldn't be surprised if it only stayed together because I believed hard enough.

I got into Big Sister and didn't bother to take off my jacket. I briefly shuddered from the cold and could feel the goosebumps already forming on my arms as I rubbed them over my sleeves. The heaters primary function seems to be only making my hands and feet unbearably hot. Somehow heat never seemed to transfer to the rest of the car, a mystery I'm sure our best and brightest would love to study if only they were given the chance. Given the choice between cold fingers and a warm body or searing heat on my hands and a cold body, I opted for the layered option. At least the interior was cloth; I didn't want to think about how cold leather seats would be right then. The thought of rich, Corinthian leather in Big Sister made me giggle. She's a fancy lady, and she wants nice things!

Unfortunately, I needed to find food, and forgot to leave something in the car earlier. There's almost always a bag of nuts of some kind, maybe a protein bar. Who am I kidding? A candy bar is far more likely. And the nuts are the chocolate covered variety. I'm also a big fan of those dark chocolate covered Acai berries, but I usually opt just to get whatever I can. I'm not picky with junk food, and it's not like that does the trick anyway. I need actual food. Making myself fictional and then making myself, well, I don't want to say real. That doesn't seem right. We can just say when I come back. When I come back, I am unbelievably hungry. Given the current contents of my stomach this wouldn't seem possible, and yet, here we are. As much as I needed to get home and sleep so I could get to work, I wasn't ready to concede just yet. I took another look at the back seat, glove compartment: nothing. Oh, well. You figure things out. Like the feeling of never wanting to eat again in your life and needing to eat immediately. That kind of thing.

Putting the key in the ignition, I paused and thought about George. I don't know why. Maybe it was the unholy chemistry experiment currently being performed in my belly. That was a horrible reason to think of someone. He'd been a lot of fun. George was the kind of person who felt like he really should have been more social; like if he was entertaining someone, he was in his element. But he also seemed lonely, and maybe he was the type who let others come to him. Alone on his porch for who knows how long, and along comes a weirdo in need of a ride. I didn't know a thing about him prior to meeting him and he'd given me no indication of what life was like for him before I came along. I didn't seem to be interrupting anything, and when I thought about it? He couldn't offer to spend time with me fast enough. I was useful to him, but that didn't make him any less kind or generous or charming. There's nothing wrong with feeling alone and needing company but not knowing how to reach out properly. Damn, I hadn't expected to relate to him as much as I was at this moment. I felt like I had made a friend and for an instant, the cold didn't seem to touch me.

As I drove, I decided to lose myself in recollection. A few hours ago, I spent an entire day with someone, which felt time travely, but no more so than what you might experience on a long international flight. No, stop thinking like that, that way leads to anxiety. What had happened? Well, he had taken me into town, for starters. When I asked him where we were, he would only tease me and say, "Not West Bowlby." Sure enough, we had breakfast as he had promised, only it was much heartier than I'd expected. I was expecting an English muffin and fruit.

You know, I always just assumed English Muffins originated in England, but I realize now that I honestly don't know.

Regardless there was no muffin, English or Regular. Instead, without seeing a menu and just a simple, "Two, please," from George, I was brought a large ceramic plate crowded with food items all competing for real estate. Three poached eggs, what appeared to be half of all the bacon in town with George naturally receiving the other half, a flame grilled mushroom that could have replaced my hat in case of a downpour, and a splatter of baked beans. By splatter it looked like a summary execution of a twenty-five-pound kettle of baked beans and our plates had been positioned to catch the bean splatter caused by the exit wound. I really thought these beans were thrown across the kitchen to a waiting plate at the very least. Somehow all of this was to be comically washed down with a delicate and pleasant smelling cup of dark, floral tea. I almost enquired if it was English Breakfast. I held my tongue. I was apprehensive about the food challenge, but one look at our hostess let me know everything one needed to about the perils of not clearing one's plate.

We laughed. We bantered. We walked on actual cobblestone and visited a gazebo in a park, something George took for the equivalent of front row seats at the Hollywood Bowl. I wasn't as excited for the structure, but his excitement was contagious enough for me to be excited. I had the exceptionally bad idea to sprint across the grass in the park, something both George and I almost immediately regretted. We went for a pint, and it was actually a pint! It was almost strange how quickly I was welcomed there. George managed to know the one spot where getting day drunk was more than acceptable.

And then there was the bookstore! I almost cried when I walked inside, it was that astounding. I snaked between tall shelves that led into other shelves so that every way you walked you'd be facing a book. Every corner filled with aspiring writers, deep in conversation about characters or philosophy or how their story was the one that would change the world. George insisted on buying me a first edition of *Jane Eyre*, all covered in burgundy leather. An offer which made me choke. I tried to decline, but he insisted. Something for the train ride home, he said in response to my lie about catching a train in the evening. My heart sank, both at the lie, however necessary it was and at the knowledge that I couldn't bring objects home with me. This wasn't a token of friendship that I could keep. Still, I smiled and gladly accepted the offer, for the gesture if nothing else. The gesture was infinitely more meaningful than the book itself and days like these were not the kind you ever completely forgot.

He borrowed a fountain pen, briefly and apologetically from one of the writers, and wrote:

To ELANA-

IT'S A GOOD THING I DON'T NEED ANOTHER

PAIR OF GLOVES OR A HANDKERCHIEF.

SAFE TRAVELS,

GEORGE

It was a day that seemed as if it would never end and I wasn't sure that I had wanted it to. But it had, and now here I was, alone in the middle of the night, cold and comfortable. Nauseous and ravenous. Wondering about food options, because even the most stalwart taco trucks had given up for the evening. I'm sure a Del Taco somewhere was probably open, but I wasn't exactly certain where I could find one on a straight shot home.

Worst case I could maybe find a 24-hour gas station with a hot dog in a warming tray. That didn't sound appealing in the slightest, but it wasn't like I was flush with options. Maybe a donut spot? It was the strange time of night in LA, a rare window where no one could be found. Every street was empty. Bars close at two and everyone sane was in bed by three. No one was on the road to work until five at the earliest. Only the people who really must have messed up at something would be out on the road.

Yes, hello, hi. I'm self-aware, yes. Ugh, my stomach was protesting now. I'm going to have to hit up a drive thru if I really want to—

SPLITCH!

Okay, that woke me up. I'd seen the bug coming. An ugly thing, blue and maybe a bit of yellow; shiny even in the night. Maybe a June Bug? Whatever it had been, it was now a spectacular mess on my windshield. I'd just hopped on the 110 too, damn it. Two seconds later, and I wouldn't have—

SPLITCH! SPLITCH!

Two more! "Are you kidding me with this?" I said out loud to no one. My frustration lasted only a moment as I saw them. Maybe thousands of the bugs coming from the sky, shimmering carapaces in the lights of the freeway which gave the mirage of a wave heading straight at me. I slammed on my brakes; it was a pure panic move. I'd never seen anything like what came next, and I don't know anyone who would want to.

Hundreds of dead little exploded things covered my windshield in seconds. The swarm had completely blotted out anything else in the sky before I could react and they slammed into the vehicle like a tsunami. I'd like to say it sounded like microwave popcorn, but the sound of popcorn never made me feel hollow. The wave of flying insects continued madly past me, ignoring their fallen, and as soon as it began it was done. I might have screamed a little, or I might have just wanted to. It was a small miracle my windows had been rolled up; I don't want to think too hard about what that would have looked like.

Well, I'm not hungry anymore.

I was breathing hard; my hands seemed locked on the steering wheel. Remembering that I was stopped in the middle lane of a freeway was enough to make me get it together, and with some effort of will, I loosened my grip just enough to turn the wheel properly and roll down my window. It was impossible to see through my windshield, and the wipers weren't doing a thing except making a bigger mess. I turned on the hazards and poked my head out the side just enough to get myself off the road to clean this up so I could just get home. One of the little creeps hit my windshield just hard enough to give it a little crack. Wonderful.

I got out of the car, cursing my lack of preparedness for this situation. Nothing in the trunk to really clean a windshield of bird poop, let alone the primordial soup now slowing dropping down towards the hood. Maybe I had a rag or something in my bag that would get me enough of a view that I could at least make it to a gas station or something. My hands stopped moving after half a second inside my bag. In disbelief, I have to assume. I willed them to pick up the foreign object that my hand had found.

"That's not possible!"

My voice was harsh and shallow. I knew what it was, but it still wasn't real, not until I'd seen it. I wasn't sure I wanted to, but I knew that I had to. I cradled it into the nook of my wrist and felt the skin of the thing with my fingertips. I lifted it, fingers trembling. I brought the gift, so thoughtful, up to the light for inspection. It was a book, one that I wasn't supposed to have.

A first edition of *Jane Eyre*, all covered in burgundy leather.

All things considered, being thirty minutes late to open *The Book's End* wasn't that bad. It hadn't rained, but the mist and moisture in the air were enough to make the streets wet and in LA that counted as rain. Any kind of water on the road instantly adds fifteen minutes to your commute, wherever you're heading to, wherever it is you've come from. This was on top of the fact I'd somehow managed to squeeze in an extra twelve hours or so into the day and had barely beat the sunrise on our race to bed. I'm still not certain how I actually woke up.

Oh right, the terror!

I could be curled in a wide-eyed ball, trapped in an anxious panic about how I might have broken the universe by managing to bring back an object that shouldn't be real from a place that shouldn't have ever existed. But I only did that for an hour or so before passing out, so I think I'm good.

I wasn't sure if it was still just exceptionally chilly from the night before or I was cold because I hadn't slept much or eaten at all. I was mostly dressed in what I wore the night before, save for a change of shirt and that was only because I'd somehow managed to stain it with bug viscera and that was just plain nasty. It gave me the chance to pull over an old acrylic sweater vest on top of a thick cotton button up shirt, so the layering was real right now. I'm twenty-four, anything I wear right now passes for cool, is a lie I've decided to tell myself. I'd also managed to nap in a wool cap which I've since refused to take off for the remainder of the day. Warm hair good, hat hair bad.

The Book's End is a charming little bookstore which straddles the unenviable location of mid-city, mid-Wilshire. Not West Side or East Side, centrally located to where nobody wants to drive. We are the place on the way to the destination, not the destination itself. We buy and sell books. Every type of book you can imagine, we have it. Or had it. Or we'll get it for you. We have books stacked precariously in some areas, neatly displayed in others.

We also sell coffee, tea, and small pastries, because I guess selling books isn't enough to keep the doors open. I'm no barista, but I think our regular customers have come to expect what they get with my skill level. I'll grind your beans and pour hot water over them or whatever, but don't expect me to draw leaves in your foam. We also sell board games, knick-knacks, and even some magazines. So really, everything you'd find in a chain bookstore but in a quarter of the space.

When I got there, there were no angry customers impatiently waiting out front, which I took as a small miracle. Quietly canonizing myself as the patron saint of being on time because no one can prove otherwise, I entered the store and was barely acknowledged by the two permanent resident cats, Koala and Jameson. Koala is a layered gray polydactyl, almost certainly more fur than cat. I don't think he's ever gone more than five minutes without either eating or furiously licking someone. Jameson is an orange tabby whose purr was as deep as a kettle drum. He was mostly lazy until he wanted love, then he would dash over to you, running in time with the movement of your legs, trying to be exactly where you wanted to step; as if each footstep were a chance to run up against you.

At the moment, the two of them were spooning on the counter, completely oblivious to me. They weren't always visible. If you could see them, excellent. If not, who knows where they could be? Outside, on a shelf, under a chair; there was no pattern to their behavior. I didn't want to shove them off, but that's exactly what I had to do. The store needed to be open, and besides, no cats where we served food. In theory. I gave them both a scritch behind the ears as a show of my good intentions, but once off the counter, they scurried away to their important cat business.

The routine helped me keep my composure. Brewing coffee added an aroma to the air. Turning on the lights added clarity to my vision. Flipping on that ancient radio we kept around brought the noise of static and song to distract me from myself. Preparing the register and wiping the counter gave my hands familiar motion. The fudge cupcake overdosed my tongue with the sugar of a dozen sodas. Don't judge me, we happen to sell them, and I was still hungry from the night before. I took a big swallow and felt it move the entire length of my torso, and my stomach ached in agreement. Wow, I hadn't realized just exactly how hungry I was.

This all calmed me down though, as it usually does. My own personal method for clarity is to occupy all five of my senses until there is no more room in my brain to over analyze my current problem. Touch, smell, taste, sight, and sound are all powerful on their own, but no one ever seems to concentrate on them all at once. People recall how the amazing aroma of fresh bread in their grandfather's oven would fill an entire home or how beautiful their partner looked when they first fell in love with them, but those memories are always a facsimile. They are missing critical components to creating a very real experience.

When you read, you don't hear the characters. When you listen to music, you don't see the musician. And when you focus only on the strongest of your senses in any given situation, you create an incomplete memory. You saw the golden brown of the bread, tasted it, surely. You heard the familiar clank of the old stove opening and felt the soft warmth of it as you tore it in your hands. Remembering all of this is harder now, and even though you remember the pleasant scent of that loaf and even the emotions that came with it, you have a hard time describing what that scent actually is. Giving all five senses equal purpose is difficult to balance and leaves no room for anything else. At least in the moment.

I opened my bag, and sure enough, the copy of Jane Eyre was still there, still bound in burgundy leather. I was reasonably sure it would be, but you never know. I hadn't changed much of my clothes or showered from the night before, so it was entirely possible this was still a dream. It wasn't, but I thought I'd tell myself that anyway.

I placed the book on the counter, and with a clear mind, I pulled up a chair and tried to figure out how I did this. I saw the grooves and texture of the book's cover itself, and I focused on them, studying them. I traced a finger along those grooves, feeling the tiny peaks and valleys. I opened the book, letting the pages cascade, hearing the familiar sound of heavy paper and smelling one of the greatest scents in life, a new book. I thought about licking it. No one was watching, so maybe just this once? No, I went back to the cupcake.

I let all these things happen at once, and I asked myself that simple question: How, book? Simple, but it also opened up other questions immediately. How do you exist? You are a book, and you are real and how are you even a thing? How did book? How... are... a book... even? Book. Boooooook!

Crap. I had nothing.

This continued for the better part of an hour. At one point I even poked the book with my finger a full hundred times in a row. Hard. I counted out loud. Koala was, for a brief window of time, curious enough to smell the book, but having given it the all clear he jumped free of the counter and vanished again into the depths of the store. Didn't he see me just try that? Dumb cat. His sudden departure made me laugh at the ridiculous nature of cats and just like that I was out of it. With a fresh mind, I realized that cat had reminded me of another friend who was around one minute and then gone the next.

When I was a child, I had a friend named Lucia. I still consider her a friend, but no one would argue that she's the same person anymore. Lucia was taken from me and placed into a mental health facility so she "Could take the summer and recover." It's been over a decade, and I guess she's still in recovery.

Lucia was my first friend that I can remember who really understood me. When we were children, she sparked my love of stories and would take me on adventures. We would sit in my room, and we would tell each other the stories that we had read. I was animated and excited as any child, I'm sure. But when she would tell me of the stories she read, those tales would bleed into something else. She would insist that these things happened to her. She regaled me with stories about her friend the mermaid who wanted to be a human, the boy in the jungle with his animal friends, the nasty boy with the tin soldiers, and another soldier who saved a princess with the help of his magical dogs. The mermaid was her favorite. According to her, they would spend time together on a rock in the ocean, telling each other about their homes and their lives. And I knew that it couldn't be real, but I wanted so badly for it to be that I gave in with my whole heart and just accepted it. These were her friends. She believed in a mermaid and toys coming to life and talking animals and me. In her world, her utterly fantastic world, I was every bit as exciting as any other piece of it.

Sadly, for Lucia, my excitement for her stories made her bold, and she wanted to share that excitement with the world. Lucia wanted everyone to feel as special and as excited as I had. Her parents tolerated it until the teachers did not. The other kids made fun of her. Some of them did worse than that. Lucia became insistent, even a little dark in her response. Of course, they were real, why would she lie? Most children would retreat into themselves. I was one of those children, but not her. She was actually insulted that anyone wouldn't believe her and was more than willing to fight someone over it. In time, everyone decided they had just about enough of her stories, and she was sent away. And that was that. No big moment, no goodbye. Just one day she wasn't at school, and that was that.

You can imagine my guilt, fear, and yes, even excitement when I learned I could do exactly what she had said she could all along. I've kept quiet because I've seen firsthand what happens when you sound crazy. I'll tell you. They treat you like you're crazy. To this day, I don't know if Lucia could really do whatever it is that I do, but I also don't know that I want to. These days she's medicated and lifeless. Her energy is gone. She's allowed visitors, but it's like spending time with a shadow. If she really was able to travel in the way that I do, that means that something incredible was stolen from her and I don't know if she'll ever get it back. And if she couldn't, it just means that my friend had her youth stolen from her because she committed the unholy crime of being a child with an overactive imagination. I'm not sure which is worse.

The door opening brought me back, which I found oddly welcoming. The clarity was making me remember things that I didn't want to remember. I made a small promise to myself that I'd visit Lucia again soon. "So how late were you today?" I heard Claire before I actually saw her. "Half an hour? Maybe?" I answered. No need to lie, I didn't know that it would accomplish anything.

Maybe I could have lied a little bit. Claire was obviously not pleased.

"Dude. We need that morning rush. Our regulars aren't going to come here for morning coffee if they can't count on us to be open in the morning. At the place they would like to buy coffee. Regularly. You realize you'd be fired anywhere else for how often you're late?"

She sighed and let her bag drop on a table with the staff picks which incidentally for this month, were *Howl's Moving Castle* which happened to be a favorite of mine from middle school. A child gets turned into an old woman and has to fight a witch in a faraway castle. *Our First Murder*, a series about two old women who inherit a detective agency and it's every bit as funny as it sounds. And a trade paperback collecting an old western comic book called *One Shot Juanita* about this bounty hunter who wields a demon possessed gun. These were my choices. Claire, deciding that one of us had to try and push the newer stuff, had out *Willful Machines*, which I think is about a kid whose dad is the President and also there's a computer trying to murder him? I hadn't read it, but Claire loved it, so it was on my list. *Passenger*, a new series that I gather is a time travel love story. And lastly, *The Edge of Forever*, which was yet another time travel book. As a bonus, she put out a copy of *Brandon Bird's Astonishing World of Art*. For someone so grounded, she sure loved her sci-fi.

I noticed the beads of water on her leather jacket as she removed it and shook out her hair, which currently was an alarming fuchsia. I hadn't actually opened the curtains yet, but I guess it had started to rain finally. My guess though was that if I had opened the curtains, it might have already stopped. Such is rain around here.

Claire had inherited the little building we now worked in when she was barely eighteen years old. Like me, she didn't have parents to speak of, but unlike me, she had a surprise inheritance waiting for her when she became an adult. And Claire did exactly what I probably would have done in her place: she bought just about every book she could get her hands on from every yard sale and book drive in the state. She borrowed an old Chevy Suburban and went on road trips with her friends trying specifically to fill the car with books. More often than not Claire convinced people just to give her boxes of paperbacks that had been forgotten about in attics and garages for free.

When she had enough, or long before it actually, she filled shelves and tables with a very unorganized collection of gently used books, each holding in it a little part of her youth and a portion of her adventure. The shelves were rescued from curbs or cobbled together by stacked wooden crates or made from various pieces of wood found wherever one finds wood. She had her friends with her, and she knew she could do anything, the least of all being her dream of owning and running a bookstore.

In time her optimism began to fade as friends took advantage of her. They used the building for bands to practice in or to hold parties, never cleaning and usually breaking something. People she thought were her friends using the loft space to crash for free rent while they tried to find themselves or work on their art, but in reality, were just trying to avoid growing up for as long as possible. The gonzo approach she had taken to starting a business felt less like a cool, modern hippie tale and more like a giant mistake as the bills began to mount. Property taxes, utilities, and all the other tiny little ways to fall victim to crippling debt began to pile up. Her freedom became a noose, and she was able to see with a bit more clarity each day that her friends weren't going to help her at all. They probably weren't even friends.

Almost as a matter of necessity, people were cut from her life. She chose the dream over the popularity. She sponsored reading programs at schools and volunteered with animal rescues, helping out in the neighborhood and getting her business out there. She managed somehow, in spite of Quantum Theory and God, to work 25 hours a day, 8 days a week, 366 days a year. Soon she was alone. Well, not alone, but alone in the sense that her community was her family. Her regulars were her friends, if only in short bursts. In time she recovered. She made real friends, not just customers who smiled politely or predators who smiled vacantly. She made friends who smiled as they looked her in the eye and were both concerned and proud, envious and admiring. People like me.

I respected her. I was in awe of her journey. I was in her debt for letting me carve out a living in a place that I loved. I was still late to work.

"How did you know I was late?" I asked, trying to deflect from the lecture I knew I deserved, vaguely aware of the uncomfortable couple of minutes I just spent in my own head.

"Olivia made a post on Facebook that you woke up drunk in her bathtub at four in the morning. And then you didn't answer my call or text this morning. I thought you might not make it in at all. Coffee?" Wow. Olivia was really not careful with her social media at four in the morn—oh, that's right I woke her up. My fault.

Claire asked that in a way that made it seem as if she had less sleep than I did. I poured her a cup and didn't say anything; I was also not exactly surprised that Olivia immediately posted my life online, if she didn't I'm not sure anyone would know I exist. She takes pictures of me for social media the way some people take pictures of their dog. And the way she described it is not exactly what happened, but it's not like I can tell anyone that.

"Why didn't you stop by?" I asked. "It would have been neat to hang out." Not a lie, but it was another deflection.

"Because I'm twenty years older than anyone else there—" she started.

"Not true, you're only like thirteen years older than me."

"… and because I had work in the morning," she finished. Ouch. "Thanks."

She was referring to the coffee. I hoped.

"Whoa, what's this?" she asked, now changing the subject herself. "Did someone sell us this?"

She set down the coffee and picked up my copy of *Jane Eyre* with the care one might show a newborn, yet examining it like a crime scene. "This is in remarkable condition. How much did we pay for this?"

"We didn't pay anything. This is mine," I said in a weird mixture of defensive and proud. Claire gave me a look of disappointment.

"Elana, you can't just buy books from customers for yourself without asking me first, this is still a business." I wanted to be hurt at the accusation that I would do that to her, but I had already screwed up enough for one day that I didn't feel I had the right. I let it go and stayed on topic.

"No, really, look." I took the book from her with considerably less care than she was expecting, and opened up to the inscription.

"Who is George?" She asked, her forehead creasing slightly. "And why did he mark up the book?"

Oh… I hadn't prepared for this question.

"He's a friend." Not a lie, just a new friend.

"A friend?" She asked closing the book. "I know your friends; I don't know George. How do you know George?"

"From that trip that one time." In my head, the D20 just landed on a one.

The side eye from Claire was strong enough to be considered front eye. "Is he on Facebook or anything? And what kind of monster marks up a treasure like this with an inscription? Does he hate books?"

The front door chimed as a couple of college kids walked in the door. I don't know how strongly I believe in fate intervening with timely distractions, but I'll gladly take them when they come. They ordered drinks and a lemon bar to share, officially marking the beginning of the day. I slipped the book back into my bag under the counter and put on a smile, getting to work. Contrary to popular belief, we actually do have customers. My mystery would have to wait.

5

I'm in my element at work. Social anxiety is just about the worst thing I've got going for me, but when someone comes to work, it's never an issue. This bookstore is as firmly a place that I can call my own as can exist. The irrational panic that someone is talking about me or the unrelenting feeling that I've wandered into the wrong place, the need to hide in the bathroom or pretend I know what to say while my body tightens… none of that exists here. In this store, the strangers come to me and I'm not trapped by social niceties, left to wonder if I'm staying too close to a friend or when I'm allowed to leave or if anyone has noticed how long I've been in the bathroom. I was here first, I'll be here again, and I am surrounded by what I love.

And maybe that is why I felt so unsure when this young man walked in. Was he young? It was hard to tell. I could have sworn at first glance he couldn't have possibly been older than me, twenty-two at most. When he was out of the doorway, I thought I had to probably double that number. That's rough. And his eyes! They seemed to bounce around to everything in the store, wild and assured at the same time.

The cats left immediately. Jameson loudly hissed, I'd never seen him do that before. They were normally better about customers, but he might have just owned a dog or something. His hair was unruly, almost like a still frame of a brush fire, but a very dark brown, almost black. It stood in stark contrast to how well he seemed put together. He was dressed well, that suit could have been pulled off a rack earlier today, but his clothes were all out of place as if they belonged to a character he was playing and didn't fit him in a way that had nothing to do with measurements. His body moved like an animal that had been taught how to walk in a polite society but rebelled against the idea anyway. I stopped staring long enough to speak.

"Can I help you?" I tried asking in a way that didn't have the subtext question *"What the hell, dude?"*

"Just looking," he said picking up a seemingly random book from our staff picks, before glancing at the back cover and putting it back down. It took me a moment to realize he glanced at it upside down and didn't bother to flip it over. "On second thought, maybe you can. I've been just dying to read a particular book, but just can't find it."

Several of the words came out of his mouth with extra letters attached to them. "I've" sounded almost aggressively Irish. Probably Irish. To my ears, it sounded like "Aohy've."

"What's the title?" Hopefully Customer Service Elana would overpower Weirded Out Elana.

"Crome Yellow."

I hoped my surprise hadn't registered, but since I was surprised at my own surprise, I probably showed something.

"Oh! The Aldous Huxley novel that—," I began, trying to recover.

"Isn't *Brave New World*. Yes, yes," he cut me off abruptly as if it had been the tenth time today he'd heard that and then looked suddenly aware of that fact. "That is what you were going to say, isn't it?"

I took half a second to open my palms behind the register out of his view in an attempt to let my frustration go. "I suppose so. Let me see if I can find a copy in the system."

I turned away from him and pretended to look on the computer, but really I was already rubbed the wrong way by this guy and was ready to blow him off. "So why *Crome Yellow*?"

"Research," he answered, placing his hands in his pockets and scanning the ceiling before he continued. "Truthfully, I've been meaning to get into it for a while now."

"Sorry, looks like we're fresh out," I said, feigning sympathy. "You're welcome to look in the bulk used pile, or maybe the library has a copy you could check out."

I couldn't be certain, but for a moment it felt like his smile was replaced by something much worse. A kind of righteous anger. It was so quick though that I couldn't just chalk it up to exhaustion. And just as suddenly the smile was back, and he extended a hand to me.

"Well, it was a true pleasure meeting you," he said, his voice a little too friendly. "I'm sorry, what did you say your name was again?"

The back door swung open, loud enough to make me jump. "I'm back from Costco, can you give me a hand with the car?"

Claire came around the corner carrying a big pack of muffins that she was going to try and pass off as freshly made, and possibly vegan. She studied us for just a moment before switching the weight of her pastries to her other arm and extended a hand out to our customer.

"Hi, I'm Claire Van Amberg, owner of the shop. I'll be happy to help." He seemed to take her hand reluctantly. "Elana, I think my trunk is open if you wouldn't mind?"

"Well, thank you for your help, Elana," he commented on my way out.

I felt weirdly grateful to have an excuse to leave and began to get the week's supplies unloaded. The cases of water bottles were the worst and always just barely at what I was able to lift, but I definitely wasn't complaining today. It took about ten minutes or so, and when I was done, I returned to the front of the store, opening a bottle of water. That weird customer was gone, and Claire studied me again.

"So your gift giver is a stalker now too?" It felt like less of a question and more a line of investigation.

"Oh god no, definitely not!" I said that a bit too loudly and quickly. "I've literally never met that guy before. Unlike you, he actually is twice my age probably."

"Oh, okay," she said softening her stance. "Expensive suit, but didn't know how to wear it, just seemed like the type to purchase a rare book and then scribble in it. Creepy guy though, right?"

"I know! Weird as hell! What was his deal?"

"He said he was looking for a book, but you told him we didn't have it," she answered, turning the monitor towards me. "Except that we have five copies. Nobody wants *Crome Yellow*, I'm always surprised when someone has read it. I'm about to donate four of them to a school or something."

I stared at her, slowly sipping the water.

"So, why did you tell him we didn't have it?"

"I don't know. Really." I was being honest with her, mostly. "He just really creeped me out I guess. Sorry, I wanted him gone."

"It's fine. You were alone, it happens. I promise I'm not mad." She was reassuring me, and not in her usual frustrated manner. "Remember, if you ever feel unsafe, the pepper spray is under the counter. I'll toss this; I thought it was for you." She started to throw away a business card that the man had apparently left, and pure curiosity made me stop her. It was simple. White, normal card stock with Navy blue letters that read:

BRES MODRED
GARDENER
(310) 555-6462

My brain seemed to click around something he said. What kind of gardener needs literature for work research?

Work was done for the day, and it was Claire's turn to close up. I didn't feel like going home, but I also wasn't feeling like staying at the store any longer than I needed to. It wasn't uncommon for one of us to wait for the other to lock up, even if it just meant taking a nap upstairs in the loft. All day long Claire had been suspicious of my book and to a larger extent my story, and trying to obfuscate the truth didn't feel right. That Bres guy showing up certainly didn't help anyone. I waited until she was busy with a particularly pushy customer until I offered a quick goodbye to avoid any more small talk before I left. I made it to my car and had no idea where to go next. I quickly pulled away from the shop and had driven clear out to West Hollywood before deciding that I was willing to brave the traffic if it meant treating myself to a meal at Cafe Mak. I told myself that traffic wasn't that bad. It's amazing how well you can lie to yourself.

Forty-five minutes later I was hunting for parking. They have spots, but at this time of day, everything was taken which meant I had to get lucky. I could have parked behind someone in their lot, but I hate leaving my keys with anyone. The traffic was a good thing. It helped to kill time, which was kind of the point, and because of that I also managed to burn through another episode of what was increasingly becoming an insurmountable number of podcasts I've been told that I just had to listen to. New rule: I'll check out your podcast if you will read a book of my choosing. Your podcast has two hundred episodes, and I have to hear all of them, but you can't read one of my books? What the junk is wrong with you?

So, make that fifty-three minutes. Everyone decided now was exactly the time to reach out to me, and I mean everyone. Claire sent a text saying she hoped I wasn't mad at her, which I didn't respond to and knew if I thought about it for more than a moment I'd feel awful. My friend Teague invited me out drinking which didn't sound like the best idea. Logan actually called me, which set off a mild panic attack within my chest. I had forgotten that my phone wasn't just a computer and texting machine but also, well, a phone. Calls were usually avoided if I could help it. The phone rang while I sat in my car, dumbly staring at it. Why was he calling me? I rarely heard from Logan. Any Logan related activities were filtered through Olivia. That wasn't because I didn't like Logan, they were just a couple, and I heard about anything going on between the two of them from her.

Still ringing. What if Olivia was hurt? What if they broke up? Some news wasn't meant to be sent over text after all. Was he mad at me? I didn't do anything, why would he be mad? He wouldn't be, something must have been wrong!

I hurriedly hit the accept button and raised the phone to my ear.

"What happened? What's wrong? Are you two okay?" I nearly shouted into the phone, my heart racing.

The voice which came back was cheerful and laughing. "Hey, Elana! I'm here with Olivia, say hi?"

"Hi!" I heard Olivia shout over what was probably the speakerphone.

"You're fine?" I asked, confirming the answer I already knew.

"What? Yeah. We're cool, sorry, I just thought a call would be quicker." I could hear in his voice he was embarrassed to be calling me now, realizing he'd just engaged in some ancient tradition that no one followed anymore like challenging someone to a duel, or inviting them to an ice cream social, or asking to borrow an AOL Free Trial disc.

"No, you're fine, I promise," I reassured him. "So what's up?"

"We're just planning out my thing, and I needed some details from you, is that cool?" He asked hopefully.

His "thing" was his birthday, which he was planning himself. Which meant another party like the one they just held, just with the benefit of being a month and half from now. Of course I was going to go, I couldn't just stay home from that. I told him everything he needed, which was for some reason my shoe size among other details, and I gave friendly goodbyes to the two of them. Having survived that harrowing ordeal, I got out of the car and headed inside the cafe.

Cafe Mak was old. Maybe not as a cafe, but certainly as a structure. Easily a hundred years old, but it was never meant to be a place of business. It was originally a home, back when the ceilings were built high and wooden floors and brick walls weren't an expensive feature, that was just how houses were made. Even sectioned off as it was, each room had its own feel. One corner had a small library filled with books in Korean, Japanese, and English, and a wall of wine bottles and old board games. Some areas felt more quiet and formal. Some were claustrophobic and social. Some were wide open and almost too big. The walls had fireplaces and fountains which were now only ornamental, having long ago been walled over. An "Out of order" sign was taped to the wall outside of the restroom where a fireplace once stood, which made me laugh. It's a good thing they mentioned that, someone might have tried to use it otherwise, leading to permanent consequences. The patio felt like an escape, like the section of a social event where a friend eventually finds you and says, "So that's where you've been!"

Luckily my favorite spot was open, a small little corner in the back behind an antique wooden changing wall, painted with a mural of a cafe in Paris. I think half the time this table is open is because no one expects anything back there. Four chairs and a table, all for me. They normally only let you sit here if you were a party of four or more, but they seemed used to me and knew I'd move if they needed me to. I settled in and pressed the call button, ordering a basket of fries and lemonade. The Tiramisu tempted me, but I probably shouldn't have been spending money on eating out in the first place, and besides, that was a lot of food. I was there for the atmosphere anyway. This was my happy place. Or one of them. An earthy building where I could be left alone to read. As long as I ordered food, that is.

Several books sat in my satchel that I managed to snag from the dollar pile, but the one I was in the mood to read was a copy of *Dragonsong*, one of the Pern books from when I was a kid, that was practically falling apart. This was the sort of fantasy I grew up on. Come to think of it, this was probably the kind of fantasy my mom grew up on. If she'd liked books when she was younger. Weird. I wished I knew what she grew up on.

I unhooked my bag and curled up on the chair, digging my hip into the cushion of the seat, excited to get into my book, just not literally. No traveling this time. The story was easy to relate to: A young, weird teenage girl has an artistic talent (in her case, singing) that no one wanted to foster. So she runs away from home and ends up living in a city that likes that sort of thing. It's not too thinly veiled or anything, there are dragons in it. Dragons are never a metaphor for anything.

The fries and the lemonade seemed to evaporate, and before I knew it, it was relatively late. This place would stay open until around the time most bars would close, and the blessing and the curse of this cafe was that the staff would not bother you until just about five minutes after they all wanted to go home. And if you were say, caught up in the magical world of Dragons, Songs, and maybe even Dragonsongs, you just might find yourself heading home late enough to worry about waking up your roommate.

Sharon, the roommate in question, was thankfully passed out hard. Her room smelled faintly of pot, and her laptop had gone into rest mode. I quietly shut her door and made my way back to the couch in the living room. The TV was left on, and I was too awake to go to bed but too tired to change the channel. I settled in for some mindless garbage in the form of *Four's a Crowd*. The show itself is widely offensive and definitely a product of the early eighties. It's about some guy, his name doesn't matter, and I don't remember it. He lives in Santa Barbara, and he can't afford rent, so he rooms with three women, but he needs to dress as a woman because his pervy landlord offers up cheap rent, but only to attractive ladies. It's mostly played for laughs and the landlord is clearly the villain, but it never sat well with me. This was a show for hipsters and grandmas.

I noticed something odd. At first, I thought it was straight up exhaustion. But then it happened again. And again. A waitress introduced herself as Jennifer, but her name tag clearly read "Elana". Then some letter magnets on a refrigerator clearly spelled out my name. Finally, a man walked through the background in a white T-shirt with what looked to be a message handwritten in permanent marker on it that read, *"HI, ELANA!"* I began to feel sick.

EMPTY THREAT

I looked online for a character named Elana on the show. Nothing. This was obviously about me, wasn't it? It couldn't be, this show was thirty-something years ago. I wasn't even born yet. I've never been in this show either, not even one like it. Can someone else do what I do? How would they even know to communicate with me? I had too many questions, at least four or five half fragments of questions for every complete one that occurred to me, but all of them arrived at the same conclusion despite how desperately I wanted to arrive somewhere else.

I did my best to steady my breathing, before saying the words out loud to make them real enough to convince myself of them. I had to investigate.

Barreling through the sleepy diner with the velocity of a toddler unaware and unconcerned with how to stop, I slammed into an all too attractive waiter, knocking over the comical amount of food he'd been carrying. That was just before tripping and then rolling over an occupied table and managing a full front flip. I didn't know that I was capable of literally flipping out, only figuratively.

I completed my pratfall in the center of the room for all to see and somewhere in the back of my head, I heard a laugh track that I was positive no one else could hear. In the category of things I was positive that everyone had heard, were the murmurs and comments. "Where'd she come from?" "Is she okay?" "Oh my God." "I guess breakfast is ruined." That kind of thing. I couldn't wait to be out of there.

I should back up a moment. I'd like to say that upon realizing what must be done I fearlessly leaped into the show, ready to investigate and get to the bottom of things or whatever cliché you liked here. Takin' care of business. I liked that one at the moment. But no, that's not even remotely what happened. For starters, there was enough hyperventilating that Sharon woke up and tried to coax the problem out of me, became silently frustrated when she couldn't and decided to try and solve the problem with ice cream. Then I feigned composure long enough for Sharon to go back to bed, before pacing in and out of the apartment, contemplating the very narcissistic idea that I was important enough for someone to send me a coded message on a TV show that came out before I was born. I also realized how little I understood how that would even work. Then I did my best to dig up a period outfit appropriate for the '80s, and you can piss off if you don't understand how that would be calming. And only then did I jump into this world. The first opening I saw was in the opening credits, which made things easy.

"Are you alright? Let me give you a hand," the waiter said, trying to help me up. The question hit me in a way that it shouldn't. I don't know that I'm ever right, let alone literally always right. I wasn't about to say that, though.

"I'm good," I said, accepting his help. I felt more confident about that answer. Probably good, maybe right. He seemed content to blur the meanings together.

"Thanks," I said on my feet again. "Oh my God, you're—" I couldn't find the words. I'm not often, or really ever for that matter, star struck. That's not what this was. I just now realized why this dude's handsome face stuck out to me even as I crashed landed in this story. This was Hugh Kilter! He was considerably younger than he was when I last saw him in anything, but age aside this was definitely him.

"Chad! Get this cleaned up!" an older, harder voice shouted from near the kitchen.

"Sorry," Chad the waiter said to me. "I have to get this taken care of. You're sure you're good?"

I nodded in response. Pretty sure. The nod made him grin, and that made me grin. "Okay, you should go."

I didn't stick around to protest and immediately left the restaurant, recognizing it from the outside as I did. It was one of the establishing shots from the opening credits for one of the stars. Don't ask me which one. In fact, please don't ask me anything about *Four's a Crowd*. As far as I know, the diner wasn't used anywhere else in the show, but I couldn't be certain. I only ever watched the show when nothing else was on and even then was never exactly enthused by the idea. It was one of those shows that I think most people kind of know in the back of their minds exists, but no one could ever pin down a narrative arc or even tell you how many seasons the show lasted or anything else about the show of any importance.

As I walked, I became acutely aware of a few things. For one thing, good or no, I was definitely uninjured, and I feel like I should have been way more messed up. I tested all my limbs, rolled my neck, and did a little hop. All solid. My landings are unpredictable, and this one was a winner. I hit that poor guy pretty hard. He had no way to see me coming either, and it felt like I was flung at him by a giant. And outside of my ego, nothing had been hurt. Second, I caught a reflection of myself and only just now understood that I don't understand the eighties. I looked like Cyndi Lauper if she had been savagely attacked by Debbie Gibson and somehow had much bigger hair and also looked nothing like Cyndi Lauper.

"Needs more sitcom, less '*Time After Time*,'" I said to myself, still kind of impressed with the look I pulled off. Certainly not about to blend in anytime soon, but I could have fronted a glam band, though.

What really struck me about this place though was the air. Or if not the air, just, everything. There was a different quality to this place that had nothing to do with the year or the scenery. It just felt different, not even off, just not the same. It was hard to explain, but easy to concentrate on given the fact that I was aimlessly wandering down a shoreline street in Santa Barbara. The anxiety I felt before entering was being replaced by mundane acceptance as it became apparent that I didn't have a plan beyond going in. I'm not sure what I expected to happen exactly. I didn't know who or what I'd be looking for. I wasn't even entirely certain there was a "Who" to begin with. I freaked out and got dressed up for nothing which sadly was not the first time I've said that.

I took a walk out onto the warm white sands of the beach, mostly devoid of people even on a day as perfect as this one. I made it about halfway to the water before I resigned myself to the waste of time I'd gone through in coming here and yelled in frustration at the sky before lying on my back, sliding my small pork pie hat from the top of my head to cover my eyes from the sun.

"I own too many hats," I said to myself, trying to release the tension. I became aware of how much sand I'd have in my clothes and my shoes and dug my shoes in deeper not caring. The sun would eventually bake the exposed bits of flesh I was feeding it, but I didn't care about that either. There was a sense of relief at not having to deal with anything on this side, but also frustration at how worked up I'd gotten. This had seemed so big, so recently. And now I was lying on a beach.

"Elana?"

The voice was male, and I didn't recognize it. It froze me solid. Nausea spread through me. I didn't know how to respond, so I didn't.

He asked again, "I'm sorry, is your name Elana?"

Okay, so he's not going away. Come up with something. "Yes?" *Nice.*

The man barked a laugh that made me spring to my feet. Maybe the verb "spring" is generous. I did whatever that thing is where you fall upwards, made worse by the fact that I was unbalanced by the sand so I fell back down. He offered me a hand up, which I instinctively took and immediately withdrew the moment I was on my feet. I clutched at my hat with both hands to prevent dropping it as I forced it back on my head. A sense of dread began to fill my stomach, the kind that comes with the unknown when someone knows your name who shouldn't. A barrage of questions spilled out of me, quickly losing steam.

"Who are you? How do you know me? Why did the… thing?"

"Easy," he said, trying to calm me. "My name is Paolo. I'm the one who has been sending you messages all these years. I can't believe you finally came."

Paolo was middle aged, dark skinned with perfectly messy hair that looked incredibly soft. He wore short, white shorts that seemed like they could only be considered a fit in the eighties and a short sleeved wool polo shirt that seemed too tight in the chest and the arms. His smile was perfect and ridiculous.

"What do you mean years?" I asked. "I came as soon as I saw my name in the show."

His face lit up with understanding. "Ah. Yeah, time doesn't always work the same between worlds. Particularly in a sitcom. Which episode did you enter?"

I had to think about it. "I don't know… John Faller was freaking out about some new opening at this theater."

"Season six, at least," Paolo said, seeming to understand suddenly. "That's the problem with reruns; they're not always shown in order. John wasn't managing a theater for a long time. I've been sending messages since around season three."

I had no idea what he was talking about and told him as much. He suggested I return to his home to speak further, which I absolutely wasn't ready to acquiesce to just yet.

"That seems like a lot of trust you're expecting from me for a dude who just sort of semi-inter dimensionally stalked me, kind of, I guess." I wasn't sure how to classify my discomfort. "Exactly why would I follow you home?"

"Because, Elana," he began, his smile starting to fade, "you never know who is listening. And what we have to talk about shouldn't be said over a cup of coffee."

"We're pretty much alone on a beach," I said motioning to the small handful of people who weren't exactly within earshot.

"Yeah, I see that," he replied sharply. "Like I said, you don't know."

I cautiously followed him to his home, which happened to be a pretty decent apartment. Much larger than mine, actually. The living room was covered in soft pastels, and beach themed swaths of color. On the wall hung a painting of palm trees on the beach at sunset, with two dolphins leaping out of the water. It was displayed without a hint of irony. The television was enormous, the carpet shag and white, and god help me there was actual neon trim around the walls. Actual. Neon. Trim. It was like he lived in Windows 95.

"This is the most '80s thing that has ever been," I said in awe, suddenly questioning the very idea of good taste.

"Yeah it is!" Paolo said quite proudly. "How about a Fresca?"

I waited to see if he was quoting anything or if he was sincere. He opened a Fresca. He was serious. "No, thank you. How does this place even exist?"

"Are you asking me to explain object permanence?" he asked, hopefully less serious about that question than he was about that Fresca.

"Okay, revision. *Why* does this place exist?"

"Kids these days just don't understand cool," he lamented with a shake of his head. "Want to hear something awesome?"

Before I had a chance to point out the absurdity of that question, he popped a cassette into a tape deck (his stereo was, of course, huge), and a very synth-heavy song began to play. "All right, we should be okay to talk now."

"Is there a chance someone is listening even in your home?" I asked, half worried at this point. "And if they were, would music really dissuade them from listening to us?" Whoever "They" were.

"You never know," he said gravely.

"Yeah, you said that earlier," I pressed. Before I could continue, the front door unlocked and I swear to god, Jodie Reese walked through the door with groceries.

"Oh honey, you're home. Give me a hand?" she asked, casually kicking the door closed again with the small of her foot. Paolo smiled and took her bags as she gave him a quick kiss on the cheek. "So, who's your friend?"

My mouth must have been open, as Paolo sensed the awkwardness and tried to force out his words. "Sweetie, this is, umm, Elana."

Jodie smiled wide in disbelief and stifled a laugh.

"No way!" she finally exclaimed, smacking me hard on the shoulder. "You know, I was beginning to think you didn't exist! I'm Becky by the way; it's so great to meet you finally!"

She offered both of her hands to me, fingers stretched out to their limit. I took one of her hands and asked, "You know me?"

All in a moment I knew far too much. *Becky Sayers was born in Mona, Utah. Her parents were kind, and her life was idyllic. She enjoyed summers at the lake and orange flavored candies and dancing alone and boys with messy hair. When she wanted to go to school out of the state, everyone had been sup-*

portive. Her Dad had given her his old pickup truck, complete with instructions on dealing with sticking gears and the virtues of regular maintenance; and she drove to the west coast. She wanted to be an attorney or an opera singer or a marine biologist. Her love for the possibilities of life was boundless. While on her road trip to school, her parents died back home in a car accident. She didn't even find out until a few days after it happened. They were so proud of her, but she felt so guilty for leaving them. Maybe if they still had that old tank of a truck, they'd have been fine. Maybe she would have been in the car instead of Mom or Dad, and she would have avoided the accident altogether. At the very least one of them would still be alive, and they both deserved to be.

Before leaving, making friends had come so effortlessly for her, but now she couldn't bring herself to connect with anyone. Her roommate in college might have been the closest thing to a friend, and most of the time Becky merely felt tolerated due to proximity and for the sake of good roommate relations. All seemed hopeless. Until one night she met Paolo. Paolo was different in how he saw the world. He made her feel like there was more to see and do. And the way he looked at her when she spoke made her feel like he was genuinely interested in everything she had to say. Like her words had weight. Like she was the most important thing to him. Like he'd known her all along, and she was better for knowing him. And when they finally married, she'd found a partner. When he told her he was from somewhere else, she knew he was telling the truth. He wanted to protect her. He wanted her to keep him here. She could feel it in her bones. She was prepared to live a long life with him and they would.

My hand snapped back, not from pain, but something else. I didn't want to be touching her. "I know you!" I blurted out, not thinking. And I did. I knew too much. I felt ill.

"Ohmygod!" Becky shouted, drawing her hands back to her mouth. "I am so, so sorry. I totally forgot!" She looked at her husband. "You were right, she is just like you, isn't she?"

I wanted to say something, anything, but the words wouldn't come. Paolo looked, what was that look? Exasperated maybe? "This is my fault dear, can you maybe give us a minute? We'll need to talk."

Some hurried and concerned apologies later, Becky left the apartment, and I sat down to regain my composure. Paolo seemed less concerned.

"So you're like me?" I asked finally.

"I told Becky that I was an alien from the planet Castrovalva in the Andromeda galaxy," he answered.

"Holy crap we're aliens?" I asked much, much louder than I'd intended.

Paolo recoiled in surprise. "No! Of course not! It's a—look, keep quiet, okay? We're humans. From earth. But *an* Earth. Maybe the first Earth. No one is certain."

I just stared at him, unable to process one of a thousand questions I needed to ask like my brain ran out of memory and the desktop of my mind crashed. "Take a moment," he offered, relaxing his posture. "I'll answer whatever questions you have."

I tried to center myself. The soft velour of the couch on my fingertips. The poor but unique sound of a cassette tape playing '80s jams. The taste of that tiny bit of sand from the beach in my mouth. The smell of the ocean prevalent even in a closed apartment. The sight of the soft sharpness of angular neon and pastels. I allowed myself to become calm.

"What are we? How many of us are there?" I asked in an even tone.

"That's a big one," Paolo said, leaning back into his corner of the couch. "We are travelers of a kind. Among other things. And as for how many of us there are, I couldn't say. More than you're about to imagine, but less than you'd think. I'm sorry if that sounds cryptic, I just really don't know the exact answer. We are most definitely not alone if that's what you're asking."

I wasn't content with the answer, but I could already feel my mind starting to spiral back out of control. "What did I do to your wife? Why was she so understanding of that? I've never felt anything like that in my life!"

"You Knew her," he explained. "Or you Know her. Whichever term you prefer. It's one of the things we're capable of; you're pulling microscopic bits from The Knowing. When someone offers themselves willingly, we learn their stories. Some of the big things, some of the small things. Usually, the parts that matter to them, but not always. It's possible to share your story at the same time with them if you're so inclined. It's not always completely reliable, however. People lie to themselves. They block out the bad, or romanticize it. They taint their past with nostalgia. You need to be careful with this because some people hold on their past too tightly. When you take on their past, you can also take on their pains and their fears, and you won't know what you'll be able to handle until you suddenly can't."

He was right. Even now, I felt tremendously sad at the death of her parents. I didn't know them, and yet I missed them. He said The Knowing like it was a thing or a place and I had questions about that, but I decided to come back to that before I lost track of the existing questions I already had.

"You're married to an actress," I said, trying to approach the question carefully. "I know her, from like my daily life, and her name isn't Becky Sayers. It's Jodie Reese. She's won awards. Everyone knows who she is."

"No," Paolo replied with a tightness in his voice. "You met Becky, not Jodie." I said nothing, giving him a moment to take the hint and explain on his own. "Okay, let me start over. Imagine all of the people. Ever. Well, humans at least, but that's an entirely different conversation. So, humans. Generally, we can agree on the basics: Two eyes, a mouth, nose, ears, a pair of arms and legs; you've seen humans before, you know what I mean. Think of how many different possibilities and variations there must be! It goes on forever and ever, right?"

"Of course," I replied, focused in.

"No, it doesn't. Like most things, there's a limit. People get repeated all the time. Sometimes they're more recognizable than not, but we end up with... I don't want to say doppelgangers, but you get the idea. And for some reason, certain people get repeated more often than others." He was correcting me as if I were a child.

"So does this mean that there's an evil Elana somewhere?" I asked, already picturing the possibilities. "Dark Elana? Nega-Elana? Sorry."

He shook his head. "No, it's okay. This is a lot to process. And I never know how anyone is going to take this answer, but the answer is no. There is almost certainly just one you. Travelers don't get repeated. You might see someone with a passing resemblance to you, but it's not you."

"So that's what we're called? Travelers?" I asked.

"It's not an official name or anything; it's just something we can do. We're all people, but you did just travel here, and I'm sure it wasn't easy for you." His answer made me think. Actually, it had been quite easy once I got past the existential terror of falling into a TV show, but I didn't feel that this was the time to correct him.

I started to catch on. "So then Jodie and Becky are—"

He interrupted me. "Two completely different people." There was a sharpness to his voice on that, like it was a closed matter. I wanted to let it go, but...

"But she's not real," I pressed. "None of this is, not really. It's fiction!"

Something showed on his face, a flicker of shock maybe. He paused for a moment. "You truly don't know, do you?"

"Know what?" I felt strangely unsure that I was ready for the answer.

"This world, nearly every world for that matter," he said the words, but I knew what they were somehow before they left his mouth. "They're real, Elana. Exactly as real as your own. Fiction exists, but not in the way you define it."

And then I was gone.

7

"**O**kay, so this one time I was in Vegas and I met this woman,"

I was pulled under a gigantic blanket, sinking into Olivia's couch, trying to hide from the world as she told me a story. I don't think Olivia has ever actually been to Vegas.

She continued, turning her body towards me on the couch. "So she tells me about this great place to get a drink and says we can meet there later. Oh yeah, but she also tells me about this awful place to get a drink that's supposed to be further down the road. So I start walking that way later, and I end up at the bad spot for a drink, and that's when I realized I Mister Goodbar!"

She took a long, exaggerated pause where she wanted to laugh, but wanted me to catch up as well so we could laugh together. I didn't get it at all.

"Oh, right! I was supposed to mention that her name was Candy. Or that she sold candy? I screwed up."

Olivia forgot for a second I was sitting next to her and began to do pun math in her head. She was trying to cheer me up in the worst possible way. That was kind of her, and I didn't have the heart to tell her what was up with me.

It had been a couple of weeks since I'd last traveled. Or opened a book. Or watched anything on TV. There were a couple of times after our meeting that I tried to pick up a book, but I couldn't enjoy them. I would consistently see openings, I would always feel the pull to enter, and it just didn't feel like they belonged to me anymore. If I were to enter into these worlds, I'd be a pretender. Or worse, an invader. The characters I was reading about were no longer just concepts and ideas but rather flesh and bone. It was like reading hundreds of obituaries only to watch those people die in real time, one by one, seeing their triumphs and failures only to see the inescapable reality of death time and again. I was surprised to finally realize exactly how prevalent death was in fiction. Even if no one died in these stories, lives were still ruined just for the sake of advancing the plot or showing how powerful the antagonist was or some equally stupid reason. How could I enjoy that?

There was one particular time. I had been reading an old fantasy novel by Roger Zelazny. He wrote this old series of short books which were always high in absurdist space fantasy but played completely straight. Not my favorite, but not my least favorite either. I've never actually made it through all of them. I'd been in the middle of one, *The Hand of Oberon*, and I couldn't stop seeing openings. It was taking all of the willpower I had not to enter. Then on one particular opening, right when I thought I had the timing down on resisting, I was struck harder than I had ever been before. This was not a gentle invitation; it was the sensation of having your back to the ocean and being swallowed by a wave with all of the impact and lack of preparedness that implies. Still, my defenses were up, and I resisted, and I found myself for the first time caught between here and there. It felt like I was encased in sap that was being sucked into a vacuum. All around me were conflicting colors of indigo and turquoise and pearl. In every direction were shapes and trees and stars and people and it all changed moment to moment. It couldn't have lasted longer than a second or two, but it took everything I had to power out of it and with an effort of will I was once again home and in my bed. I slammed the book shut and flung it on instinct, terrified of what was inside. But it just lay there on the ground, a simple book. Pages and ink. Nothing special.

It was then that I did everything I could to avoid this happening again. I started to take long drives for no reason, the music I listened to told their stories without lyrics. I tried to go hiking and exercise in places that I had to get to physically. I wasn't particularly good, but it kept my mind and body busy, eating up precious hours to get me through the day. I did volunteer work on my days off wherever I could find it. Animal shelters, the LA Mission, the senior center; whatever I could find. I even began to sleep a full eight hours every night with the thought that if I were asleep, I wouldn't have to worry about being entertained. None of it was truly working; however, my mind kept drifting.

I was starting to run out of distractions, and surprised at how small my world felt in such a small amount of time. I could tell everyone around me was starting to see something was wrong as well. For one thing, I hadn't been late to work once, something which made Claire suspicious. Olivia kept coming up with reasons to have me around, even when I could tell she'd rather be alone. I could always tell with her; her concern was outweighing her desire for alone time. It hurt me that was I was doing that to another person, even if I could appreciate how lucky I was to have someone like that around me at all.

Paolo had shaken me. How could he not? The idea that everything was real was more than enough to... I don't know. Freeze me? It's just too big. Put aside even more personal things like the tragic death of a side character or something along those lines, what does this say about every disaster movie or zombie TV show? And who else knows about this? If you were a writer and you knew what you wrote would actually happen to someone, somewhere, how could you tell those stories? Maybe it doesn't even work in that order. Maybe the writers are writing from a place of vision. A thing happened somewhere, and they're historians, just showing the world what happened. Does that mean there truly is no such thing as creativity? Either way, it seems like there's no good answer here. Like I said, too big.

While I was lost in thought, Olivia had gone to the door for a food delivery. I hadn't even noticed earlier that she had placed an order or that she had left the couch until she returned and handed me a hot, white clamshell case. I knew what it was before I opened it: Spaghetti Aglio from *Folliero's*. It was more garlic and red pepper than pasta. I'm surprised that I didn't just smell the delivery car before the door even opened. She was hitting the comfort food hardcore for me right now, which left me to wonder: Just how messed up did I appear right now? I tried to ignore the question and focus on my feast, and because of that, I missed another key event.

Olivia plopped hard onto the couch next to me, remote already pointed at her television. "All right nerd, I got your favorite food and *Eternity Pilgrim* ready to go. No more bad time for you!" It was said with mock authority.

I couldn't even protest as the screen came to life and the cold open of an episode of one of my favorite shows began to play. I wanted to yell no, or to grab the remote, or for a localized meteor strike to hit just this very particular part of her home, but it was too late. The show had begun, and I couldn't look away.

I remembered this episode well. It wasn't one of the bigger episodes or anything. I wouldn't call any episode of *Eternity Pilgrim* a filler episode really, but some are clearly more memorable than others. That just happens. This episode featured a Procyon, one of the lesser known monsters from the show; that was left behind from the rest of its clan. And somehow it ends up in the storage room at this huge department store, moving between walls as it terrorizes the occasional employee or stray customer until at some point the Pilgrim catches wind of it and decides to investigate. Eventually, the Procyon dies, mainly due to exposure from the atmosphere on earth. It just wasn't designed to live in our environment and had been doomed from the start. The episode really just existed to give the Pilgrim reason to be on earth in current times to set up for a larger plot. He's on a pilgrimage through time and space; sometimes you need to write in an excuse for him to be somewhere.

This was the cold open. I couldn't look away. Two women, one older and one younger, were chatting about a sale. Both were decidedly British, as you'd expect from British television. They needed more shirts from the back. The older woman asks the younger employee to be a dear and get them for her.

Oh, no. Oh, God no, I remember this now! The younger worker, she smiles and says sure. She's off soon anyway; she doesn't mind helping. The Procyon is back there. It is so many things: Confused. Hungry. She steps into the back. I'm crying suddenly. She's facing away from the corner. The Procyon lurches from behind her. Teeth are bared. She senses something behind her. She turns, and her eyes go wide. She wants to scream, but it's too late. The opening credits play. I can't breathe. I can't. I hurt everywhere. The Pilgrim is now eating a banana while looking on a monitor in his ship trying to find his comrade who is lost somewhere in time. I almost throw up.

I'm vaguely aware of Olivia asking me if everything is alright. How could it be? I'm furious and confused. What had that woman done to deserve that? She went to work. I only saw her for a moment, but she had been kind to the elderly. She seemed friendly. She was a person! Now she's a footnote. I felt hot, then suddenly I began to feel a chill. Like a breeze? No, air conditioning? Was I standing?

"Can I help you?" a British woman asked, older than me and concerned.

I looked up, wiping away tears to see my surroundings. This was the store! From the show! Did I travel? Then, I saw something that flared every nerve in my body. The younger employee, walking towards the back! I couldn't think about anything else just then; I had to... what? These were characters! I'd seen this already! What would happen if I interfered?

"Excuse me!" I shouted without thinking. That was much louder than I knew I was capable of. The older woman in front of me stiffened. The younger woman jumped slightly, startled. She turned towards me.

"Yes?" she asked, smiling.

"I need help!" I tried to make it sound like a request, but I practically screamed this. I wasn't thinking the situation through, but it was too late.

"I'd be happy to—" the older woman started.

"No! Her!" I snapped. I wasn't in control. I could feel it, all of it in me swirling. The panic, the uncertainty, and the fear. I needed this to happen, but I needed control first. "Sorry." I managed to use a proper indoor voice now and began to mumble. "Sorry. Sorry. We're just much closer to the same size, is all. I'm sorry." We were not the same size, it was evident.

"I'm happy to help, but we're in the children's section," she said. I noticed the actual clothes around here for the first time, and sure enough, they were for toddlers. "I love this, by the way!"

I was still wearing a onesie with panels of a comic book printed all over it. Thankfully there were no spaghetti stains from my recent meal, which I was certain had spilled somewhere back in Olivia's living room.

"Oh. Thank you," I said, wiping away the last of the tears from my eyes. "It's from *The Avatars of Justice*. It's a comic book. I like it a lot."

She suddenly looked at me with a new expression, the smile leaving. "Is everything okay? You're crying." The way she asked I could tell I was her full focus and she wanted to help me. I almost laughed at the idea and then felt sick again at why that might have been morbidly funny.

"I'm fine now. It's nothing. It's nothing," I said, more quietly than I would have liked. I was mortified.

"Marilyn," she said past me to the older employee. "I'm off in ten, so I'm just going to get some coffee from the break room and take off early, okay?"

"Of course, dear," Marilyn replied, and I could hear the concern and understanding from her as well.

"Come on," she said to me with a comforting rub on my shoulder. "There's a break room where we can talk."

We walked out of the department area and eventually down a corridor that went past a pair of bathrooms. The department store was fairly big, and that seemed to be expected. It was several floors, and from what I remembered of it from the episode it carried clothes for everyone you could think of, shoes, luggage, tools, appliances, and electronics. We weren't walking past any of that, though; these corridors seemed to run behind the showrooms. I couldn't have been sure if the walk was long or if I was just feeling numb and uncomfortable.

We finally arrived in the break room, a windowless place that sat in the corner of one of the buildings. It looked like it was a spot that regularly held two or three dozen people at a time for lunch, but for now, it was empty save for the two of us.

She motioned to the room in a way that suggested I choose our table, and I did. "So what's your name?" She asked me with a smile as we sat.

"Elana," I replied, still numb. I felt like a child in the principal's office.

"That's an excellent name, Elana. Very pretty. I'm Charlie." Her introduction was friendly with sympathetic overtones, despite having no way of knowing what to be sympathetic for. "Sorry to get you out of there like that, it just seemed like you needed a minute."

I nodded. A quiet moment. It felt like Charlie was waiting for me to say something.

"I'll get us coffee, okay?" she said, standing up. I think she was just uncomfortable and needed to do something.

I nodded again, understanding that feeling. She walked away towards a big, automatic coffee maker. The kind that needs to have special packets put into it. Something felt different. In the air, in me, I couldn't tell. Not right or wrong, just different. That's when it hit me that for the first time, really the first time I directly involved myself with characters in the middle of their story.

Charlie was dead a moment ago, largely forgotten by the universe. Now she was making me a cup of instant coffee. It was like breaking an heirloom when the owner wasn't there to scold you yet. I had no idea what I'd done. Was this good? It had to be, right? Charlie was humming. It's not usually a bad thing when someone is humming.

Without thinking I bolted upright from my chair, sending it backward into another chair with a crash. The noise startled Charlie enough that she dropped the coffee as her mouth went agape, trying to think of something to say to me. A thought gripped me like ice, the idea that the monster was still in the breakroom and I left an old woman alone with it. She was probably going for those damned shirts any minute now. Charlie said she was almost off, meaning someone would be there to replace her any second, and someone else would take her place if I didn't act.

I'm not the monster fighting type, I'm not stupid, but I saw a fire alarm on the way in here. I had to reach it as soon as I could, and this onesie was not meant for speed. I dashed through the halls, I practically fell into the alarm I got there, shattering the glass with the tiny hammer and tripping the alarm. An obnoxious, deafening noise signaled to everyone in the building they had to leave. That didn't solve the problem long term, but it helped for the moment. I collapsed to the floor, spent and past overwhelmed by how much of a mess I'd made of things. So much for not getting involved in the story.

"Yeah, that ought to do it," I said out loud to myself. I blinked, and I was gone, back in Highland Park, face to face with a wide-eyed Olivia.

There was a long moment where the only thought in my head was that I regret everything, and for the dumbest of reasons. I had every chance in the world to let someone else in and to show someone that I trusted them by showing them what I could do. Olivia would have probably been at the top of that list. Should be at the top of that list. And she got to find out by watching her friend suddenly blink of existence in front of her and then, well, I don't know what she saw. Her carpet stained? It was stupid, but I looked down at the food. Still in clamshell, no mess. Huh, that was a good thing. Maybe things were alright after all.

"How the—?" she started, words trying to pour out of her in a panic, which immediately sucked me back into a panic. I couldn't help it, I spoke over her.

"What did you see?" It came out as a defensive shout; as if I was trying to hide something.

"No, you don't get to—"

"You're right, I just—"

"Where did you go?"

"I was in the—"

"In the—?"

"Yeah, and I—!"

A thought hit me like a bucket of ice water being poured from the roof of a ten-story building. "We have to watch the show! Where's the remote?" I shouted, searching the couch and flipping over my blanket. She held her hand towards me, still holding it. I snatched it from her desperately and restarted the episode.

"Are you going to talk to me?" she asked. Or demanded. One of the two.

"Sit down and watch!" It was half mania, half command. It worked, and she sat next to me, and my eyes were focused on the show in a way that I couldn't remember since I was young. The cold open began. Two women were talking about a sale. They needed more shirts from the back.

Something is different. There's a shot of the Procyon in the storage room. The younger woman, I know her name is Charlie now; she turns around because of some disturbance. The viewer can't see it, but it's me.

Damn it. I must have been a wreck, she looks perplexed. Another shot, now from the point of view of the Procyon looking out through the doors of the stock room. You can see Charlie, and she walks away. The Procyon is confused and wanders away to another part of the stockroom. The last shot is the older woman, looking concerned and resigned to her job. Suddenly a fire alarm sounds, causing the woman to jump a little. Opening credits. Theme song.

I let out a loud whoop of pure exaltation. Olivia recoiled at the sound of that and was already off balance when I tackled her into a hug.

"Okay," she said. "Just let me get the—"

Her free hand made it to the remote, and she paused the show. "There. It's okay." She returned the hug for a moment before asking, "What's happening?"

I told her everything. Absolutely everything. Things she probably didn't need to know. It was like I was dying by keeping everything inside. I revealed my fears, my concerns, but also every beautiful thing I've ever experienced using my powers. She had questions. I don't think she believed me at first, but not in the sense that I was lying. She actually couldn't believe in the idea of making yourself fictional. I didn't blame her. it's an insane idea.

I told her about Lucia and when we were children. I told her that I believed Lucia, at least at the time and that the idea that she could jump into those stories as well wasn't the craziest thought, she just talked about it years before I had the chance to experience it first-hand. She wanted to know if this was something I could teach. I told her the truth, I didn't know. After all, how do you teach someone to see something? I told her about my first time, as well as my second and third. At first, it had been so terrifying. I somehow knew less then than I know now if that is even possible. I just remember not knowing if I was going to be able even to make it back. I thought maybe I'd been dosed or something, or that my life was coming to an end and this is what a coma felt like. I told her that if I ever looked unusually tired, that was probably the reason. Once, I went missing for three days and missed a day of work. Claire had questions, so I'd said I was super sick and she eventually let it go. But if I ever seemed really out of it, it was probably because on occasion I was packing 36 hours into a 24-hour day. And Oh my God, the food! She was usually too polite to mention my eating habits, but I knew she noticed.

"It's like doing this burns ten thousand calories on the way back!" I told her. "I am starving every time. Actually starving."

I even told her about my copy of *Jane Eyre* and George and the bugs. "Wait, that was actually on the news," she said to me, pulling up an article on her phone. I skimmed through it, reading about how something about a bug called a Tansy Beetle, previously an endangered species, had been found by the thousands all over Los Angeles. No one was quite sure how they got here or in such large numbers, but some believed that maybe they were brought over by boat on accident and started breeding during the trip.

Well, that's dumb. Then again, it was more reasonable than the possibility that I brought them back from a hundred years ago and a different universe.

"So you must have brought back those bugs with you!" she said, excited by solving a puzzle.

"I'm on the fence about that. It's definitely possible, but I think the bugs thing is actually a coincidence," I told her, explaining the bathroom incident. "When I came back, I think we both would have noticed thousands and thousands of insects in your house."

The bathtub is her moment where things click into place.

"I knew that didn't make sense! I'd been to the bathroom, and you weren't there!" she said somehow relieved. "I knew I just didn't see you."

"Yeah, opened a portal. Maybe. Or teleported. Unmade? Something."

"I'm going to hit you with like, every question right now, is that okay?" she asked. I nodded, but my thoughts were on food. The garlic was stronger than ever. "All the questions. Every single one. Are you sure?"

She follows my gaze to the food. "You want to eat first, don't you?"

"I really do. And can we watch the rest of the episode?" I ask. "For reasons?"

"Yeah, totally," I quickly agreed.

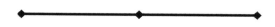

The rest of the episode happened exactly like I remembered it. Nothing broke as far as I could tell. I don't know if "broke" is the right word, but everything remained in one piece. Well, one piece doesn't feel right either, but I'm not going to get anything else done today if I can't move past the mere verbiage of reality.

"Good episode," Olivia said carefully. "Fun the way the Pilgrim saved the day from the thing, alien, guy." Another pause. "I'm only asking because I'm genuinely not sure, but did we watch that episode again because you just really wanted to see it or because it was connected to whatever you did earlier?"

I literally jumped to my feet as I answered. To be honest, it kind of hurt my ankles a bit but I was too excited to care. "Both! Sort of. You get it, right? You understand?"

"... No?"

"No, of course you wouldn't, but that's okay. It really is, and I'll tell you!" I must have looked insane to her right now. "Because nothing happened! We didn't blow up the world!"

"Was that a concern?" Olivia asked, genuinely concerned.

"Maybe. Probably not, but that's not the point! I saved that woman! And nothing bad happened!" I was practically yelling at this point. "I can save them, Olivia! I can save everyone!"

The thought must have dawned on her because she slowly started shaking and realization spread over her face. "So that clerk, you actually saved her life? She was dead?"

"Yes! Charlie! Remember what you saw?" I pressed. "Do you remember both intros?"

"I do! She died and then you came back and then she didn't. Hold on!" Olivia pulled out her phone and seemed to scroll through YouTube clips and fan pages. "I don't see anything about the intro where she died! It doesn't exist! How is that possible?"

The sick feeling in my stomach, the one that told me I'd done something terribly wrong tried to come back, but it was overwhelmed by the elation of the feeling that I was somewhere new, somewhere I wasn't supposed to be, and I was there anyway.

"Best answer? It doesn't matter. Not even a little bit. Charlie is alive because of me. And if I can do that, what do I care if the world remembers things a bit differently? They don't understand the show the way you and I do!"

"It's actually crazier than that," Olivia said, still looking at her phone. "Charlie has been announced as the new comrade in the next season. 'New Pilgrim, new Comrade, same pilgrimage.' Apparently, fans are calling it a brilliant piece of foreshadowing. Some hate the idea, but some fans hate everything."

I thought to myself that's not technically what foreshadowing means, as I looked on her phone. I let it go. "Even better!" I exclaimed. "She will do wonderfully!"

"Okay, but hold on a second," she said. I recognized that look. This was getting to be too much for her. "Think of the very real world implications here. This actress is now going to be on a TV show full time because you saved her fictional character in a TV show. By jumping into it. But at some point, writers must have sat down and decided they wanted to use this actress and they wrote stories with her in them, developed a character for her, even just getting the press release signed must have required a few people to say okay before it went out. So how did it go out if you just did this?"

I started to answer but Olivia seemed on the verge of having a freak out of her own. She shouted, "You altered reality! What if I'm supposed to be a painter?"

"You're a terrible painter," I said sadly. "I love you, but really—"

"Or what if I'm supposed to be French?" she continued, her breaths now coming quickly and shallow.

I didn't know where to start with that. "What?" I asked. It was all I could manage.

She really looked like she might have been on the verge of hyperventilation now. "So, like, I'm half French now, I just meant like, if I were actually in France and... I don't know, okay? Just, how would we know if you changed things in the real world?"

"That's the point!" I nearly shouted. "I did change the real world! This one and that one!" Why was my mouth so dry all of a sudden? "Whatever else happened, I saved someone."

"Yeah," Olivia agreed. "Yeah, you did."

"Yeah, I did!" I echoed. "I saved someone's life!"

I felt like singing! My body seemed to want to burst with pure sunlight. My face stretched in a smile so large that it hurt which only made me elated. "I know what to do! I see what I'm supposed to do with these abilities or powers or whatever! I have a purpose, and I'm going to live it!"

I embraced Olivia in an adrenaline fueled hug before gripping her hands. "I'm going to save them! I'm going to travel until I don't know which way is up and I'm going to eat so many burritos because the food is a part of it and when it's done I will save them!"

"Who?" she asked, searching my face. I gave Olivia a long look with a knowing grin. I knew my purpose now.

"Everyone."

"I promise that I'm not complaining," Claire said to me as she prepped the week's online orders. "But you're clearly in a different mood. What gives?"

It was one of those amazing Los Angeles days that got overcast in a way that seems to happen nowhere else. I had pulled back the heavy curtains on all of the windows for the day, and bits of sunlight were leaking in despite the distinct chill in the air.

"Am I?" I asked. I could feel the smile reach my eyes as I sipped my tea. Mood aside, I'm definitely someone who likes a warm beverage on a chilly day. Jameson seemed to yawn in response. It could have also just been an ordinary cat yawn.

"You just seemed really out of it the past few weeks. You hadn't borrowed a single book. Now, look at you!" She gestured around the shop. "You've been early every day this week. The place is spotless. The coffee even tastes good! What are you doing differently?"

"Salt and vanilla extract!" I beamed. Now that she mentioned it, I did a hell of a job cleaning the place, actually. We almost looked like a proper bookstore.

Claire's eyebrows rose at that. "Wow, really? Salt?" She eyed her cup in amazement. "The point is, the benefit to the shop is undeniable, but the real difference is in you. You've just thrown yourself into everything. There's hardly anything left for me to even do here anymore."

"Well thank you, I guess I have been feeling better lately. You're not trying to go home early, are you?" I teased.

"My shop, we open and close on my say so," she said flatly. "And no, I'm just curious. You're my friend, and I get this sense like... like events are happening in your life that I know nothing about."

There was a turn in the conversation. Genuine concern crossed her face. "You don't *have* to tell me if you're not comfortable, but I want you to know that whatever is going on, good or bad, you *can* tell me."

I felt a twinge of guilt at that. Claire's eyes were on me, and she wasn't looking away. I felt like I'd already made this mistake once, and I was going to make it again.

"It's just life," I said. "I promise you that I'm okay. I have these moods sometimes, but right now I'm in a good place." Nothing I said was a lie, but I couldn't help but feel rotten about having good news and not being able to share it, but what could I say exactly? *I've embraced chaos, Claire. I've decided to rewrite history as a full-time hobby. I am definitely not an alien, an '80s sitcom character told me so.* I laughed unexpectedly at that.

"Being in a good place is funny?" Claire asked.

"No, just, remember that video where that guy takes a mannequin to that vegetable garden and messed up 'This Charming Man' until he's yelled at to leave by all those seniors?" It was a funny video, but not what made me laugh.

"This Farming Man? It really wasn't that funny. Those people are old, they just want to garden in peace. They probably don't even know what YouTube is."

"They're old enough to remember The Smiths though," I countered. "You'd think they'd get it."

"I'm old enough to remember The Smiths!" she shot back.

"Oh dang, really?" I asked, suddenly remembering Claire's high school photos. That makeup haunts me.

"So are you! Morrissey still performs," she sighed. "Without a shirt and it's kind of weird and he sort of looks like someone's uncle who refuses to cover themselves while they grill in the park. But he's not ancient or anything."

"I could get corn tonight!" I began to sing, my body a poor imitation of British, sad boy flourish. I never finished because Claire threw a muffin at me.

"You're fired," she said, sipping her coffee. "Not really, this coffee is delicious. And sorry about the muffin, that was kind of aggressive."

"I was eating that." I pouted.

"Then have another on me," she said, pretending to ring up a sale.

I decided to have a somewhat serious discussion with Claire, opening up as much as I could at the moment. "Listen, you know I love you, and I'm incredibly grateful to have you as a part of my life. There will always be times that I'll want to come to you, but my brain is kind of broken. I do things without knowing why. I'm irrational, and I don't always relate to everybody. I have times where I want to cry or stop existing or just want to know that I'm not the only one who feels lost."

Claire seemed to stiffen at the sudden shift in the conversation, not looking at me with sympathy or down on me, but taking in every word. I continued. "You're one of the few people I really feel I can talk to and I hope never to lose you, but there are times that I don't feel I can talk to anyone, and that includes you. I understand this is irrational. Consciously I know this doesn't make any sense, but it just is what it is. The best I can hope to do is wait for that moment to pass. It can last an hour or a month, but I'll always appreciate the patience you show me. Cool?"

Claire looked like she wanted to cry and didn't say anything as she stepped forward to embrace me. It was the best possible thing she could have said, and I held her back, grateful for her understanding. The bell of the shop chimed just then, signaling the arrival of a customer. Neither of us looked up; the customer would just have to wait.

Olivia and I rolled down the 118 in my roughly car shaped metal box. She had her phone in the middle of a cup, amplifying the sound. I wasn't always certain who she was playing, but this was pleasant. Funny thing about my car is that everyone is always quick to point how dangerously close to evaporating it was, and yet at least half the people I knew didn't even have a car in the first place. So when we had the idea, well, when Olivia had the idea to visit Lucia; my car was the only real option.

Lucia's hospital was not convenient at all. Located in Ventura, it was a bare minimum of an hour and some change to get there, and my car wasn't excellent on gas. Or getting there. It wasn't a good excuse, but if I'm being honest, it's definitely something that has prevented me from making this trip more often. The 118 significantly extended the distance if not the time, but I'd much rather drive through the unexpected closeness of farmland and open sky than sit on the 101. With how congested it always seemed to get, it was probably a wash in terms of overall time spent in the car anyway now that I think about it. Besides, there was this one little stretch when it stopped being a freeway, and if you were lucky, you got to ride alongside the train, which was fun. For me at least. I might just be boring.

The drive and the silence gave me time to think about the past couple of weeks. I'd saved people three more times since Charlie, but honestly, it was starting to get a bit more dangerous. The first one took place in a supernatural detective novel. There had been a string of murders related to witches, and while I couldn't get to them all due to the fact they were talked about in the past tense, I got to the scene where a room was being investigated before it happened. The woman, a witch named Janice in her thirties who mostly hid that fact from the world, thankfully immediately believed me and got to safety in time. There was a flow to the book and other events were going to take place one way or the other, it was just a matter of keeping her away from the action until everything else caught up. Living as a witch meant she was open to the idea of getting killed by a witch hunter. I changed an entire chapter of the book, but outside of that, the rest went along the way it was supposed to. The wizard detective saved the day, Janice is back to work at her cubicle and relatively safe for the moment. As safe as one could be in a world filled with monsters and magic, but she's at least prepared.

The second time was a whole lot bigger. I saved an entire bar full of people. It was a relatively straightforward plot; an insane super villain had gas canisters on a timer filled with lethal gas. Initially, in the comic, a couple of dozen people died and it had been treated as a footnote. The hero investigated, found out fairly quickly who was behind it, had a showdown and they were arrested. This time I just called in a bomb threat and the building was evacuated. When they searched the building the canisters were discovered, superhero recognizes the work, still stops the bad guy and nothing really changed outside of the lives of those people. That one definitely felt good, but I think I got a little cocky going into the next one.

The third and last time was saving a child from being killed by a werewolf. Some twelve-year-old kid who wandered into the wrong part of town. It seemed like no matter what I tried; he kept on a path towards being at that old garage on the worst possible night. I told his parents he was sneaking out, I slashed the tires on his bike, I even tried to give him food poisoning, but he must have an iron stomach (Yes, I technically tried to poison a child.) He was still out there after everything. I ended up having to put myself in harm's way, going where I knew a freaking Werewolf was going to be and I scared him off before things got ugly. I blinked myself out of that world and back into my own while the werewolf was lunging at me. I didn't sleep for two days straight after that. Olivia was there to cheer me on the entire way, even helping me come up with the strategy before going in. We were making a great team.

I stretched hard when we finally arrived, popping various joints and likely giving me a full extra inch of height. At least it felt that way. It had drizzled on the way up, but now the threat of rain had subsided.

"I don't think Big Sister got enough of a shower," Olivia remarked, looking at the mud which had caked onto the car. It rained enough for the dust to turn into something worse, but not so hard that the car had been cleaned. Nothing had ever fully removed the bug carnage from the windshield either, that was going to take work.

"Just as well," I replied, closing the driver's side door. I rarely locked it, unless I had something inside. No one was taking this car. "I think maybe the dirt might actually be holding her together."

"Hold up a second," she said, stopping to turn towards me. "Are we sure this is a good idea? I know you two are close, but you're not certain Lucia is the same as you and I'm definitely not a mental health expert. This is something else, though. What if we make her worse?"

I took a moment to consider that. "I don't have the correct answer for you. And you're right, this is a huge guess, but if Lucia can do what I do and she's even considering that she might be crazy, she deserves to know she's not alone. You can stay out here if you want, but I'm going to talk with my friend."

Olivia looked resigned and said nothing more as we walked up the ramp to the hospital. It had been a while since I'd been here, but I've never been comfortable past these doors. Lucia was allowed visitors, and we could spend time together in the common areas, but this place still felt like a prison where the only crime was being different. I'm not saying that there weren't people here with legitimate needs, but I never really felt like Lucia belonged here. It felt like a slow death for her.

The lobby was mostly empty. No one sat in the waiting area chairs watching the daytime TV. Three women sat behind the reception area, two of them doing some kind of filing. "Can I help you?" one of the nurses asked us. The pleasant tone of her voice didn't reach her eyes, despite the creased wrinkles in her face that exaggerated her expressions.

"Visiting Lucia Cruz?" I'm not sure why I made it a question. Olivia wandered into the waiting area to check out the TV. The nurse grimaced and clicked a few keys on a keyboard.

"I'm sorry, there's no patient by that name. Are you at the right facility?"

I felt punched by the answer. "No, I'm positive she's here. Long-term patient? I haven't been to visit in a while, but this is—"

"Why don't you have a seat and I'll look into it," she said cutting me off. "Name?"

I hesitated.

"Your name?" she insisted.

"Elana Black," I replied, mildly perturbed.

"Someone will be right with you," she said, swiveling her chair away from me.

I walked over to Olivia who was watching an old movie, one of those middle of the day local television shows. I recognized Lee Marvin and Burt Lancaster, but I wasn't familiar with it.

"So, weird thing," I began.

"Yeah?" Olivia hadn't looked away from the screen.

"They have no record of Lucia," I said.

That got her attention.

"Well, it's a mistake, right?" She was squared up with me now with that look she got when she was ready to solve the problem, whatever it was. "Did they check the spelling?"

"I didn't get that far. That nurse brushed me off, told me to wait." Didn't seem too shocking, hospital staff isn't always, well, hospitable.

"Yeah, we just drove an hour and a half, so that's not going to work for me. Come on." She stood up and walked back towards reception briskly. I followed but was surprised to see everyone gone.

"Hello?" Olivia called out, leaning behind the counter.

Something was off. Why did all three of them leave? Their filing work looked abruptly abandoned. "This is weird," I muttered out loud.

"Rude, for sure," Olivia agreed. "Not exactly weird."

"Listen to that." I told her.

"To what?" She asked. "I don't hear anything besides the TV."

I jogged over to the remote in the lobby and hit the mute button. I might as well have been hitting mute on the world.

"That's weird, right?" I asked again, a little panic creeping into my voice.

"It's quiet, yeah," she agreed. "Where are the rest of the hospital sounds? No PA system, no machines, nothing."

I nodded towards one of the aisles leading towards the back and made my way over to it. Olivia walked beside me and I could sense she was also getting nervous. This was wrong. All of it. I peered into a couple of the rooms. No one was in any of them, though there was plenty of evidence that someone had been quite recently.

"We should probably go," Olivia cautioned. I was about to agree when about a hundred yards down the long hospital corridor I heard a sound.

Footsteps. Clicking on the floor, slow and deliberate. A man, dressed all in black rounded the corner. Perfect suit, insane hair. I'd seen him before, but where? He smiled, and it was terrible and devoid of mirth. He brought his left hand from behind his back, and with a flick of his wrist, he was holding a scythe.

The realization was the stuff of nightmares. I recognized him. I know who this was. Bres, the creepy customer from the store.

"Run!" I shouted, gripping Olivia by the sleeve and nearly pulling her down. We bolted back the way we came through the empty hospital and into the lobby. We stopped abruptly as we looked out below into the parking lot. Maybe two dozen people all wearing perfect suits of a solid color stood at the ready. White, Black, Red; whatever color they wore was solid from head to toe. And they noticed us.

10

Beyond my car and a handful of others probably belonging to employees, the parking lot was largely empty. Except, of course, for the gang of angry looking people in monochromatic suits about fifty yards away, including some wielding knives and batons. As if coordinated, they fanned out in different directions while two individuals, a man and a woman both in red, marched straight up to the main entrance not far from us.

"That doesn't look right, does it?" Olivia asked as we both stared.

"Everything about this looks definitively wrong," I agreed. "Come on!"

We ran back inside. The hospital lobby was our quickest way out, but we were not about to leave given what was outside. Directly ahead after the nurse's station was a corridor where Bres was presumably waiting. That left two options: the other hallway to the left or wait in the lobby and hope nothing horrible happened. I made a nod down the opposite hall, and Olivia seemed to agree with my leadership. Neither of us had to point out the elevator at the end of the corridor to each other, there was really no way to go but up given that we didn't see an immediate way down, and we didn't have much of a head start on whoever that was coming after us. A moment later, a pair of footsteps joined us without a word, gaining speed. We just reached the elevator doors when a sharp sting in my calf sent me tumbling forward, knocking Olivia over on the way down. We both hit the floor of the elevator and Olivia quickly reached up and swiped her hand hard across several of the numbers and the door close button. We saw the two red suited figures charging at us, trying to reach the elevator in time. The doors closed (more slowly than I wanted them too), and I finally let myself breathe when they did. I looked up. The camera had been ravaged into a mess of wires and cracked glass. *No witnesses. Awesome.*

The elevator stopped on the fourth floor first. I looked at Olivia questioningly and she shook her head, saying, "Further up. Let's go. We need to hide."

She stood and offered her hand to me. As I got up, my leg burned and I could feel the bruise already forming, but I was otherwise fine. I still couldn't see what actually hit me, though.

We stopped at the fifth floor, and I looked both ways before exiting. I limped a little at first, but my fight or flight mode was working overtime, and it wouldn't last long. We found an office unlocked a bit down one of the halls and ducked inside, shutting the door behind us and turning off the lights on instinct as we did. We crouched behind a desk and took a breather. Olivia already had her phone out and her expression was grim.

"No service," she said flatly. "You?"

I pulled my phone out of my coat pocket. The sudden illumination was a bit much for my eyes to handle in the dark, but I could see right away what I was afraid of.

"I'm dead too," I sighed, turning the light towards the desk. I found the landline and picked up the receiver, but there was nothing there either. "Well, guess we're not getting any help."

"Who the hell are these people?" Olivia demanded, keeping her voice to a harsh whisper.

I took another breath before I replied. "Scary guy. Weird hair. He came into work a while back, creeped everyone out. He didn't have a, what was it? Did he seriously have a scythe?"

"Yeah, he did!" Olivia incredulously confirmed. "And he seemed entirely too comfortable holding it!"

"That he did. His name was Bres. He was looking for a book. We blew him off."

Olivia nodded in acknowledgment. "Okay, now we know, maybe next time you sell him the book. What do we do next?"

"I need a minute to think," I told her trying to steady my breathing. "Just a minute."

Okay, five senses. I'm largely in hysterically calm mode anyway, but I can get through this. All right, what's first? Just pick a sense. The sight of—no. No good. The leg is aching too much. Okay, start there. Breathe in. And out. In. And out. Match your breathing to the throbbing.

"We could set a fire!" Olivia's eyes lit up as she said it.

"What? No, we're not burning down a hospital!" I exclaimed, genuinely surprised at the fact that her first idea was arson. Damn it. I had to start over.

"No, it would be a distraction!" she reiterated, proud of her eureka moment.

I tried to center myself before I replied. "We would be in the building. Surrounded by people with ill will. You're not thinking this through. There's a lesson about frying pans and fires that you might find applicable. Now really, I need a moment."

Well, I was distracted now, if not exactly in the way Olivia intended. It was just enough to forget about my growing leg bruise. *All right, where can I start. There's not much to see, nothing to in the air to taste. God, even my hearing is off from the throbbing reaching my ear drums. I just need one sense to start, though.* I began rubbing my hands over the coarse carpet. That was a good place to start.

There was a crackle and pop over the hospital PA system, and a familiar voice came crackling over every speaker.

"Hello, Elana Black! And I guess... Elana's friend? What's her face? Eh, not important!" It was unmistakably Bres, though now he sounded more like a game show host. *"Ladies and gentleman within the sound of my voice, I'd like to offer you my sincere thanks for your assistance in this matter. And, on a personal note, good hunting!"*

I didn't need the clarity of senses. The situation was clear. I turned to Olivia and quickly said, "They're going to sweep the hospital and it won't take them long to search the first few floors and when they get here, if we're still here, we are done."

"This probably won't work, but if Elana's sidekick would like to turn her in, we promise to let you walk right out the front door," Bres said over the PA and then paused. *"No? Well, it was worth a shot, right?"*

I opened the door a crack and poked my head out, thankfully not seeing anyone else. It also immediately occurred to me that had anyone else actually been out there we would have been instantly screwed. That was kind of a stupid move. I should plan better.

"All clear," I whispered, feigning confidence. No reason for us both to know I had no idea what I was doing.

"Wait!" Olivia hissed at me, grabbing my shoulder. "I have a plan. A real one."

Her expression was grim.

"Does it involve fire?" I asked. Even I didn't know why I was cracking jokes right now.

"Look, the power isn't off, just the phones, right?" she began, and I acknowledged with a nod. "And this guy, he said it himself—He's not interested in me. We've passed rooms with televisions. I've seen a few books sitting out. You could just—"

"Absolutely not!" I nearly yelled, locking eyes with her and giving her my full attention. I could feel my face flush and heat up. Elsewhere, Bres continued his mad, arrogant monologue but I'd tuned it out. "Those people have attacked us and somehow they made an entire hospital staff disappear! I am not leaving you alone with them! Are you out of your mind?"

"No, they attacked *you*," Olivia corrected, concern obvious in her voice. "I just happened to be there. But what about, you know, trying to take me with you?"

That hadn't even occurred to me.

"I don't think I can! I've never tried it, and I don't know what would happen. You could be killed! I've brought something back with me once—"

"Twice," Olivia said. "Beetles and the book."

"Two different things, but same instance," I said. "But I don't know how I did it. Every other time I've tried to bring something back, it just evaporates. Or... something. What if I end up in another world and you're here alone? Or worse, what if you disintegrate? Now's not the time to experiment!"

She considered this while Bres continued over the intercom. *"You know, if you two die today, it will only be your fault, Elana. You did this. Your death will be, well... mostly forgettable, wouldn't it? It's not like you've done much with it so far, have you? But your little friend there, she'd die just for being your accomplice. Shame."*

Hearing the word "die," my blood ran cold. I wouldn't let that happen. Olivia gripped my shoulder, and I jumped as she locked eyes with me.

"Elana, look at me. Look," she said sternly. "Neither of us are going to die. We'll both get out of here, okay?"

"Yeah, sure, okay," I replied meekly. Why was she trying to convince me? I kind of felt like it was my turn to do something convincing.

Our conversation must have gotten someone's attention because I'd no sooner heard the footsteps down the hall then Olivia pulled me back into the office we'd originally ducked into before throwing her phone down the opposite hall, ricocheting it around the corner. Two men in red suits must have fallen for it, as I peeked through a crack in the open door I saw them dash past our room and around that corner, both of them holding what looked to be ceremonial daggers of some sort. Curved greenish blades that shimmered as they moved.

I could hear them stop for a moment, maybe to inspect the phone. Then the footsteps continued and faded away down the opposite hallway. "That was your phone!" I whispered in harsh disbelief. Who just throws their phone like that?

"The stairs, come on!" Olivia hissed back, grabbing my arm. We ran as silently as possible. When we got to the stairs, she peaked her head inside, gave a glance up and down, then motioned for me to follow. We made our way up a full floor before we heard movement above us. With no other choice, we ducked into the sixth floor, opening and closing the door as quietly as we could. No one was waiting for us, fortunately. Without waiting an extra second, Olivia dragged me into a small examination room.

"All right. Okay. New floor. That's something. We just need to figure out what we do now." Olivia said pensively; I wasn't sure if she was talking to herself or me.

"Can we stop for a moment?" I demanded. "Where is all of this coming from?"

"Well, I don't want to die, and one of us had to do something!" she snapped back with a mirthless laugh.

"I was going to figure something out!" I began to protest. I stopped, seeing how Olivia's expression changed.

"Are you serious? Have you seen yourself?" she asked. "You're sweating. You're literally shaking. I had to physically drag you away from danger. Look!"

She spun me around towards the direction of a mirror. I couldn't believe it; I was a portrait of panic. My left hand was actually shaking and wouldn't stop. "I'm trying to keep us alive! I am not at all equipped to survive this, but we *both* can't be petrified. I'm scared too, but whatever. Unless you're either going to get it together, or get a new superpower, you just have to trust me."

I took a few breaths. I couldn't let us die here, so yeah, it was time to make with my best superheroine impression.

"Right. You're right. I'm better," I said with a couple of quick hops to release some of the tension. "You're right. We got this."

"That's fantastic because I have no idea what to do next," Olivia replied with a sigh.

"You know, my superiors seem to think you deserve a warning," Bres interrupted over the PA system. *"I don't. I don't think there's a damn thing any of us can say to get you to stop really, so why bother? You insist on leaving a bloody mess everywhere you go. Hell, you've already figured out the Cruz girl, so you're not likely to stop, are you?"*

"What he's talking about?" Olivia asked.

"No clue," I answered. "He's probably just trying to get under our skin, right?"

"Right."

"I have a plan, but it's desperate and stupid." *And largely based on television because I've never really been in this situation before.*

"I'll take it," Olivia replied.

"This is pure speculation, but I think the higher up we go, the more spread out they are. There are multiple ways up to the higher floors, and they're probably sending people up, but they're going to be gathered on the ground since that's the only feasible way out. We're not getting out the front, but if we can get to the roof we might just be able to, I don't know, flag someone down or something. Or just lock everyone inside and wait until they leave or maybe they'll just, I don't know, burn down the hospital themselves."

"The stairs are still blocked, how do we make it there in the first place?" Olivia asked.

"This is the dumb part," I continued. "We send the elevator down to the first floor. There's like, a thirteen percent chance that they bite. Before you ask how I came up with that number, don't. This probably isn't going to work, and I'm going to get us killed."

"I'm not scared at all," Olivia said, about as sarcastically as I've ever heard her.

I shrugged. "Let's do it."

As we left the room, Bres spoke again, and it took everything within me not to yell at him to shut the hell up.

"You know, when people talk about forces bigger than them, they often speak of things outside of their control like shadowy government agents or earthquakes, or God, or any number of other stupid things they could have just planned for."

I hit the button on the elevator. I could hear the movement in the staircase. It might have been working.

"And while you indeed have been messing with forces much bigger than yourself, something I'd love to make you pay for; I want you to be assured that those are not the forces you need to be worried about."

We stood still, quietly, until the footsteps faded away. I threw open the door and we dashed up the last flight of stairs to the small ladder leading to the roof. The hatch was even un-locked, our luck was actually picking up.

"The only force you should worry about, the one who de-cides if you live or not, is me. And Elana... I am so much bigger than you."

As I pushed the hatch open, a gale force wind sent me hard to the ground, taking Olivia with me and, ironically, knocking the wind out of both of us. I found it oddly funny for half a mo-ment, but as I looked up, the wild-haired silhouette framed by the sunlight pouring in through the hatch removed any humor.

"The smaller they are, the harder they fall, eh?" Bres gloat-ed into a wireless microphone, his voice still echoing from the PA. He floated down to the ground somehow, as if he had al-ways been standing in mid-air, but there was no time to be shocked by this. "Good enough, all. Go home; I'll handle the rest."

Olivia was still down, but I tried to get to my feet, my legs shaky (maybe from the shock, maybe from the fall, I don't know). The instant I was upright, Bres sharply pointed a finger in my direction. Immediately, something I couldn't see slammed into my stomach, harder than I could ever remember being hit. I didn't even make a noise as I doubled over; one just wouldn't come out of me.

"You've got to learn, Ms. Black, that your actions have consequences. The world will always demand balance. That's the job it's given me."

As he said that, a sickly red glow began crawling up his fin-gers, growing brighter, extending further from his skin with each subtle flick of his hand. A sick grin spread over his face as he gestured at Olivia, releasing a fireball towards her.

Even before the flame left his hand, I was on my feet again. I'll never know where I found the energy to move as fast as I did, or remember what I screamed as I moved, but I somehow threw myself between the fire and Olivia, squeezing my eyes shut in the process. Through my closed eyelids, I saw a bright flash of blue and red competing with each other, followed by brilliant black and then... nothing? No burning, for a moment not even any sound.

I opened my eyes and blinked rapidly as they adjusted to the light again. In front of me stood a bright shimmering half sphere crackling with sparks, like a curved wall of electricity. Around us, the stairwell had been scorched. Bres for his part looked amused. I remembered to breathe, and then the half sphere evaporated.

"Nice," Bres said flatly. Then, with a casual wave of his hand, he excitedly said, "Let's see you do it again!" Another burst of wind knocked me down next to Olivia, who seemed to be awake and alert again finally. Bres stood over us, looking... disappointed? "Like I thought," he remarked as he slowly, deliberately walked down the stairs, leaving us. "You're done, Elana. This is about as easy as it will ever get for you. Next time you travel, I start making bodies, and they're going to be ones you'll recognize. I trust that threat wasn't too thinly veiled for you. Farewell."

There was nothing to do but watch him leave. We were helpless, but alive.

11

We took our time getting to our feet. I didn't see the need to rush. I'd never been attacked like that before in my entire life. Come to think of it; I don't think I'd ever really been attacked. The longer I sat, the more I realized how dangerous that situation had actually been. Two dozen people, at least, somehow managed to empty a hospital and came after me, specifically. They had hunted me down. They'd carried weapons, and clearly, had horrific intentions. And if that wasn't enough, my stalker had... I don't know, magic? Super powers? Unreal. How were we still alive after all that?

I became more aware of Olivia who, like me, was slumped against the wall and breathing heavily. I was in a car accident once in high school, struck by a drunk driver in the middle of night. We actually went through a rail and off the side of the freeway. It sounds much worse than it actually was, everyone walked away. How I felt the day after that crash was close to how I felt now. If the adrenaline was masking the pain like it had after the accident, I could only imagine how we were going to feel in the morning.

"You okay?" I managed to say to Olivia between my own gasping breaths.

She shot me an exhausted, pained look that said, "Really dumb question." Then she winced.

"Yeah, I know," I said apologetically. Neither of us really knew what do next. We just kind of sat in silence for a while. My hyperawareness was fading, being replaced by a bizarre calm. I was unaware of how long we even sat there by the time, couldn't have been more than a couple of minutes; before I heard movement and the typical sounds of a hospital resuming below us. That felt like as good a cue as any to get up, and that was not without difficulty. Our first stop was to head back to the fifth floor to try and find Olivia's phone. None of the staff paid any attention to us, and sure enough, her phone was right where she threw it, though now with the added feature of a cracked screen.

It was surreal. Everyone seemed to be going about their daily business as if nothing had happened. Was everyone just pretending? That seemed unlikely, but most of the people milling about weren't giving any indication they knew what just happened. I wanted to say something to someone, anything, but what good would that do? If they were pretending, then they would lie, and if they weren't…

Instead, we gingerly made our way to the elevator and rode it down in silence. The knowing expression and the sick grin on the nurse's face as we made our way through the lobby erased any doubt in my head about whether or not they had been involved. This wasn't a safe place; it was a snake pit. We were leaving defeated, and she knew it. "You two have a nice day." She didn't break eye contact with me. My skin crawled.

We got into my car wordlessly and I drove. I didn't bother to check the map and I was distracted, so 15 minutes later it was evident pretty quickly that I made a wrong turn when we found ourselves on a particularly twisty road away from our usual scenic route. Olivia looked at me strangely as I suddenly pulled off into the dirt on the side of the road near the farming fields, surrounded by nothing. She looked even more concerned when I burst into a cackling laughter.

"What's happening? Why are you laughing? What is this?" she asked anxiously. I couldn't answer, I was still howling with laughter. "I mean it; this is scary. Is this you going crazy? Do I need to drive?"

"You...! You...!" I couldn't get more than a word out. Tears were streaming down my face, my cheeks burned, and I thought I might pass out if I didn't stop soon.

"Okay, me. Yes. What about me?" Olivia asked, focused on me.

"I can't believe you threw your phone!" I finally shouted before erupting in more laughter.

"Are you serious right now? We almost died!" Olivia shouted. She seemed offended maybe. Annoyed at the very least.

"And you... and you cracked the screen!" My ribs already hurt before this but now they were pure agony.

"I kept you alive, idiot!" Olivia said shoving me.

"Oh God, I need air!" I gasped, rolling down my window.

"I mean it! Stop!" she pleaded.

I wanted to, but I couldn't. "There were just so many other things you could have thrown!" I managed to wheeze out.

Olivia chuckled at that finally. "Well, I couldn't use it if we were dead."

"I'm surprised you can use it now!" I said, finally managing to stop laughing for a moment.

Olivia had a massive grin. "You should have seen your face when I did that."

"Oh yeah?" I replied. "How did it look?"

Her face went blank for a second, and she gave me the widest-eyed dead stare I've ever seen on her and her jaw went comically slack. A full two seconds of silence passed like that. Then we both burst into a cathartic mutual laughter that lasted far longer than it had any right to.

It took forever to find a Walgreens, but when we did it felt like an oasis in the desert. What I really would have liked about then would have been several alcohols and a coma, but I still had to drive us home, so I settled for good old fashioned liver-killing aspirin. I asked the pharmacist the best way to score a prescription for morphine, but I don't think she appreciated the joke. I also bought two large bags of chocolate covered blueberries, a liter of Dr. Pepper, and one of those beef sticks that are almost as tall as I am. I felt absurdly hungry for some reason, like I would feel after traveling back from another world. Maybe getting your ass kicked just works up an appetite. Or just the act of not dying makes you appreciate food. I wouldn't know, this was kind of a first for me. I felt weirdly rugged for some reason all of a sudden. It's like, I was just blasted by what I can only assume was for real, legit magic and now I am driving home. Bruised, but alive. It makes sense that I feel spectacular, actually.

Olivia was aghast at how famished I was and I felt that I must have absorbed her appetite into my own. Two appetites, one tiny stomach. Literally not the craziest thing I'd heard today, but I was hungry. The jerky was gone before I left the parking lot and I could feel the food making all the hurty things less hurty. I was humming to myself which seemed to make my friend both confused and amused simultaneously. "I'd like to ask what next, but I can totally wait for you to finish chewing if you'd like a bit of time." She said.

"Was dah?" I replied through a mouth full of Blueberries. Enunciation was not my strong point when I was chewing. She just kept looking as I swallowed. "Sorry. Are you sure you don't want any?"

She cautiously took a single berry from the bag. "I asked you what our next step is."

"Sleep for a week? Drink away whatever the heck just happened?" I mused aloud. "I'm not sure why you'd assume I'd have any kind of plan after that. We lived, I'm not sure why we'd press our luck right away."

"Do you hear yourself right now?" Olivia asked incredulously. "Did you completely forget why we went in the first place? Lucia! She's apparently been kidnapped!"

Oh damn!

I did somehow manage to forget that, actually. My good mood made a full retreat, and I felt like the worst human alive for a moment.

"Yeah, there it is. It's good to remember, right?" she asked, reading my face.

"Don't hate me," I said, honestly apologizing. "Somehow between the magic and the army of besuited assassins and blocking a fireball with my mind, it completely got away from me. I can't believe I didn't think about that! I was just happy we were alive."

"Well, our friend is in trouble!" she yelled at me. "What are we going to do about it?"

I drove a couple of minutes more in a tense silence. "I don't know," I finally replied, almost too soft to hear over the sound of my car. "We don't know anything. We don't know where she is. We don't even know who those people are. We have absolutely no advantage over them. We have nothing."

Olivia seemed to shrink at the sound of that. Her tone softened as she muttered, "When you say it like that, it sounds hopeless."

"It is hopeless!" I insisted. "A guy threw fire and wind at us! What can we possibly do?"

"Call the police?" she suggested. It was a reasonable and inevitable suggestion. But...

"What do we tell them? The truth?" I asked, a little more condescending than I would have liked. "How do you think Lucia was locked up in the first place? Why do you think I didn't want to tell anyone about my ability? Even when I did want to tell someone, you for example, I knew I couldn't."

"Yes, you could have!" Olivia insisted.

"No, I really couldn't!" I nearly shouted. "I've known you since small times. And you knew Lucia. I know you weren't that close, but tell me the truth: did you believe her?"

My friend sat in silence next to me, and the distance between us in the seats felt too close for an odd moment, but I wasn't going to break the silence for her. She needed to answer this, and I was willing to let this be uncomfortable to make a point.

"No," Olivia finally said. "We were kids though, and she seemed sick."

"She seemed sick because no one believed her," I said coldly. "I did, but that was about it. Imagine it. That young and you just wanted everyone to be happy and know the same love for the world that you had. And then you're called a liar by everyone you know. You never lied, you know your world is real, but everyone insists that you just wanted attention or, worse, that you're sick. Too young to know or even have the capacity to really speak eloquently about your experience, to know how to make your case. There's just what you know, and what everyone says you're supposed to know. Of course she seemed sick. You all made her that way."

I caught it almost as soon as I said it but I couldn't take it back, not fully. I could tell it stung Olivia.

"Not you, exactly," I said, trying to take the edge off my words. "Just everyone. *You* couldn't have known. You weren't cruel about it as others were, just… you know what I mean."

"Well, we're not kids anymore, and no one is going to accuse *you* of any of that," She said firmly. "I have your back. So why don't you stop making excuses and do what you know you need to do!"

"And what's that?" I asked.

"We're going to see Claire."

I hadn't expected that. I should have, but I didn't. I tried not to show it, but I shuddered inside. I stared at the road ahead, but this time it was Olivia's turn to let things get awkward. When I didn't reply, she pressed.

"Right now. No more stops. No more hiding in your room for weeks at a time. And no more of these stupid blueberries! When we stop this car we are going to see Claire because you are going to trust her more than you've trusted me, do you understand? She gave you a job, she knows when you're not at your best, and she's done nothing except treat you like family. So together we are going to her, and this is your chance to give Claire the same trust she's given you!"

I felt small. Olivia was right, after all. I either loved and trusted Claire or I didn't.

"Okay," I said simply.

"Okay," Olivia replied.

The remainder of the drive was by some miracle both traffic free and mostly quiet. We pulled into the parking lot of The Book's End and I cut the engine, not moving for a while. It was dark, and the lights inside the place reminded me for an instant of a lighthouse.

"It's going to be okay," Olivia said, her hand on my back as she gave me a reassuring rub. "It's the both of us. You're not alone. Claire and I both love you, and regardless of anything else, she will listen to you."

"I know what she thinks of me," I said, not wanting to hear the words out loud. "I have a job here because she thinks I can't really make it anywhere. I'm directionless or worse. I have this job because that's just who Claire is. She helps people unable to take care of themselves."

"That's not true," Olivia said. Her words lacked conviction.

"It is. I'm twenty-four and I finished school two years ago. I should have a real job or at least be in grad school. My life should be together." The words were coming out faster now. "I needed my friend to give me a job in a bookstore and even she thinks I'm a screw-up."

"You stop that immediately!" The sharpness in Olivia's voice made me jump a little. "That is not how you get out of this. You work here because you love it. She gives you a job because she believes in you. This is her life! And she entrusts it to one person: You. If it weren't for you, she would literally live here and sleep in the loft, because she is sure as hell wouldn't hand the keys over to someone else. So get in there and show her the same respect!"

I wasn't entirely convinced, but I had to leave the car sooner or later. Even getting out of the car I still stood in the parking lot, looking into the little shop. Through the window, I watched Claire for a moment, and right then I could appreciate what she is. She hadn't noticed us yet, and so she hadn't stopped her tasks to wave and welcome us in. I watched her dart from task to task, and just then I understood what Olivia meant. There was so much to this shop that no one appreciated. Paying all the bills, keeping the whole place stocked and figuring out what to buy and what to sell. The trips to the store, dealing with annoying customers or even just pleasant customers when you don't really want to talk to anyone. I took a full minute to appreciate all the sacrifice she must endure for the sake of living the dream. Any minute it could all go away. A few bad months. A poor decision here and there. She makes it all work, and the person she trusts to keep her sane, the person she chose to trust her livelihood with was me.

Of course, all of this appreciation was just another way of stalling.

I took a step forward to walk into the shop, and Olivia joined me, the little bell chiming to herald our arrival. Claire looked up at us with a smile meant for customers but allowed it to slip into mild confusion.

"Oh. Hey! What's up?" she asked, before looking back at the inventory. "Wasn't expecting you two in here today. How was the hospital?"

"Not good," I said slowly, unsure of how to jump to the end of that story.

"Sorry to hear that. Is your friend okay?" she asked, turning to look at me again and showing genuine concern.

Claire was really throwing this conversation off the rails before it even began. I started to answer before the shop phone went off and Claire held up a finger.

"Book's End," she said pleasantly into the phone, putting the smile back on immediately. Olivia gave me a nudge and a look to reassure me. Clair continued, "Yes, we close at eight on Saturday. Great, see you tomorrow!"

She put the phone away and looked up at us. "I know you're off today, but can I get a hand with this? I want the floor cleared off before I close up."

Olivia and I both helped her move several boxes into the back room, which removed some of the clutter at least.

"Isn't this more of an after-hours sort of activity?" Olivia asked when we made it back to the front of the shop.

"Normally, sure," Claire said, turning off the various appliances and getting food stored for the next day. "Have you seen the cats by the way? And oh yeah, I have plans tonight."

"Cool, what are you doing?" I was sort of hoping that changing the subject would run out the clock and we could have this conversation another time.

"Sorry, just a bit rushed," Claire replied. "Did you need something or did you just pop in to say hi?"

No such luck on running out the clock. I was kind of hoping she'd be too busy to talk to me, but that's unlikely. Didn't hurt to try. "If you're busy, we can always talk later."

"No, she can't," Olivia interrupted. "Elana has something to tell you."

"Sounds important." Claire stopped what she was doing and faced me. "What's up?"

It took a second to steady myself before speaking. "I know this is going to sound crazy, so I'm not going to give you the whole speech I gave Olivia. I'm just going to say it." I paused and somehow that didn't magically make everyone go away. So … I just said it. "I can become fictional. I don't even know if that's accurate anymore, but that's kind of the best way I have to describe it at the moment. If I'm reading a book, I can see things and then move into them and then I'm in the book and…"

Everyone was quiet for a moment. Claire had a tired look on her face; it was difficult to figure out what she was thinking. "Fantastic. Lock up for me please, I'm late now."

I was stunned. "You don't believe me, do you?"

"No, I don't." She sighed. "I just... do not know what to do with you anymore."

"Hey, this is serious!" Olivia practically yelled. "We almost died today! It sounds insane, but she wouldn't lie to you!"

"How did you almost—?" Claire's eyes seemed to glaze over as her focus shifted to Olivia. "Whatever. No, I don't think she'd lie to me. She probably believes it, which scares the crap out of me. You're the one I'm actually frustrated with right now."

"You're not serious!" Olivia was taken aback.

"Her, I can see believing that, but you?" Claire began. "Letting her live this fantasy? Why aren't you helping her?"

"I'm right here, and I don't need you speaking of me in the third person and I don't need help! I can do everything I said I can do!" I was shouting now too; this isn't how this was supposed to go.

"Fine. Prove it."

Claire walked past me to a pile of books she was sorting. She turned and tossed a book my way. "Here. Make use of this. You didn't want to sell it, let's see some use out of it."

"Fine, I will!" I snapped back. I looked at the book. *Crome Yellow*. "And you know what? This will be easy! I've been in this one! I made a friend in there and everything!"

Claire looked at me like her patience was about to wear out any second and motioned me to get on with it. I took a seat and started reading. I read and... I didn't see the original way. Nothing happened.

"One second," I said.

I skipped forward a bit and tried again. Chapter two, surprising Priscilla.

Still nothing. Okay, skim a bit. Chapter three, that awkward tea party. Nothing was happening. *Still nothing!*

"I don't understand," I murmured, closing the book.

"We'll talk about this tomorrow," Claire told me gently, though I could hear the strain in her voice. She looked at Olivia and, with a less gentle look and tone, said, "We will too."

Claire left the store with one last reminder for me to close up for her. I could hear her pulling away, the sound of her motorcycle sputtering to life and then growing distant as she left.

"Are you okay?" Olivia asked after an awkward moment of silence.

"No! I'm not!" I shouted back on the verge of tears. "Why couldn't I go in there? Did they do something to me?"

"I don't know," Olivia replied helplessly. "There's so little that I do know."

I gripped the book hard, frustration starting to take hold. "You always want me! You've pulled at me! You've even scared me!" I screamed at the book, rapidly flipping through the pages. "Now, let me in. Let me in!"

"Elana…" Olivia started, her voice full of concern.

I was flipping through the pages now almost faster than I could read. A sentence here, a sentence there.

"Let! Me! In!"

Something happened. Or it had been happening, and I hadn't noticed. A swirl of conflicting colors. Pearl. Indigo. Something darker. The way in wasn't inviting; it didn't gently warp the world around me, replacing sensations with others. It sucked me in like a riptide, violent and sudden; it flung me as if I were a stone skipping across a lake. There was a sound of water boiling over, and then darkness.

12

There was only one thought stuck on replay over and over as I fell through the tunnel, surrounded by what my mind could only process as tendrils made of emotion and memories and imagination. I didn't know how I knew what I was seeing, but it felt like the knowledge was just there at the tip of my brain somehow. And almost as suddenly, I had another piece of knowledge: I wasn't falling, I was being propelled.

It was then, for some reason, that I felt the helplessness of being terrified about somehow literally everything about this situation. When I could manage a breath finally, I shut my eyes and screamed.

An instant later I bounced off something soft, but still hard enough to knock the wind out of me, before I rolled hard on the ground. I was still struggling to get air into my lungs, and the crackle of electric pops in front of my eyes was preventing me from seeing what was going on, but I heard the voice clear enough. An Englishman, flabbergasted, yelling at me.

I'm probably not dead. That's good.

It took me a moment, but I was finally able to make out what he was saying, and my sight cleared up. My chest burned, but the oxygen felt better than I'd ever remembered.

"Are you on drugs? I said out!" The man yelled at me.

I got to my feet and looked around. The man was wearing a three-piece suit, and his tie was huge, but it was in perfect proportion to the mop of hair on his head. He had a mustache, dirty blonde like his hair, and it looked like it might be alive. He wore yellow-lensed sunglasses, despite the fact that we were indoors, though I don't know under what circumstances those glasses would be useful. They would make terrible sunglasses, and they didn't look to be prescription. Maybe he just enjoyed looking stupid?

"That is a lot of plaid," I said weakly. I was still having trouble breathing; I probably shouldn't have wasted oxygen insulting a man I'd never met before.

"That's it. You're done," he said gripping me by the arm. I wanted to fight back, but he either worked out, or I hadn't gotten my strength back or both.

"Wait," I asked, trying to stop our movement as he tried to walk us out of the room. "Where are we?"

"You are leaving," he said impatiently. "I have a house to show and I'll never sell it with junkies and squatters laying about."

I saw what I hit, it was a couch, thankfully. I had knocked it over. Just on the other side was a fireplace and having that to stop my momentum would have been significantly more unpleasant. The house was big, and this was just the living room.

"Am I in Crome?" I asked, quickly.

The man stopped. After another moment, he let go of my arm and said, "No one has called it that in a long, long time. I didn't know anyone remembered that name."

"Yeah, well, what else would you call it?" I asked.

The man adjusted his glasses. "Frankly, no one has called it anything at all in quite some time. No one has lived here for nearly ten years. I was hoping to change that today."

"Ten?" I asked suspiciously. "What year is it?" Ugh. Did I just ask what year it was?

"Ah, yes. I forgot. Drugs," the man commented to himself. "Would you like to show yourself out or would you like my assistance?"

"No, I got it." I hoped the sarcasm was clear in my voice.

"See that you do," he replied with equal sarcasm, walking towards the door to open it for me. "Good day."

I stepped outside, and the sun hit me square in the eyes. Parts of the landscape looked familiar, but this was not the Crome I remembered. It certainly wasn't a quaint, idyllic 1920's English countryside manor. My first clue was the Mini Cooper with the Union Jack painted on the roof. Also, the paved roads. I could be a detective. I'm very into clues lately.

A sickening thought occurred to me: I might have somehow gone into the future in this world. No... No, that most definitely didn't make sense, the sixties or seventies or whenever I was didn't exist in that book. It would make sense that they would exist eventually, but how did I get here? Oh my God, George! Before I realized it, I was in a dead sprint in the general direction of his home. I had no idea if he was there or if his house was even a house anymore, but I knew I needed to find out.

I had run all of five minutes before I thought my heart was going to burst, but I didn't stop. Every bump and bruise also made its presence known, but that wasn't enough to get me to slow down either. The car pulling alongside me though was as good a reason as any.

"Is anything the matter, dear?" an elderly woman, kind in her eyes, asked me through a rolled down window.

"I don't know," I replied truthfully, gasping for air. "I'm trying to find a friend. I don't... I'm not sure if he's still around here or not."

The woman saw me sweating and panting. "He must mean quite a lot to you to have you in such a state," she pondered. "Why don't you ride with me and we'll see if we can find him together. Would that be all right?"

I nodded vigorously and sat in the car, feeling the burn of my sudden cardio workout. The old woman pulled off the road and parked the car. "Take your time, dear. Tell me about your friend when you're ready."

A couple of deep breaths and one hacking cough later and I answered. "His name is George. I don't remember his last name. He has a barn. Very nice man." I was still panting, forming longer sentences would take another minute. The older woman's lips seemed to tighten as she tried to think.

"Oh!" I cried out as a thought occurred. *I just hope I still have it.* My hand dug into my book bag, and I instantly recognized what I was looking for by touch alone. "I have me this!"

I pulled out my copy of *Jane Eyre* and flipped the cover back to reveal the inscription. The small woman leaned across the seats to steal a look, and her face visibly blanched.

"Oh, my," she said quietly and then repeated it a bit louder. "Oh, my! I expect I know who you're going to see. And I expect I know why. We mustn't delay." She looked crestfallen.

"Has something happened? Do you know who this is?" I asked.

"Oh dear, you're looking for George Newton, and you were right to be running," she said, starting the car. "George doesn't have long. Or so I hear."

I sat in silence for a moment, not knowing what to say to that. It was about everything I could have feared. I tried to think about the silver lining. He was still here, alive, at least for the moment. By a stroke of luck, I'd met someone who knew him who was willing to take me to wherever he was.

"So your name is Elana?" the woman asked me.

"Yes, ma'am," I replied without thinking. "Elana Black."

"Lovely to meet you, Elana Black," she replied with a nod. "My name is Mary Bracegirdle. A pleasure."

I stiffened, recognizing the name. Mary seemed to notice and looked in my direction, but didn't immediately comment. "You know," she said after a moment, "this may sound like a coincidence, but I believe I knew your grandmother. Or at least knew of her."

I remained still, and getting nothing from me, Mary continued. "When I was quite young, much about your age I suspect, I fancied George. It was but a moment in time, it came, and it went, but George told us of a medium who came to him one day like someone out of fairy tale. A bizarrely dressed young woman. A drunk he suspected, but fun. Unique. He told me she was the smartest person he'd ever met, that he'd always hoped to see her again one day."

She looked at me again, and I felt my cheeks grow hot. "We all laughed at him, of course," she continued. "No one came up here if they didn't have to, not in those days at least. I knew one fellow who tried to ride a bicycle on these hills, if you can believe it. Half of us didn't believe George; and the other half were confident she'd never come back. I mention this of course, because that woman shared your name, as I suspect you share it now with your grandmother."

We continued down the road and I noticed there were considerably more homes along the way than I remembered. They seemed to get in the way of the view. She went on. "I don't mean to speak ill of anyone of course, and if my suspicions are correct, I would assume you knew her better than anyone. There was one thing that always bothered me, though; I'm hoping you can solve an age-old puzzle. As the story goes, George said he met a lost medium who wandered to him from Crome. Priscilla, God rest her soul, resolutely denied anyone of the sort had come to visit her. It was a point of contention if I may speak plainly. In truth, that book is the first piece of evidence that'd I'd ever seen on the matter. George signed a copy of *Jane Eyre* just like that. He was always so proud of the joke he'd made."

I felt tears welling up. "So, what sort of woman was your grandmother?" Mary asked expectantly. "What became of her? And why are you here now?"

"I knew her pretty well," I lied, wiping my eyes with one hand. "She was reckless. She traveled a lot, but honestly, I think she mostly worried about herself until things were just about too late. I swear, she was luckier than she had any right to be. She had friends, but they'd get into trouble just by being near her. She liked George, though. A lot. This book was one of those things she treasured. I don't think she would have given it up for anything. That has to say something. I think she probably regrets not getting to know George better."

"I'm confused dear," Mary said. "She regrets not knowing him?"

"Regretted," I corrected myself quickly. "My apologies."

"Not at all," Mary said sympathetically. "She sounds like she was a wild soul."

I nodded but disagreed internally. In less than a day, I had lost track of Lucia, almost gotten Olivia killed, disappointed Claire, and now I had apparently missed the past fifty something years of a friend's life. He'd been from a different time and a different world, but he'd shown me kindness, and we'd connected. The experience hadn't been any less real.

"I think George will appreciate seeing the book again, just knowing that your grandmother always kept it will bring him some comfort," Mary said, pulling over in front of a familiar-looking home. "You're a good girl for doing this for her."

"Thank you," I replied. What else could I say?

"We're here," she muttered. A young man about my age sat on the same porch I'd first seen George. He looked considerably less inviting and much less likely to buy me breakfast.

"Thank you again, Mary," I said quickly unbuckling my seatbelt, eager to leave the car.

"Give George my love," she replied sadly. "It's been some time for me as well, and I don't know that I'm ready."

That cut deep within me. If not now, when? I had the feeling that was a story she wasn't willing to tell me or maybe anyone ever again. She seemed so frail for a moment, and I could only nod. "I will. Goodbye Mary."

"One last thing," she said, and I poked my head back into the car. "Do you know what your name means?"

I tried to remember. "As a child, I always heard that it meant 'Torch.'"

Mary seemed to chew on that for a moment before she answered. "I suppose it has more than one translation. Goodbye, dear," she said, and pulled away. I watched her drive off for a moment.

"If you're here for Grandad's money, he hasn't got any," the kid on the porch snapped to me.

Part of me wanted to punch him in the nose immediately, but instead I just said, "I'm not here for anything. I'm here to see George."

"First names then, is it?" he asked. "Well, go on back then if you're so close." As I walked towards the fence, he made kissing noises and barked out a hollow laugh. "My name is Simon, by the way! So sweet of you to ask."

I stomped past him, and he promptly ignored me and went back to his seat.

George had a sprawling backyard, somehow bigger than I expected from the road. There were several trees, one larger than the rest. The bark seemed heartier with a fuller color, and it produced fruit. Pears, in fact, dozens of them ready to be plucked and ate right off the tree. And there, on the other side of the yard, sat a frail old man. I spied him before he saw me, and I knew who it was right away. For a second that I'm not proud of, I wanted just to walk away. He hadn't seen me yet, and that wonderful memory was still whole.

"George?" I asked just above a whisper before I could give myself the chance to do otherwise. A delicate head turned in my direction. A wrinkled brow raised in astonishment, his eyes could not have gone any wider. I walked closer, slowly at first and then with more purpose.

"Elana?" he asked in disbelief. "You said you were a medium. You never said you were a witch!"

I wanted to cry. I wanted to be happy to see my friend. I wanted to apologize. I just smiled and held back tears. George feebly raised his arms to greet me in a hug. I didn't think he was able to stand, at least not without help. I fell to my knees and gave him about as big a hug as I felt that I could without hurting him. He looked at me with a mixture of joy and disbelief. "It's really you! How is this possible?"

I locked eyes with him. "I'm so sorry, George. I never meant to be away this long."

"Hey there, what is this?" he asked gently. "No tears, no apologies. Why don't you just have a seat here and watch this sunset with me? Besides, you're ruining my grass."

We both chuckled at that as I got off the ground and sat down on the reclining chair next to him that matched his own. "I know you said sunset, but I think it's maybe two in the afternoon."

"And I don't like to miss a minute of it!" he laughed. We both did until his laughter turned into a coughing fit. "Oh, don't look at me like that, I'm old. I'm going to cough sometimes. It's allowed."

I almost feigned ignorance, but it wouldn't have done any good. We both knew what I was thinking. "I'm sorry, I couldn't help it. This is just such a shock."

"It's quite all right," he said, relaxing back into his chair. "I'm just happy to see you here at all. This is one of the better surprises I've had this year. The other surprises were less good."

"I really did mean to come back a lot sooner," I said, no longer sure which of us I meant to comfort. "I treasured that day we shared."

"As did I!" George said with a sudden spark. "You know, I told everyone about you, but they didn't believe me!"

"I know," I said with a grin. "I ran into your friend Mary on the way up here; she gave me a ride."

"Oh, Mary," George whispered thoughtfully. "I do wish she would have come by and said hello."

"She asked me to give you her love," I said, continuing to feel better about where we were.

"Is that right?" George asked.

As we sat in silence for a bit, a thought came to me. I did have something to share with my friend. "So, I'd like to show you something, and I don't know how I'm going to do it, but I have a feeling that if I'm supposed to figure it out, then I will. Is that okay?" I asked. George didn't take his eyes off the view, but he nodded. "Okay then. George, give me your hand. Please."

He looked at me and extended his hand towards mine, and almost as if to catch it, I clasped his firm, but gentle grip. I could feel decades of memories pouring from him, but I embraced it this time, accepting it and willing my mind back through the channel we'd created. It felt like the first moments of giving blood, a part of me leaving steady and controlled. Vulnerable and ready.

And I saw it all at once. *George had been alone, but never for long. Raised in a house that he was to inherit. His parents had come from money, but in the boring way where proper investing took hold and paid dividends. When they passed, they had left instructions for young George to be looked after in the home by his nanny, Hilda, until his eighteenth birthday, at which point George would be given the deed to the land and the house, as well as his inheritance. Unlike others, he would come to know, George never felt the need to hold onto the things and before leaving the attorney's office instructed half of the fortune be given to Hilda for her years of kindness. Hilda was now able to travel home to be with her own family, and though her appreciation was genuine, George was alone. He had understood from an early age what it meant to have others leave, and he always felt it was his duty to help others. No matter how much he gave, the income never seemed to stop, so while he was never poor, he was never wealthy either.*

One day, a strange woman walked into his life and reminded him that fun was something that could still be had. Just as suddenly as she appeared, she was gone, though George never gave up the idea of seeing her again.

George became a whole person, no longer suffering and serving the needs of others, but living life and infecting others with that same joy. By chance, he met Mary Bracegirdle. Rumor had spread that she'd been jilted recently, but George didn't care for rumors, he wanted to know who was in front of him. Theirs was a whirlwind romance, lasting but a blink of an eye in comparison to the rest of their lives. It wasn't that they were incompatible, they just met at the wrong times. The promise to always remain friends was kept, but only in the most technical terms. Shortly after an end, there was a beginning for George.

Celeste, from France. He rarely saw Mary after that, despite her close proximity. He'd never stopped having love for her, and her for him, but her stubbornness prevented them from having what they once had.

George and Celeste had two children: Ewen, for her father, and Lana, for his mother. Besides, Lana sounded pretty close to someone else who'd taught him to live, and it seemed like a happy coincidence. Their lives were pleasant, and they had become known to the town as the family who would survive anything. Until Ewen had become old enough for war. Until Ewen never came back. The family stopped surviving. Celeste, once so bright and cheerful was now a shell.

A few years later, when she took her car over a cliff in the middle of the night, no one was terribly surprised, and not everyone had missed her. George still had Lana, but even she was now a woman and could not be asked to stay forever. And so she didn't. She moved to Germany where she married Aldrick and started a life together, one without George in it. And just when everyone thought they were too old to begin, they made George a grandfather with the birth of Simon. But as these things go, it was only another few years before Aldrick died of liver failure and then a year later, Lana died in her sleep, complications of a heart defect that had always been a worry but they always hoped wouldn't be. And so, Simon came to live with George, and the two had never seen eye to eye. George was old now and having outlived just about everyone; it was his time to be diagnosed with—

I loosened the grip as tears once again welled up in my eyes. "A month?" I shouted, unwilling or unable to control myself.

George was beaming at me with pride. "You've been helping people!" His smile made him seem like a child at that moment.

"Mary said you didn't have long, but, a month?" I told him. "It's not fair!"

"Oh hush up on that," George reassured me. "I'm dying. So what? I've probably got less than a month if I'm trusting my gut."

"Not funny," I cried.

George placed a hand gingerly on his stomach. "No, I suppose it isn't. But Elana, I am just fine. We're all dying, some of us just get to do more stuff than others before that happens. But you!"

"I'm not going anywhere," I reassured him.

"That's very kind," he said with a pat on my hand. "But it's not my point. I will be happy for every moment you spend with me, but when my time is done, I want you to keep moving and appreciate your own life. We were never supposed to meet, and I am grateful that we did. But I have lived so, so much longer than you. I have met so many people and created so many memories. My life was full! I fell in love. I had kids! But do you know what else I did?" I did. I did know what else, but I let him say it anyway. "I made the people around me happy! I helped whomever I could and made their lives better when I was able. And if that's not the point of everything, what is?"

"I'm not ready," I muttered to him.

"Neither am I, but I'm doing a remarkable job of pretending," He replied.

I sniffed back a tear and tried to relax with him. There was still time, but I just didn't want to even take a chance that I'd miss the sunset.

13

My trip back to The Book's End was easy, almost gentle. I touched down onto the floor as if guided by caring, ethereal hands. Olivia was half-asleep in one of the reading chairs, her jacket repurposed into a blanket; she bolted upright when she saw me return. She ran to me, her jacket falling to the floor without a thought.

"Where have you been?" she demanded, still waking up, her mind catching up to her body. "I've been here all night, worried!"

I gripped her as hard as I could and just wept. "Four days!" I shouted, my throat sore already from the heavy sobs. I shrank into Olivia while my grip tightened like a child afraid of losing their mother. She was rigid from the surprise, but after a moment began to stroke my back, remaining silent. I couldn't stop crying. "It's not fair!" I cried. "It's not."

"What isn't fair, sweetie?" Olivia asked me carefully, continuing to pet me like a cat.

"He was supposed to have a month left. Doctors are wrong all the time, right? 'A month' means 'six months.' 'Six months' means 'three years.'" I could hear my voice shaking. "I was with him for four days!"

"Who?" Olivia asked, not letting go. "Who were you with?"

"George! He's gone!" I cried.

"George? George from the book! Did you see him again? What happened?"

We sat down in the reading chairs, and Olivia waited patiently for me to get steady enough to continue. "I went back to Crome. But it was a different year. Sometime in the '70s I'd guess. I found George, still living in his old home, but he was so old and very sick. He remembered me. I told him I'd stay with him as long as he would stay with me. We only met the once, but he remembered me after all those years. His wife was gone, so were his kids. His grandson didn't care. He was supposed to have a month!"

I started crying again, Olivia said nothing. I could feel her radiating pity, but being unable to translate that sadness into words that could do anything, she merely sat there.

"I'm going to fix it," I said finally with a sniff. "This is my fault. All of it. I'm going to go back, warn him about Ewen and the war. Or I don't know; I'll do something! I just need to remove one of those horrible dominos, prevent that chain of events from happening the way it... if I just..."

"None of that was your fault," Olivia tried to reassure me. "You weren't even there."

"It *is* my fault!" I screamed hoarsely. "Where's the book? I'm going to fix it!"

Olivia was startled enough by my voice raising that she just pointed to the counter where four copies of *Crome Yellow* sat.

"Okay, I can do this," I said snatching a copy and marching back over to a seat. "I just need you to be quiet. I need to concentrate. I don't know how this is going to work after last time."

Olivia nodded. "I'll get us some coffee from down the street and give you some time, I don't understand how to turn on this equipment anyway. Hopefully you're not here when I get back."

The bell jingled as she left, and I started reading, carefully, focusing on each word, so I didn't have a repeat of last time. Olivia must have taken her time getting back, or maybe she just had a problem finding a spot that was open in the middle of the night, because I was easily a third of the way through the book when I noticed the coffee on the table. I hadn't seen so much as a hint of an entrance yet. After two and a half hours, I hadn't touched my coffee, and I finished the book. It was just a book, hollow and meant about as much to me as a story being retold at a party for the eighth time.

"It was the book. I must have done something to it when I traveled," I said defiantly. "I need to try with a different copy."

"Elana," Olivia started to say as I tossed the book onto the table and made my way towards the counter. I suddenly doubled over in pain, gripping my midsection. "Elana!" she yelled.

"It's fine, I'm just hungry," I said wincing as I stood. "I just forgot to eat when I got back. Can you get me a snack? I need to try again."

"Okay, if you're sure," Olivia said hesitantly, helping me to my feet. I got another copy, one that looked practically unused, and when I sat back down Olivia handed me a chocolate chip cookie as big as my fist. Half of it was gone before I finished the first page.

"The sun is coming up soon," Olivia said weakly. "I know you don't want to be bothered, but—"

"Then I have time before the store is supposed to open to get in there," I said, not lifting my eyes from the page. "Now *shh.*"

I got lost in the reading. But not literally this time. I don't know how Olivia kept herself busy while I read. Another couple of hours later and I was so frustrated that I had to stop myself from ripping the book in half. "I don't understand it!" I yelled, slamming the book against the table.

"What's happening when you try?" Olivia asked.

"It's like the whole thing is dead!" I said, falling back into the padded chair with a grunt. "There's nothing! It's like looking for an elevator on the floor of a swimming pool."

Olivia thought for a moment and grabbed a book off the dollar pile. "Here, look inside this," she said, tossing the paperback in my direction. Some sci-fi book with a picture of a spaceship on it.

"What are we doing?" I asked.

"Troubleshooting," she said. "Just start reading."

And so, I started reading. It wasn't good, but after the first couple of pages, I could feel the pull. I clapped the book shut. "Well, this one works."

"So, it's that story, not you," Olivia concluded. "The story of that title, regardless which edition or copy you read."

"But I still don't know how to get back there."

"Maybe you're not supposed to?"

"… but I know someone who might," I said, ignoring her question. I got to my feet and chugged the now cold coffee. "Do me a favor?"

"Yeah, anything," Olivia said, standing as well.

I dug into my bag and tossed her the shop keys. "Cover for me this morning. Claire won't be happy about it, but it's a cash register and a few books. There's a bed in the loft if you want to nap before we open. However you want to play it, I believe in you."

"I mean, I'm going to screw this up, but sure," she said. The cold air hit me through my coat as I opened the door and heard the little bell jingle. She called out after me, "Where are you going, though?"

I briefly turned in the doorway to answer her as I left. "Santa Barbara."

I practically ran into my apartment before realizing that there was a zero percent chance my roommate was awake yet. Any disturbance before noon and she would hate me. I slowed my steps and took a peek into her room. Sharon had left her door open, as usual, but thankfully she was out cold. I quietly shut her door and made my way back down the hall. I was starting to think we might never actually see each other again with the hours we were keeping.

Finding an episode of *Four's a Crowd* on demand proved harder than I would have expected. I'm not sure why I thought it was okay to just hope that I'd randomly find the show on precisely when I needed to, but it sure would have been convenient. It wasn't showing up on TV again until two am tomorrow, and even then, it was an older episode. Paolo had mentioned that I came in sometime around season six, so I needed something later than that or I'd be repeating my conversation. And even if he recognized me, I'm not sure how that would have played later on when I did enter the show. Would Becky and Paolo have already known me? And wouldn't I know it by now, given the otherwise linear series of events which got me to this point? Then again, I know for a fact that I've changed history already, albeit in less than significant ways.

"Congratulations, Cerosa Vadis," I mumbled to myself, suddenly remembering Charlie as I opened my laptop. "Everyone knows who you are now. Oh, and your otherworldly double wasn't gruesomely murdered by an alien, that must be so great for you."

None of the streaming services had the show, and at this point, I wasn't even surprised. I should really stop expecting things to go easy for me. None of the video sites had episodes either, just clips and that didn't feel safe somehow. The best I could come up with for specific episodes was buying them for a buck ninety-nine each, and there wasn't a guarantee I could jump into all of them. If I wasn't careful, I could find myself out of as much as ten, even twelve dollars. Given that I currently had forty-two bucks in my checking account, the stakes were reasonably high.

I figured it was better to be safe than sorry and I went with the first episode of season seven that I could find, "The Man Who Would Be John."

Well, that sounds terrible, I thought to myself, not even bothering to read the synopsis. I couldn't have cared less. The episode began to play, and within moments I found the opening again, in almost the exact spot I saw it the first time. I felt more prepared for what may come, and as I felt pulled into the show, I braced myself for the landing and merely hopped a few awkward steps as I landed in the restaurant this time. Different crowd, fewer people than before, but the same Chad.

"Whoa, easy!" he said, maintaining his hold on the tray that I nearly knocked over. "Hey, you were here before!"

"That's right, Chad, good to see you too," I said, taking a step back for personal space.

"That was some mess you made you last time," he said with a smile. "I almost didn't recognize you when you weren't in costume. How have you been?"

It took me a second to realize what he meant, and when I did, I had to let it go. I couldn't even be mad, I looked ridiculous last time, and I didn't bother trying to blend in before I made this trip. "Doing okay, but I'm in kind of a rush to get—"

A short, heavy-set man came out of the kitchen yelling before I could even see him. "Damn it, Chad, do I pay you to wait tables or do I pay you to chat up the ladies?"

Aw, screw it. I'm in a sitcom, right?

I took a glass of soda from a tray and sent the contents directly into the eyes of Chad's manager. Chad for his part looked at me, his mouth agape.

"As I was saying, I'm in a rush and not really in the mood to chat, but will you do me a favor?" I asked him. He nodded yes in pure shock. "Get out of here and do literally anything else. This job sucks and your manager is a jerk. Have you considered acting?"

"No," he replied, eyes still wide.

"Huh. That's weird," I said. "You should consider it. Take it easy."

I made my exit as quickly as possible, trying not to think about how unlike me that was. I wasn't planning on coming back anyway, and maybe I was just in a mood. I made a tacit agreement with myself right there that until I got to Paolo and found a way to get back to George, nothing was going to get in my way. I counted myself thankful that Paolo lived near the beach and I was pretty sure I could find his place without a lot of effort. A good fifteen minutes later and I was at the complex which housed his apartment. As luck would have it, security gates weren't exactly a big feature back in the eighties, so I was able to walk right up to his door.

If I had any sense of self-preservation at that moment, I would have probably thought something was amiss given that his front door was ajar. But then again, tacit agreement, so I didn't. Instead, I flung the door open with the full weight of my shoulder and shouted. "Paolo! Where are you? We need to talk!"

I heard movement from down the hall before Paolo dashed into the living, an incredulous look spread over his face. "For the love of—!" he spat. "Are you serious? What are you even doing here?"

"I need your help. I'm trying to get to a friend and... Uh, why are you wearing that?" It took me a second, but I recognized what Paolo was wearing. Red suit, very crisp, but a bit loose in the chest. Two piece. Button up shirt, no tie, an extra button on the shirt undone. All of it was red, even the shoes. There it was. I guess I found my sense of self-preservation.

"What does it look like?" he said sadly. "I'm going back to work."

I took a step back towards the door to try and put a little more distance between us. I hoped he hadn't noticed. I carefully asked, "Paolo, where's Becky?"

"Safe," he replied. "Or so they tell me."

"And who are they?" I asked.

"Do you really need me to say it?" he countered.

I took a breath. "No, because I really don't want to believe it," I said, not taking my eyes off of Paolo. "And because I really didn't come here to fight you, I need your help."

Paolo's laugh was hollow, more from disbelief than joy. "Well, you'd better start believing, because this is me. I was wrong to think it would ever be different, I was a fool to think they'd let me just be." He started to walk in my direction and I tensed up, but he moved past me into the kitchen. "Are you sure I can't interest you in that Fresca?"

I refused to relax, and he took the silence for its own answer. "Suit yourself. You know, from what I hear you're not much of a fighter anyway. And yet you still seem to get around okay, even better than okay in fact. You're here without a scratch on you. You're cunning." He mulled over the thought. "Though I'm not sure which is impressing me more right now:

That you haven't bolted out the door or that you're still asking for my help."

"Who says I'm not a fighter?" I said, trying to sound brave.

"Three guesses," he replied opening his drink.

"Bres," I said matter of factly.

Paolo visibly shuddered at that. "The less I speak with him, the better. No, try again." I paused. Who else could it be? "Wow, really? You don't know? Come on, who else do you know dressed like this?"

"Jason?" I nearly shouted, temporarily forgetting how dangerous the situation was.

"Winner," Paolo said, raising his drink in my direction in a mock toast. "And that deserves a prize, so I'll tell you what: You have about—," he briefly paused then to check his wristwatch, "—three minutes and forty-seven seconds before everyone arrives. Until then, ask whatever you came to. This will be the last time we speak as friends. Besides, just because I'm back in red doesn't mean I need earn these colors just yet."

Since I had to take him at his word, I just immediately asked, "How do I get back into *Crome Yellow*?"

"Why would you want to?" he asked. Then he blanched and narrowed his eyes as he said, "Wait. Why can't you?"

"I don't know. Believe me, I've tried," I answered. "I went back and found myself forward by about fifty years, and then I watched a friend die. I need to go back and fix things."

Paolo laughed hard at that, nearly choking. "No kidding?" he finally asked with an astonished grin. "Wow, I don't think anyone thought you'd screw up this badly this soon."

"What do you mean?" I demanded.

"It doesn't work like that," he said. "For one thing, you don't get to go back and fix things. When you enter a new world, it is malleable. But make too much of an impact?" He slapped his hand down onto the counter suddenly, and I was surprised that I didn't even flinch at the dramatic gesture. "That's it. That's your anchor. You made your starting point. Time marches on; you just get to go with the flow. Make your decisions wisely, because there's no such thing as a do-over."

No... No. I pressed on. "How did I get so far ahead in the story in that case? *Crome Yellow* took place around 1920, and I was at least fifty years ahead of that."

He shrugged, spinning on his heel through the kitchen as he shouted with authority, "That! I genuinely don't know. You ever see a child make a mess on such a grand scale that you're no longer mad, you're just impressed? That's you right now. Don't let the Directorate find out. They'd run experiments on you forever."

"So you can't help me?" I said, frustration welling up from my stomach.

He sighed and shook his head. "Kid, no one can help you. I don't even know who would know where to begin. Your friend is beyond help. I will tell you one thing, though, and I have no reason to lie to you about this. When I tried to make contact with you, at least at first, I genuinely was just a fan. I thought I was out from under their control and I wanted to help. I was sloppy, though, and they found me. And if the choice is between you or anyone else and Becky, I'm going to do whatever it takes to protect her. So just know, whatever happens next isn't anything I'm going to be happy about. I'm going to apologize to you now for how good I am at what I do."

My frustration was turning into anger. *This smug, arrogant—!* "How did Jason know to spy on me in the first place? And where did Bres take Lucia? And what the hell is with this color scheme you people have going on?" The questions came out of me in a stream of annoyance, each word a demand for the truth. As I ranted, a sound like Tupperware opening, barely audible, occurred just outside of the apartment, causing both of our heads to move in its direction.

"Sorry, Elana," Paolo said with regret. "Time's up." I looked back in his direction just in time to see the steak knife leave his hand and fly towards my face.

14

"*Ohmygod!*" I screamed, shutting my eyes, a vision of home flashing in my mind's eye. An instant later I felt weightless for about a second and a half before landed hard on something hard, hearing a sickening crack.

I opened my eyes to find I was back in my apartment and on my couch. My heart was trying to pound its way to freedom. I was panting, and after a second I moved my hands to see what was broken, only to find that I had landed on my open laptop.

"No, I can't," I said, praying it still worked. "I really can't afford... *Gah!*"

I found the culprit of the crack I'd heard: one of the hinges on the monitor had given way. What did it say about me that in this exact moment in time I was more worried about my screen coming to life than I was about nearly having a knife buried in my skull less than a minute prior? The screen was black, but the power button was slowly blinking, meaning the whole machine was in rest mode. And who says I'm technologically illiterate?

"Please, please, please, let me..." I begged as I pushed the power button, the slowly blinking green dot becoming a solid, unblinking light. I stared at the screen, seeing only my reflection until the welcome screen literally welcomed me.

"Yes!" I shouted, savoring the bittersweet victory. This machine was now a bit uglier and probably shouldn't be moved very much, but it was on, and that was more than enough for now. I very carefully closed it up, laying it down on my coffee table like a newborn.

I took a moment to figure out my next move. Paolo had betrayed me. Or he was always against me. I'm not exactly sure what to even believe at this point, he felt like the closest thing I had to an ally, and it turns out I didn't have anyone on my side after all, except—

"Olivia!" I shouted without thinking.

I pulled out my phone; it was nearly one in the afternoon. That thought alone caused my eyelids to feel like they were weighted. How long had it been since I slept? I couldn't think like that right now, Olivia had at best a liar in her home and at worst a killer from some secret cabal… society… magic… association thing. A Gardener? Is that what Bres had put as his job title on a business card? And why would he even give that to me, just to freak me out? Whatever he was, whoever he worked for, I had no way of knowing how long it would take until Paolo told Jason that I was onto him. If Olivia walked home and into that situation, anything could happen.

I dialed her number and felt my skin grow cold when it went straight to voicemail. *Okay, she's probably just still at the store, unable to answer her cell phone. That's something people do right, turn off their phones?* I didn't feel right about this, but I had to be optimistic, so I dialed the store and held my breath as the phone rang.

"Book's End. I went to college so please stop telling me that I'm illiterate, and how can I help you?" Olivia said in a monotone that suggested she was not ready for the rigors of bookstore life and customer service.

"You're alive!" I exclaimed, stifling a yawn.

"Me?" Olivia asked. "Dude! Claire is pissed! She's on her way in right now. It turns out I can't make coffee, and it's somehow a super bad thing if you haven't read Von Gut."

"Vonnegut," I corrected on instinct. "Whatever, you're exhausted, not important. Can you meet me at my place when Claire relieves you?"

I heard a grunt from the other end of the phone. "And how would I do that? You left with the car and my phone is dead, so I can't order a ride over there. You also left me without a charger. Unless you want me to call Logan and we can all go together."

That wasn't the best news, and no, I didn't want to involve anyone else in this just yet. I really didn't want to run into Claire right now either, not while I still had to figure out how to handle this situation with Jason. "Yeah, can you make your way over to the bakery down the street? I have some uh, distressing news that you need to hear."

"Yeah, okay, she should be here in ten minutes or so," Olivia said. "Meet me in twenty?"

That didn't leave me time to rest, considering the traffic, but I couldn't ask her just to wait around either. "You got it. I'll leave now. Just apologize to Claire for me. And say hi to the cats."

"Elana."

"Right, sorry. On my way."

We hung up, and I dug into my bag to grab my keys when my stomach abruptly reminded me that I forgot something. The hunger could be considered the worst side effect of what I did, but at least I had food in the house. I grabbed a banana, but I swear that if it were possible, my stomach audibly scoffed at the idea of a single banana being enough. We had a total of five in the kitchen, so I guess it looked like I was bringing five bananas. Potassium is supposed to be one of the more helpful vitamins, right? Or is it a nutrient? One of those two, I'm sure. Honestly, if you asked me to tell you a vitamin from a nutrient, I'd need one of them to be shaped like a cartoon character and to be berry flavored. There was no way potassium was a mineral, though. Minerals are supposed to be like, rocks, I think. Maybe a potato is a soft rock.

Deep thoughts, with Elana Black. I was really over thinking the usefulness of bananas.

Big Sister roared to life. Well, not roared as much as shook, but we were off. I rolled down the windows and blared the radio, which according to NPR was an old Blues singer named Roy Brown, and he insisted we were going to boogie at midnight. Hey, I had bananas, crisp air, and a horns section; anything to wake me up and keep me up at this point, and I didn't think *All Things Considered* was going to do it. *Boogie at Midnight*, but I'm about thirteen hours too late. It's probably midnight somewhere. And wherever that is, whenever that is, someone is feeling the inexplicable need to boogie. You're welcome, the boogying ones. Those who would boogie.

It was a Sunday afternoon which wasn't a guarantee there wouldn't be traffic, but in this case, it worked out for me. All the same, Olivia was outside waiting the bakery when I arrived, so I was sure she hadn't hung around the shop to catch hell from Claire. She was about to sit in the car when she spotted the fresh pile of banana peels I had created on top of the paper bag in the space that her butt was about to occupy. She paused and looked at me.

"Did you eat all of these just now?" she asked.

"I saved you one!" I said, forcing a smile to sell it, extending the banana in her direction.

Her face flushed with what looked like a very mild bit of nausea before she answered. "Hold on just a moment," she said, collecting the peels by carefully grabbing the bag underneath and walking it to a trashcan. When she returned, I had already peeled open the last of the fruit.

"So you didn't save me one?"

"You didn't look like you wanted it," I said over a mouthful of banana.

"You're right," she agreed, sitting down and switching off the radio. "So we're just going to turn whatever that is off and okay, yeah, what's your news?"

"You might be living with a magic murder man," I answered while taking another bite.

Olivia gave me a blank look. "What?"

I finished chewing and swallowed. "Sorry, I should have made that more dramatic," I apologized. "Let me try again. Olivia! You live under the specter of a dark conspiracy! Dark forces, uh, conspire to—"

"No, stop it, I get what you're saying," she said. "I mean, what?"

"Oh yeah, so you remember that guy inside of that one eighties show? Paolo? So he's also a magic murder man, and he told me so. Or I guessed it, and he confirmed it. A lot was going on. He tried to kill me."

Olivia's eyes widened. "What?"

"Yeah, with a knife!" I exclaimed. "That he threw at my face!"

"Okay, this feels like you're leaving a whole lot of information out right now." I could see her trying to get a handle on this.

"Later, for sure," I said. "Let's just focus on the important parts right now. Like the part where your roommate is spying on us, and he's probably the reason Lucia was taken."

"That's... You're right!" she said, putting the pieces together. "He asked where we were going when we left. And right before you called, he called the store and asked when I was going to be home. It didn't even occur to me that might be weird, I never told him I was at the shop so how did he know? What a turd!"

That got a small laugh out of me. "You called him a turd."

Olivia laughed too. "I did, but this is serious!"

"It's fine, I do the same thing when I'm exhausted," I said. "You know, with the grade school insults. I just hadn't heard anyone say 'turd' in a long time."

Olivia rubbed her temples, trying to focus. "Okay, help me think this through," she said. "Jason is at home. No one else is there, and that's good? Right? For anyone else at least. So maybe we just don't go back? Call the police?"

I shook my head. "You already told him you were coming, the longer we wait, the more likely he is to know that I know about him. If he's one of them, he's dangerous. Not to mention that we don't have anything to call the cops with. And what if he has powers like Bres had? You can't exactly warn the cops ahead of time about something like that, and if you don't give them a heads up, you're potentially sending people to their deaths."

"Well, that's pretty grim," Olivia agreed. "So it sounds like you have a better plan?"

"I absolutely do not," I said resting my head back in my seat and looking at the ruined interior of my roof. "I don't even have a plan, let alone a better one. We didn't exactly get counterintelligence training in high school. And the course on defense against the dark arts was always full months in advance in college. How the hell could I have planned for any of this?"

"And giving up isn't an option. It's not like we can just drive to the mountains and hide," Olivia agreed. "I don't know which plants are okay to eat. We'd definitely die up there."

I turned my head to look at her. "The mountains? Really?"

"Yeah!" she said, proud of her contingency plan. "No one ever looks for you in the mountains."

I turned the car back on and tried my best to throw the last banana peel into the trash can through the driver's side window. I made it most of the way. Close enough. I'm sure it would biodegrade. On the concrete. "We're going to your place." I said, resigning myself to an atrocious idea.

"That seems like a really bad idea," Olivia replied.

I smiled. "I was just thinking the same thing."

"I temporarily hate you for this," Olivia continued to air her grievances, specifically at having to walk up the hill to her home. "Couldn't you have just maybe dropped me off and then walked up on your own?"

She didn't mean it, but I gave her a look anyway. "This plan is all right as far as plans go. He would hear the car coming. If we walk up, we get the element of surprise."

I had more to say, but this hill was very steep, and I was hoping to keep my breath. I also hated myself, albeit temporarily, for this plan. Olivia overestimated my cardio and took my silence as a sign to continue. "Then what? We walk into my house where a predator with unknown power is waiting for me, and we surprise him? Your plan seems to be missing pieces."

I sucked in a big breath of air and continued. "You walk in the front door and distract him. I'll sneak around to the back door and improvise."

It was Olivia's turn to give me a look. "You'll improvise?"

"Yeah, pretty much," I said. "That's what you do when you only have part of a plan, right?"

She looked like she had more to say but we were only a couple of houses away, and it wasn't like I was bursting with answers at this point. We got into position, Olivia waiting for me to get to the side of the house before she walked inside. I unlatched the gate as quietly as possible, careful to lift it as I opened it since it had a habit of scraping on the ground. I saw a variety of objects that gave me all kind of ideas. I didn't exactly have a weapon, so maybe it wouldn't hurt to have something to defend myself with. There were logs for the fire pit, but I wasn't sure I was up for wielding tree parts as a weapon. There was a slightly rusty pair of hammers on a crafting table, but those had the potential for murder, and I'm not trying to kill anyone. There were a rake and a broom handy, but what was I going to do with that? Rake him? Shoo him out of the house like a raccoon through the cat door?

Just when I thought I wasn't going to find anything, I saw them: A pair of Tiki heads probably bought for a party at some point. I picked one of them up, and I couldn't tell if it was supposed to be smiling at me or if it was constipated or if it was trying to relay some sort of threat. It felt like it weighed about five pounds or a bit more, maybe a foot and a half in length. I gave it test swing and decided this might hurt, but it wasn't going to kill anyone, so it was good enough for me.

Right then, I heard Olivia drop her keys, which was the signal to me that she was about to open the door. I hurried to the back of the house and saw Jason on the couch, arms at his side, his head back. The television was on, some sort of cop show was playing. I tested the sliding glass door. It moved, not making a sound. Jason still hadn't noticed me. My heart was pounding with the sudden knowledge that I had no idea what I was doing right now in the slightest. I got the door open and crept inside.

"Can you believe our luck?" Olivia whispered. "He's asleep!"

A guttural howl rose from the pit of my stomach as I dashed towards his still form, Tiki head held high over my head. Jason barely had time to register his surprise as the wooden statue swung down, slamming hard into the soft parts of his midsection. He sat upright immediately, trying to double over, and I swung wildly again, this time connecting with his face. A small spray of blood squirting from the impact.

Jason fell to the floor, letting loose with several inarticulate curses as he went down. Olivia jumped back in shock, her mouth opening in surprise.

"Where's my friend?" I practically screamed. The words had more force than I was expecting.

Jason coughed and winced, clutching at his now disabled nose. "Who are you talking—?"

"I will beat you into the carpet!" I shouted, raising the Tiki head again.

"All right! Stop! Damn!" he pleaded, raising his hands defensively. "Lucia, right?"

My whole body tensed at her name. Something must have shown in my face from the way everyone was looking at me. Or it could have been the spontaneous act of melee violence. One of the two.

"Where is she?" I demanded. "And why have you been spying on us?"

"Can I at least get some paper towels first?" he asked, tears welling in his now swollen eyes. "This really hurts."

It seemed like an oddly reasonable request given the circumstances. I motioned to Olivia to get something for his nose, and she came right back with half the roll. He made a gesture of thanks, and Olivia quickly backed away from him.

"All right, talk," I commanded.

He started to sit back down on the couch before I stopped him. "Stay on the floor! You... wow, you're... that bleeding doesn't look like it's going to stop. I'm going to have to help clean this later, probably."

Jason gave a look of annoyance and resignation through the mask of paper towels he was holding to his nose with one hand and sat back down on the carpet. "Well, you caught me," he said sarcastically. "Congratulations. Happy?"

The grip I held on the Tiki head never loosened. "Where's my friend?" I repeated.

"How should I know?" he asked. "I barely had time to give them any kind of warning you had figured it out."

"Figured what out?" Olivia asked, seeming to snap out of her initial shock.

"Her powers? The prophecy? Did you really not know?" Olivia and I exchanged looks. "You're kidding," Jason said, looking like the unluckiest man in the world.

"Why were you spying on me?" I asked, uncertain what he was talking about.

"Prophecy?" he offered. "Look, to be honest, we were looking at a few people, I just drew the short straw with you. There's a lot we're trying to figure out. Some of us buy into it, some of us don't, but we still follow orders, okay? You think I want to be here?"

"I don't know how to answer that," I said. "I've only really met you once, and you were kind of a jerk, and you work with a bunch of scary people, so yeah, I would honestly guess that you do want to be here. Olivia actually lives with you; she might be able to answer that better than I could."

"He's never really around when I am," Olivia replied, "and he always keeps his door closed whenever he is home, so I don't have much more to go on than you."

"This is my first damn mission!" Jason yelled. "Unsupervised mission, I mean, I'm not fresh out of training."

"There's training? And missions?" I began to ask, and perhaps a half a second in time I saw his free hand moving towards me, starting to glow with a dark orange energy. I reacted just a little too quickly for him, bringing the Tiki head down hard into his fingers, sending a burst of energy dissipating into the air. Jason screamed, but I could still hear the crack of his fingers.

"Look out!" Olivia yelled, causing me to turn my head towards the television. A tunnel appeared on the screen, and I watched as Jason was sucked into it. With a familiar sound, the tunnel suddenly closed, leaving us alone.

"Oh frick him!" I yelled, throwing my improvised weapon at the ground. "Frick him to heck!"

I let myself fall into the couch, while Olivia just stared at me. "What? I told you I was exhausted."

My friend had better foresight than I and moved right away for the remote, turning off the TV. "Just in case that's how he gets back."

"Is that what it looks like when I leave?" I asked, the colors still fresh in my head.

"No," Olivia said, sitting down next to me. "That looked decidedly different, but I guess he's in that show now?"

"Probably. I am far too tired to think about it." My eyes suddenly felt drained of light; sleep wasn't going to be a choice soon.

"Hey, so, whenever we wake up, assuming no one murders us in our sleep," Olivia said, curling up into a corner of the couch, eyes closed. "What do you say we see what he's been hiding behind that door?"

My own eyes shut as well. "That is an excellent idea," I probably said.

15

It was the shove that woke me up first, though my eyes didn't open right away. "Hey, you," Olivia whispered. "Get up. You're drooling."

I sniffed hard and sat up. At some point I must have curled up on Olivia, forgetting that she wasn't a pillow. I muttered an apology and stretched, reflexively going for my phone to check the time. It refused to power on, and it hit me that I really should have tried to charge it at some point. Given the cold and the total darkness outside, I guessed it was night time.

"Who left the door open?" I asked, standing up to close the sliding glass.

"You're responsible for the back, the front is my fault," Olivia said moving to shut the front door. "Together we're responsible for this wonderfully crisp draft."

For the moment I was grateful to have fallen asleep in my coat. It was still miserably cold all the same. "The heater maybe? We're going to get sick like this."

"Already on it," Olivia answered.

"You have a charger I could borrow?" I asked, holding up my dead phone. "And do you have an idea of what time it is?"

Olivia plugged her phone into the charger and checked its glowing screen. "Yikes, just after two! We were out for real. Look, you can borrow mine after I've charged for a bit. I'm at ten percent, okay now nine percent, and I don't like letting it die all the way, it's not good for the battery. Maybe you could see if Jason had one in his room?"

I considered that for a moment but thought better of it. "Nah, I should probably get home anyway. I need a change of clothes and I can't tell you with any certainty if I parked in a tow zone. Unless you want me to stay here?"

"I'll be okay," she answered. "As dumb as it sounds after all of that sleep, I kind of just want to go back to bed."

"Ha!" I laughed before I could stop myself. "I completely understand that feeling. I can't think of anything better right now."

"Okay, get out of here, I've had enough adventure for one day," Olivia said, walking me to the door.

I stopped in my tracks. "What about you? What if Jason or the rest of them come back?"

"Locked doors I guess," Olivia answered with a sigh. "Honestly, I straight up don't care right now. I'm willing to risk it at this point. I don't know how much more of this I can reasonably be expected to take."

"Maybe you should just come stay with me in that case?" I didn't like the sound of Olivia's answer. "It might be safer if we stick together."

"Hey, unless we're going to hide in the mountains—" Olivia began.

"Not a thing," I remarked.

"—then we're going to have to live our lives at some point," Olivia continued, ignoring me. "Because if they really want to get us, what can we do? We lost the first time out and almost died, and then we got lucky when you sucker punched one of their rookies while he was asleep. And if I can be very, very honest with you? Sleeping at your place is probably a bigger danger to me right now than just curling up under my own blankets and pretending that the whole of the universe exists under them. They're mad at you. Me? I'm an innocent bystander."

"You wanted to burn down a hospital," I reminded her. "But I take your point. Just be careful, all right? Call me tomorrow, let me know that you're okay. Don't text, call. I want to hear your voice."

Olivia hugged me firmly. "Fine weirdo, I'll call. Get home safe, okay? Besides, don't you have a roommate of your own who might be a more likely target?"

"Oh my God, Sharon!" I exclaimed. "How do I keep forgetting about her?"

"Because you're never home and when you are you lock yourself in your room because you hate the smell of weed and because you met her on Craigslist for an apartment and your main criteria for accepting it was the price?"

"Well, when you say it like that I sound like a jerk," I answered.

"Go!" Olivia commanded. "I'm sure everything is fine, I don't know what I'm saying right now."

"Fine, but we're going to search Jason's room together tomorrow, agreed?" I asked. Olivia doubled down on the Go look.

The cold was biting as soon as I stepped outside and I dug my hands into the jacket pockets and shuddered. Most people seem to associate Los Angeles with the constant sunny weather, but when we start to approach any kind of rain weather, the temperature appears to plummet. Or maybe being from the area just meant that I was just a wimp and accustomed to warmer climates. Either way, I was cold, and I had to walk to my car in the middle of the night. I had a bit of good news; my car was still where I left it, no tickets or slashed tires or anything.

Big Sister groaned to life, and I opted for the hot hands as I turned on my mostly useless heater. It was something, at least, I just needed to head straight home. As I drove, I thought about what Olivia said, and felt terrible. I don't believe she meant it to hurt me, but she was onto something. I had to worry about my roommate getting attacked right now, because of me. I'd endangered the life of my friend by doing nothing more than being close to her. And hell, not that I owed Paolo anything after he tried to kill me, but I'd probably broken up a marriage. A happy one, from her point of view at least.

And what was my crime? Trying to help people. I'd saved lives, so that meant I was in the right, didn't it? It had to. With one very recent and notable exception, I didn't make it a habit of attacking and threatening people. I just wished other people weren't paying for my actions.

I made it home, eventually, and thankfully managed to park directly in front of my building. I thanked whatever loving deity blessed me and ran up the stairs in my building, expecting the worst. An instant before I opened the door I silently cursed myself for not keeping that Tiki head. Maybe I'd found their weakness, and they were all just terrified of wooden party totems. I slammed open the door and yelled at the room, and I really couldn't tell you why. Maybe I just wanted the element of surprise again? It really didn't make any sense.

The house was still and dark, save for a few lights. The bathroom light had been left on, for one. There were ambient lights from various appliances. The soft humming light coming from my laptop, now in rest mode.

One more light joined, and that came from behind the door of my roommate's door. Sharon opened poked her head out, exhausted and freshly woken from slumber.

"Dude," she drawled, half-awake at best. "The noise. Go sleep. The hell's the matter with you?"

The door closed, and the light went out. The apartment was warm, and for the moment all of my concerns washed away. My apartment hadn't been invaded by besuited men and women of an unknown origin come to attack my Instagram famous roommate for living with a literary nerd. That thought alone made me realize that I'd had just about enough of this nonsense for the day, or maybe forever.

How is any of this real life?

I slipped out of my coat, throwing both it and my book bag on the couch, not being particularly concerned with the cleanliness of the apartment. Shoes similarly came off, and I made no effort to put them away. I plugged my phone into its charger, and even then, I barely remembered to do that. The comfort of my bed beckoned me.

I looked at the stack of assorted paperbacks I had in my ever-growing reading pile and determined that I needed to just unwind and read. Olivia was an inspiration for this; if she could sleep in her home without regard for immediate danger, I could read for the sake of reading. Because that's who I was: I was someone who enjoyed stories and characters. The medium didn't matter; I wanted to see how things played out, I wanted to see people grow. And for everything else going on right now, as insane as it was, it made me feel like I was moving forward with my life. I mean, I could also just as easily be killed or trapped in a parallel world or worse any minute now, but assuming I continued to survive, I felt that life was starting a new chapter for me.

My eyes fell on a tattered copy of F. Scott Fitzgerald's *The Crack-Up*, and the idea of reading the borderline mental breakdown non-works of a great writer at his lowest point seemed appropriate. It also felt good to read something with a low probability of traveling. There wasn't much in the way of story structure or character development, it was mostly manic cries for help in the way of essays and letters and feeling like everyone else in the world had gone crazy. I propped up an extra pillow, burrowed my way into a blanket, and started to read. I was asleep less than five minutes later.

"The stars don't look right," I mused. "Wrong color for one thing. And something else."

The sky was violet, shades of it shifting brighter and darker. The stars shone bright, but they were black. I took a moment to look around. To my right was a desert, infinite as far as I could tell. It went as far as I could see. To my left was a vast ocean, illuminated by no visible source of light. The waves were slight, barely licking at my feet. The sand felt warm, even through the protection of my shoes. I was wearing my coat, my bag strapped across my chest. I heard soft tones, repeating in the distance somewhere. I tried to make sense of the situation, but even confused I felt a calm gently wash over me, as gentle as the waves coming to the shore.

Without another option, I began to walk. The sand itself seemed to rise to meet me, making my steps as natural as walking on a paved road.

"Oh, you're here early," a genderless, monotone voice said beside me. "Welcome. I apologize for not being ready."

I looked to my right, and the desert was gone, replaced by aggressively green plains, made even more vivid by the odd night sky. An exotic cat of some kind, maybe a Lynx, seemed to mold itself to life from the ground like a chunk of clay being removed from a block and sculpted before my eyes.

"Where am I?" I asked the creature, locking eyes with it. The calm was still within me.

"Don't you know?" the large cat asked me, increasing in size as I looked on.

"Am I dreaming?" I asked. In response, the tones seemed to grow in pace. I turned my head in their direction and saw a city street, empty and decaying.

"Of course," the voice replied. "Though if we're moving here, I should change as well."

The figure moved in front of me, no longer a cat, but a slight and slim figure, with a long torso and arms, which seemed coiled and relaxed all at once.

"What are you?" I asked.

"An excellent question," the figure laughed, even as its transformation continued to that of man, ethereal green robes seeming to form out of the air and cover him, his hair growing out as he walked. "And one I will freely answer. I am Aos Si, though right now I am not even that."

"Because I am dreaming you?" I asked, and started to look around.

"If you could focus, please," the man asked firmly. "I know there's a lot to see, but if we could stay in one place for more than a few minutes, I would appreciate it. And no, that is not why, but you are asking the wrong questions."

The fact that I was still calm was in itself alarming, but I decided to play along. If this was a dream, there might be something to learn.

"Why did you say I was early?" I asked.

His eyes lit up at that. "Because it was not supposed to be your time, but the future is changing. Even if no one else notices. Look over there, what do you see?"

He pointed down the street, and my eyes followed. The road seemed bigger now, much bigger, and towering in the distance was a skyline, one particularly large shimmering building towering over everything. "Too far," he said. "Look closer."

In the middle of the street was a tree growing through the asphalt, smaller plants knocked over around it. The tree itself seemed maybe burnt, or just petrified in many places, bits of redwood shown through in patches. Many of the branches seemed to have died, though a few had leaves. One of the branches in particular grew to an impossible length compared to the rest of it, a fruit of some kind hanging off the end. A Pear? No, something else. I couldn't tell given the intersecting beams from lamps behind the branch; one pointed at the street, one at the sky.

"I don't understand," I said, still staring.

"Well, you are early, after all," the man said, circling me. "I could help you understand if you'd help me understand something as well."

Every instinct in me screamed not to answer him for some reason. I didn't know why; the offer seemed harmless.

"What is your name?" I asked him instead. He stopped circling me and met my gaze.

"I have a name," he answered carefully. "But it is not for you to know, not yet."

His stare was invasive, I didn't like it, and so I shut my eyes. "No, not yet," He said with some urgency in his voice. "You mustn't leave yet. Not yet!"

My head left the pillow as my body shot up straight with the feeling of both surprising and being surprised by a dangerous animal and then backing away, both of you managing to get to a safe distance. I got out of bed expecting to wince in pain, but I felt as fresh as ever. Nothing hurt, nothing was even noticeably sore. Perplexed, I moved my leg and stretched my calf where I'd been struck during our fight in the hospital. Nothing, not even the bruise when I inspected it.

I gave my torso a twist in either direction and found that I felt limber. No rest should have done that, no matter how long I'd been out. How long had I been out? The wall clock said an hour. An hour? That didn't seem right at all.

The phone confirmed the time once it finally came to life, assaulting me with notifications. Four missed calls with matching voicemails, a slew of messages and numerous texts, all from Olivia imploring me to get back to her. My heart started to pound.

I shouldn't have left her alone.

I dialed her number, already throwing on my coat and shoes as it rang.

"Elana!" Olivia shouted into my ear. "Why didn't you answer?"

"Dead phone!" I hissed back, mindful of Sharon's slumber. "Are you okay? What happened?"

"Oh, you have to get over here," Olivia said, and I could hear the enthusiasm in her voice. "I went into Jason's room. You're not going to believe it."

I finished slipping on my shoes and went for the door, waiting until I was on the other side to use my normal voice.

"Well, don't do that thing where you give me anxiety the whole time I'm driving there." My annoyance was probably showing in my answer. "Just tell me what to expect."

"I'm not sure what this is," Olivia answered. "Information, I guess. And a lot of it. I don't understand most of what I'm reading; you need to see it like, now."

"Okay, on my way," I replied, shoving the phone in my pocket. It was too early for this, neither of us should've been awake. Our respective sleep schedules were screwed. The sun would be coming up in an hour or so, but we were expecting rain, so I'm not sure how quickly anyone would notice. Cold and cloudy was no way to live in Southern California.

I pulled into the driveway and parked like a jerk because there was no way I was walking back up the hill again. I tried the door, and it was unlocked, so I walked in without bothering to knock. Olivia poked her head into the living room, holding a bottle of wine over her head like a club.

"Oh, you!" She smiled, lowering the bottle. "Check this out!"

We walked into Jason's room, clearly tossed, like someone was searching deep for something. "This place is a wreck, what were you looking for?" I asked.

"Huh?" she asked. "No, that's not what I was talking about, this was just how he lived. Dude was gross."

And he seemed so put together at the party too. "Okay then, what are we looking at?"

Olivia handed me a book out of Jason's crappy wire frame bookshelf. One of the motorcycle books, it was vintage for sure. There was a picture of two young people jumping a small mound of dirt. They looked like they were having fun. The cover read:

How to fix
your Yamaha
one cylinder motorcycle
Easy to understand Fully Illustrated
Save time Save money

"It is almost a certainty that I will never own Yamaha motorcycle, regardless of how many cylinders it has," I said flatly, looking at the book in her hands. "I don't even know what that means to the bike. Are fewer cylinders good or bad?"

"Just open it!" She said practically giddy from excitement. I took the book and opened to a random page, and was taken aback. There was nothing in here about engines or other mechanical knowledge; it was a training guide on something about the meditative restoration of an expended dimensional weapon.

"What the hell?" I breathed, eyes wide as I flipped through the pages.

"This is unreal, right?" Olivia asked, every bit as excited as I was.

I looked at the shelf, now not sure if the book on developing psychic powers through a vegan diet should be taken seriously or not.

"Are they all like this?" I asked, replacing the book in my hand.

Olivia walked towards his sliding closet. "Better," she said opening it. The closet was stacked full of books, a few boxes were scattered in the mess, and he had honest to goodness weapons hanging in the back. "I called dibs on his box of money," she added.

I looked over to her face now. "Box of money?"

"It was like six grand." She shrugged. "Jason still owes me for six months of rent for his part of the lease. What? Rent is expensive!"

I sincerely didn't care about the rent money right now. "Is that a sword?" I asked. Before she could answer, my phone rang. I looked down and saw that it was Claire.

"Who's calling at, like, six in the morning?" Olivia asked.

"Claire," I responded, knowing I had to take the call. "It must be urgent. I know she's mad, but if she's not asleep and calling, something is up."

I took a deep breath and slid the phone to answer. "Hey, Claire."

A familiar voice, dripping with venom greeted me on the other end that was decidedly not Claire. "Hey, yourself."

16

"Hello?" the voice asked after a silent moment. I was about to vomit. Olivia's eyes grew with concern watching me, but I couldn't say anything. "Don't tell me you've hung up already, this isn't a wrong number."

"What is it? What's wrong?" Olivia asked. I could only shake my head, desperately trying to wish away this nightmare.

"You know, if you're not going to play," the voice said slowly. It sounded like he was chewing on something. "I might just slit her throat now and be done with it."

"Don't! I'm here!"

"That's better, isn't it?" the voice asked. "Now then, we're going to play a game. You do want to play, don't you?"

It was a loaded question. Of course I didn't, but I had no idea what was happening with my friend, and I had to keep him talking. I pleaded, "I'll play whatever you want. Just don't hurt my friend!"

The voice *tsk*-ed at me. "And that is precisely how you will lose this game! That wasn't the question, was it? I asked if you wanted to play, not what you had to do to keep poor Claire Van

Amberg alive. The correct answer would be yes. Or no. I don't really care if you want to play or not quite frankly, but you will."

"Why?" I asked, tears welling up. Olivia stared with concern, not knowing what was happening.

"Because you are going to learn who holds the power in this relationship. Because for some daft reason," the voice said, "you seem to think the answer to that question is you. And now, unequivocally, unquestionably, you are going to learn that you have been so very, very wrong."

There was more chewing into the receiver. I remained quiet, waiting for some kind of instruction. "Now then," the voice continued. "Here are the rules. I am going to ask you five questions. If you get them all correct, I will tell you where to find us. Fail even one or deviate from my questions, Claire will die. Is that clear?"

"Yes," I answered. I wouldn't get another shot at this, and I knew it. I needed to be in control, not controlled. If I let my emotions get the best of me now, and they were extremely close to getting what they wanted already; then I'd have Claire's death on my hands for the rest of my life.

Take it in. Take it all in.

The smell of old takeout containers in the room. The taste of morning breath in my mouth since I haven't had a moment to brush my teeth. The feel of the pages of the book in my hand as I let my fingers absently flip through them. The glint of light from the sword's polished steel as the light in the room reflected off of it with a brilliance like crystal. The sound of that disgusting chewing in my ear. I let all of it in, accepting all of it equally, and I don't think I've ever done it so quickly.

More chewing. Gross. Good.

"Peachy," the voice assured me. "Now then, what is my name? First and last if you don't mind."

I steadied my breathing, remembering the business card he gave us the day he came in. "Bres Modred," I answered without thinking, my brain and mouth worked in unison with the correct answer.

"It does feel good to hear one's own name," Bres said smugly. "And you are off to the races!"

Olivia's hands shot to her mouth upon hearing me say his name. I gave her a look and motioned her to be silent. Bres continued. "Now tell me, what did I say would happen the next time you traveled? Exact words, please."

The exact wording was awkward, but I couldn't mess this up. I thought back to the hospital. I was already dazed as it was, it was something about stacking bodies, or...? No, I had it. "You would start making bodies, and they would be ones I'll recognize."

Bres suddenly snarled into the phone, a bestial sound, like he wanted to throttle me without restraint. "But you just didn't listen to me, did you?"

"No," I admitted, not allowing my focus to falter. "I did not."

There was a shout, like rage or of allowing fury to escape from one's lungs. "I am sorry, I'm letting you get to me in a little ironic twist. Sorry, how many questions was that?"

My lips curled up slightly at the question, Bres had been so transparent. Or he hadn't, but I was ready for him. "That was five, Bres," I said slowly. I didn't dare follow that up for fear of losing on the other terms.

Mad laughter seemed to be coming far away from the phone. Bres sounded like he was losing it over there and had put the phone down in response. "Explain," he commanded when he came back to the phone.

"You first asked if your rules were clear," I began. "Followed by the request for your name and the nature of your threat.

That was three questions. You then asked if I heeded your warning and ended with how many questions you had asked. Two more makes five."

The other end of the phone was silent, which was only serving to lead me to anger. "I won your game, fair and square," I said harshly into the phone. "Now live up to your end of the bargain and tell me where you are!"

"Well done, Ms. Black," Bres cooed. "I thought I might have tripped you up there, cannier than you look, eh? Fine, I'm at the place that sells the worst Scones in the country. Claire's quaint little bookstore, The Book's End. A fitting title, indeed. Oh, and I'd hurry if I was you, me arm is getting bushed."

He hung up and I allowed myself to let go of the controlled calm I was holding. It was like flexing a muscle and the strain of maintaining my composure was beginning to make my legs shake. My legs buckling from underneath me, I moved towards the bed just in time to not collapse to the floor. "Oh, God."

"Elana, talk to me," Olivia said on the edge of panic. "What's happening?"

I was on the verge of hyperventilating, but I knew I had to maintain for the moment. "It's Bres," I said, rocking gently on the edge of the bed. "He's back. And he has Claire."

Olivia looked at me in disbelief. "That... that doesn't make any sense. Why? She wasn't with us at the hospital."

I wished that I could say that it took me longer to realize why, but that day stuck out in my mind like an infected wound. "No, Claire met him before you at the store," I said sickly. "And there's something else. We don't have time for me to show you, but you have to take my word for this. People like Bres and me, there's something we can do. If you offer one of us your hand of your own free will, we can know things about you."

"What kind of things?" she asked, sitting next to me. To her credit, she didn't seem surprised by anything anymore. I could have said I was the ghost of the moon but also from a thousand years ago and in the future, and she would have been sad that I hadn't crossed over to the other side yet.

"Everything," I said. "And it can work both ways, you can learn about them too. I'm still not used to it, and I can't exactly control it, but it takes something out of me.

"And you're telling me you think this Bres guy did something to Claire?" she asked, catching up.

"I don't know how I missed that before," I said, blaming myself. "We should have warned her."

"That's it," Olivia said, standing up. "We're calling the police; this is too much."

"If you do that, you're killing our friend. *My* friend," I emphasized grimly. "I'm sorry, but it's true. He has her; he has powers, and absolutely no reason to keep her alive except for the fact that he's still interested in screwing with my life. We sit here and hope for the best while the cops do their job? We're planning a funeral next week."

Olivia looked hopelessly ill, and I could relate. "Then what do we do?" she asked, before sadly adding, "I feel like I'm asking that a lot lately."

I stood as well, rubbing her shoulder. "We aren't doing anything," I told her. "You are staying here. I'm going to take one of those swords and... I don't know. Improvise? It worked out okay last time."

Olivia looked like I'd punched her in the chest. "You'd really be that selfish?"

"I'm sorry," I reeled. "But what?"

She moved my hand off her shoulder and stood toe to toe with me. "You just said Claire is as good as dead if the police get involved and what? Are you just going to rush in there alone? We barely walked away from him last time, and if you go in alone, I'm going to have two dead friends in a couple of hours.

I'll be here, alone, waiting to hear that you died. You'd do that to me?"

"B-but you," I stammered, unprepared for this. "You don't have powers."

"And yours are worth a damn right now?" she asked me. "Go on then, tell me. Tell me how you're going to use them to save Claire's life."

My shoulders slumped, I felt defeated. "You're right. I don't have a chance. But I have to try. If I do nothing, that's it."

Olivia pounced on me in a hug. "You're not doing it alone, you walnut." Her breath was hot next to my ear; I could feel her heart beating fast as she pressed into my body. She let go and looked me in the eye. "I saw two swords in there. We're doing this together."

"Do you even know how to use a sword?" I asked, still processing.

"No, do you?" she asked.

"Not at all," I sighed. "We are definitely about to die."

We pulled up to the front of The Book's End. Both Claire's motorcycle and her car were in the parking lot. The curtains were drawn in the windows, which meant we had no way to know what was in there.

"So, last chance," I told Olivia as I turned off the car. "Are you sure you want to do this?"

"Oh hell no," she replied. "But I don't want you to go through it alone even less."

"Okay, let's do it. And please don't stab me by accident," I added.

"Same," Olivia responded.

I pulled my sword from the backseat. Olivia's sword was much smaller and considerably lighter. It was maybe the half the size, with a blade that snaked up to the tip with multiple curves. While hers was meant for stabbing, mine was sharper along its edges, making it a weapon intended to slice and cleave. Up the center of the blade itself were pearlescent stones, with carvings in each one that resembled sigils. The hilt was ornate steel, cold to the touch, and somehow the complicated patterns gave me an exceptional grip. I needed both hands to keep it steady; it was heavier than I would have thought by looking at it.

With a silent nod to Olivia, I pushed open the front door, the little bell jingling in the doorway announced our arrival.

"Ah, Elana," I heard Bres shout from the back. "I'll be right with you. Hey… let's have a little bit of music."

The sounds of a fiddle and a banjo rose out of the speaker, and I openly gasped when I finally saw Bres turn the corner. In his right hand was Claire, suspended in the air as he clutched her throat. Her eyes were wide with surprise, her arms hung limply at her sides, but the shocking part was that she was weightless. Not that Bres was in possession of super strength, it seemed clear that she was light as air, like Bres was holding a balloon. His grip held her down, not up.

When he saw me, though, Bres must have saw something equally shocking, as his eyes widened and then narrowed in my direction, and he started to shift to his left, taking strafing steps toward the center of the room without his eyes leaving me. The silence got the best of me, and I yelled to him.

"Let her go!" My voice threatened to crack, but my anger was escalating at the sight of my friend. I tightened my grip on the sword, pointing it in his direction with both hands.

"You've chosen a weapon already?" he remarked. "And the Vorpal Sword, no less? How did you—?"

The time for talking was over, and I cleared the length of the room, swinging the sword at him as hard as I could muster, an odd noise filling the air as it arced towards the neck of Bres; a booming *click-clack* echoed in the room. Bres for his part didn't move that I could see, but I felt the direction of the sword misdirected before a hard kick landed in my stomach, sending me rolling backward a good six feet into a shelf. It hurt, but I was relieved to see the sword was still in my hands.

The fight half of my fight or flight response took over my body, and I stood up immediately on sheer survival instinct, ready to continue. Bres made a motion with his hand, and the scythe that I noticed for just a moment, the object I must have struck, vanished. Then almost faster than I could process, his hand extended my way again, this time a bolt of fire streaked towards me. As it did, a familiar mixture of colors, blue and red mixing like oil and water, shimmered in front of me, stopping the flame prematurely. And as the flames and the hard colors dissipated in every direction, perhaps a second had passed, before a gust of wind knocked me off my feet and half a foot back into the shelf again, dislodged several books. I felt the energy drain from my body; it hurt to breathe in suddenly.

Bres grinned, that horrible grin, before he addressed me. "You haven't actually gotten stronger at all, have you? You do realize I have to power to kill you right now and be done with it. You're weak, untrained; you have no reserves, how were you planning to stop me?"

He gestured and Claire rigidly moved with him as effortlessly as a conductor's wand would have. "You barely have the battery to shield yourself the once. So, then you're not actually capable enough to choose yet, so then how did—Unless…"

His expression shifted to a panic, and he turned his entire body in reaction, just in time to prevent Olivia from running him through with her sword. A howl of pain left him, and he held

Olivia's wrist with both hands, dropping Claire in the process. Claire for her part looked as if she was suddenly reanimated, gasping for air, her face a myriad of confused emotions.

Olivia had found her mark, but only the first of the curves made its way into the torso of Bres. He grunted, only in a stalemate with Olivia for the second it took him to adjust to the sudden pain, before he struck her with a backhand, sending her to the ground, the small sword clattering at his feet. "Feck!" He shouted in frustration, ignoring the unconscious Olivia and clutching at his wound.

I was still struggling to stand up, at least thankful that Claire was scrambling away. Bres took a second look at the sword in exasperation.

"And then a Stale stabs me! With Johnny bloody Corkscrew, no less," he spat, his attention now turned to me. His expression was a mixture of acrimony and curiosity. "You didn't choose at all. These are just pieces of metal to you! Did you rob Jason? Did you and your friend manage to rob Jason of two artifacts?" he asked again.

"Maybe," I said defiantly through heavy breaths, trying not to show how defenseless I was at the moment.

"I don't know whether to laugh or kill everyone in this room," he said to no one in particular, before allowing himself a small chuckle. "I guess both."

He turned his back to me, walking back to Olivia and gripping her by the hair. He lifted her head off the ground as he continued. "You know, I really did call you to just talk this out with you. I was really just going to kill one of you to make an example, get you back in line. Now I'm going to have to kill you all and wash my hands of the situation."

The action woke up Olivia, the blood draining from her face. The scythe materialized in his hand, and he moved it towards her neck.

"Wait!" I screamed.

"No, thank you," Bres said casually, putting the blade to her neck.

My brain was moving faster than it ever had. "You really don't want to do that!" I shouted.

"Oh?" Bres asked, looking my direction. "I think I do."

I need to think of something immediately.

"I met someone," I said quickly. "Someone who you really don't want to piss off."

He had an amused smile. "I'll play. So just who would that be, Lass?"

I recalled the name from my dream, not exactly a person but a thing. "An Aos Sí," I said directly.

Rage crossed his face, and he dropped Olivia's head. "You're lying!" he spat.

Gotcha.

He was Irish and I'd heard that name before. If all the fiction is real, why not the folklore? "Then kill her and see what happens!" I shot back.

"Who was it? Give me a name!" he demanded, waving his weapon menacingly at me.

My pained smile touched both sides of my face. "We both know it is not given freely."

"Then all of you will die! You'll just get the honor of taking that secret to Hell!"

The bell to the door chimed as the front door slammed open. "Stop!" the familiar voice yelled. "These aren't the orders." I knew it was Jason before I even saw him.

"Then they need to give me better orders!" Bres shouted back, wild eyes still locked on me.

"That's not how this works, and you know this," Jason said sternly. "Car is out front. We'll get that little hole in you plugged up. Come on. You don't want to defy a direct order, at least not this one."

Bres contemplated the plea with several heavy breaths before letting loose a shout of frustration and slicing a table next to him messily in half with one effortless swing of his scythe. He marched out of the store, giving Jason a hard shoulder bump as he did. Jason walked up to me as I still sat on the ground, trying to recover. "Besides," He said matter-of-factly. "If anyone is going to kill you, it's going to be me. Now give me my damn swords."

He ripped the Vorpal Sword from my hand, making sure to collect Johnny Corkscrew as well. One more bell chime, then the sound of a car pulling off. My friends and I sat on the ground, looking to each other for answers. Nobody seemed to have them.

I'm not sure we even knew what the right questions were.

17

The room was laden with silence nearly thick enough to touch. When it finally broke, no one knew what to do. No one made a bold declaration of fury or conveyed confusion or fear with a series of questions. Instead, it was the sound of painfully thick sobs; openly weeping hard tears.

The sounds came from me, and after everything all three of us had just been through, neither of them knew what to do. My eyes darting back and forth rapidly between them, seeing their concern and disorientation growing each moment. All three of us on the ground, still unsure if we were able to stand. And before anyone could actually say anything, when everyone thought they had reached the breaking point and we couldn't be any more uncomfortable, I did something no one expected. My painful tears turned into a crazed, joyous howling of relief and exultation that hurt my ribs and reached something deep inside of me.

"What could you possibly be laughing at?" Claire finally asked, desperately.

I tried to control my laughter long enough to answer. "We are alive! We are injured, I smell like sulfur, and we lost our weapons. But we are alive!" I laughed a little bit again as they studied my face. "We didn't expect to survive, we were even all overtly threatened with death, but look! We are here!"

I laughed a bit more, followed by Olivia, who gave a small chuckle of her own. "I can taste blood in my mouth, I can still feel the bruises from the last time," she said, a twinkle in her eyes. "But I can still taste, and I can still feel!"

The two of us were barely holding it together when Claire spoke up. "I can breathe again!" she exclaimed.

There was a pause from all three of us, and then our laughter doubled. We laid down on the floor of the shop, not bothering to do much of anything except being content with our current best case scenario. We kept laughing. The laughter gave way to the occasional giggle, which in turn gave way to silent contented smiles, which in turn gave way to sleep for all of us. I don't know who fell asleep first, but when it came for me, it was sudden and all-encompassing.

Cold water. I was standing ankle deep in a wading pool, and the shock of its temperature sent a chill running through my entire body. I didn't step into the water, I wasn't dropped into it. I was just suddenly standing here and I nearly fell over trying to get out of it.

Ugh, my socks are soaked!

I looked around and realized that I was back in the same place I visited when I dreamt last. But it was different. I was in a forest, for one thing. The pool of water I'd been standing in was either the beginning or end of a road. I began to look ahead and craned my neck up to see another difference. The moon was far too close. Both of them were, in fact, and the sky was a deep emerald which gave way to a brilliant golden orange as it got closer to the horizon. I just stared at the heavens for a few moments, taking in the unfamiliar constellations. The stars weren't black, as they were last time, but clear as windows, giving me the feeling that if I were only closer, I would be able to see something outside of the outside.

Is this sunrise?

The sense that something—maybe a lot of somethings— was watching me overwhelmed me to the point where I looked back down at the road. It felt like I closed every eye by doing so. It wasn't that whatever it was that I sensed had gone away, they were just hidden. When I looked to my left, everything to my right felt like it was watching me. And when I looked to my right, everything on my left came to life.

"Is this just going to be a thing now?" I shouted into the woods. "Am I just going to keep waking up in freaky places whenever I fall asleep?"

In the corner of my eye, a movement like a swarm of bees moved to blur my vision for just an instant.

"If you want to talk, we can just talk," I suggested. When there was no response, I then called out, "Aos Sí?"

I was immediately hit by a battering ram of emotions.

"NOnonoDonotcallthemNOTTHEMstopWhatareyoudo-ingNoIcannotfacethemagain!"

It was like a thousand voices suddenly told me to stop talking in a movie theater because the consequences would be that we'd all be attacked by bears. I could tell it was the creatures, not the world, and that struck me as important for some reason, even if I wasn't sure why.

I clutched my eyes shut and forced the voices out of my head. "Fine, what do you want from me?"

The world must have sensed my annoyance, because I soon felt that same comfort and calm well up in me as before. But I didn't want it. I didn't want to feel content with what was happening. I needed to understand and be aware.

"No," I said, careful to address the world and not the eyes that I couldn't see. "That's what I need. This isn't a dream, is it? I'm somewhere."

I waited for any sort of response, and I took the silence as an answer.

"Okay, where am I?" I asked. Still nothing. "Well, let's trying something else. Why am I here?"

And nothing. I looked around. Even the eyes in the woods were still closed. Nothing even made an attempt to see me after that one. Wait. "Is that it?" I asked. "Is there something you want me to see?"

The road before me shimmered suddenly. "Well, what do you want me to see? The road? Or where it leads?"

In response, the world behind me folded from horizontal to vertical and gently nudged me as a freshly formed wall. The road itself began to decline. With no choice, I walked forward, doing my best to ignore the squishing sound and feeling coming from my feet.

"You don't have to drop me into the water next time. I would have figured it out. That I was here."

I took the hint and kept walking, feeling the number of eyes behind me grow. The forest began to thin, and in time I could see the remains of a city.

"Is this the same city I saw before?" I asked. The world wall behind me seemed to quicken my pace.

When the road ended at the edges of the city, I turned around watched as the forest and grounds fell back into place, before vanishing and being replaced by a lake reeking of stagnant water, an acidic odor permeating the air around it. The annoyance I felt doubled as I spoke to the water. "And I should move forward, not backward. I need to see the city. Got it."

Industrial buildings greeted me at first, and I must have wandered aimlessly for the better part of an hour, trying to find anything of use. The emerald sky slowly peeled back to reveal a brighter day, but there was no visible sun. Whatever was illuminating the world wasn't something that could be seen.

A thought made me shiver. Maybe it didn't *want* to be seen. That's kind of scary, more than the fact that I don't know exactly where I was or how I'd gotten there, is the thought that I don't know who or what actually lives here. Beyond the one thing I've met, which didn't want even to tell me its name; I'm aware of a lot of things here, and I knew almost none of them. A second thought made the hairs on my arms rise.

I really hope this place isn't some kind of metaphor for my social life. I rolled my eyes as I thought that. Both were scary enough without having to draw similarities between them.

The world around me offered comfort as I thought that, and this time I accepted just a little bit of it. We seemed to be able to communicate, if wordlessly. I still didn't know how, but it didn't seem like it inherently wanted to harm me, and besides, what other choice did I have but to take all the kindness I could get? I was a stranger in a strange land.

"Except not from Mars!" I said with a chortle.

Aos Sí.

I couldn't help it. It was like the words were forced into a thought in my head, a song you couldn't stop hearing when you wanted to focus on anything else. I thought it and then the world around me seemed to let me know that none were nearby.

"What are they?" I asked out loud.

No response, but I could feel some of the eyes back away in response. Well, the world didn't want to talk about it and neither did my fans, so I guess there's no point in talking about it. I'm just going to make literally everyone and everything uncomfortable.

I continued through the city, trying to find it's center, and wandered into one of the buildings on the street. I felt drawn to it for reasons I couldn't explain. From the outside, it didn't seem like anything special. Maybe some kind of warehouse, from what I could see. Windows dotted the outside, and the roof seemed high enough that there might have been a second floor.

Inside I confirmed my suspicion. An open first floor, a landing area just above a small set of stairs, and a second floor visible through a grated ceiling. On the ground floor was a single desk, not large or small, at the end of the room. I cautiously crossed the dusty floor, and as I got closer, I saw that sitting on the desk was a single sheet of paper, pristine and brilliantly white, which stood out in sharp contrast to everything else I'd seen in the city, which had seemed to be in a state of decay.

The page was blank.

"Is this for me?" I asked, reaching out for it.

The world violently shook around me, and I was pulled through the air by invisible hands up to the mezzanine, leaving the desk visible, but now out of reach.

"Okay, not for me! Sorry!" I cooed to the world around me. Out of one of the windows, I saw the opposite side of the building from where I entered, and I think I saw what I was meant to see.

I practically flew down the stairs, dashing for the back door and making my way to the street. I saw it, a little closer now. That tree, huge and dark, it almost looked like it had been burnt; it was horrible. And I glanced up to the branch; it's leaves growing in spite of everything, the fruit, nearly the size of my fist and it wasn't a pear, but what was it? A couple of thin green leaves sprouted next to it as the branch grew and reached out towards the flood lamp beams. I didn't know where to look. The rapidly growing branch, the pulsing bits of redwood which hadn't... blighted? I'm not sure what blight looks like. Before I could see the branch touch the beam, a thought suddenly struck me.

I started to vocalize it as I looked around at the buildings and the street. "This place, it isn't decaying, it's—" I turned around in time to see the things that had been following me. Every eye opened at the same time, every single one of them stared at me knowing what I knew. I screamed.

I scrambled to my feet, shock and panic obscuring my vision, the feeling flashing through me, my skin prickled. I wasn't sure which world I'd screamed in. That one, this one, or both.

"What was that?" I heard a man ask.

"Oh, that?" Claire responded nonchalantly. "I wouldn't worry about that. You have a beautiful day now, okay?" Okay, so it might have been both.

The man muttered something inaudible and left, ringing the little bell on the door with a familiar jingle as he did. I sat back down on the tiny bed with a sigh. I was up in the loft at The Book's End, still fully clothed. I gave myself a sniff, and yeah, I needed a bath. Weird, though, I felt completely fine once again. Not a single bump or bruise, I didn't even feel sore.

"Is it safe to come down?" I yelled to Claire.

"Is it safe to come *up*?" she yelled back. Fair point.

I headed down to the main floor to find Olivia still in the shop along with Claire. The place had been mostly cleaned up from the fight that took place in there just... well, I didn't know what time it was, actually. That could have been days ago for all I knew.

"How long was I out?" I asked the two of them.

"Well, it's about three now, so," Olivia said doing the math. "Maybe eight and a half, nine hours? I don't know exactly when we all passed out."

"Yeah, you seemed like you needed it worse than we did." Claire added.

"I don't remember going upstairs," I said, looking behind the counter for my bag. "What happened?"

Claire opened a drawer and pulled out my bag. "Looking for this?" she asked. I nodded.

"Around noon or so, the bell woke me up," Olivia said. "Some dude didn't know how to handle seeing us all passed out on the floor, and he especially freaked out at the little puddle of blood."

"That's right!" I said, remembering. "You stabbed Bres!"

"I did, and I got this for it," Olivia said pulling back a bit of her hair to reveal a nasty looking bruise near the back of her jaw.

"Olivia woke me up, then you," Claire added. "But you looked dazed, almost drunk. We put you to sleep upstairs and got the place cleaned up before we let anyone else in. We actually just opened again right before you woke up."

I was amazed by this. "How are you even thinking of being open today after everything that just happened?"

"Because, Elana, this is my livelihood. I don't get the luxury of calling a timeout on life when something bad happens," she said it patiently, but it sounded like a lecture. "If someone wants to give me money in exchange for whatever we have here, I need to stay open or have someone here for me. That's just how it is."

That last part was crushing. I couldn't imagine what Claire had just gone through, and she had to clean and put on a happy face because I needed a nap. "Sorry." I said softly. It was all I could manage.

Claire looked nonplussed at the apology. She asked, "Are you… did you just say sorry? Elana, that man was about to kill me, and you and Olivia saved my life! You understand that, right? You just went all big damn hero on that situation! Your coat is officially the wrong color as far as I'm concerned! No, I am in no way blaming for you any of this. If anything, you tried to warn me, and I didn't listen. If someone does something violent and awful, or just does something to harm others, that's never on you. You are not responsible for the actions of others, okay?"

I felt uncomfortable all of a sudden, unsure of how to respond to that, so I didn't.

"Come here," Claire said, offering me a hug. I took it, and then Olivia joined us as well. I wanted to cry, but didn't. After a minute, we released each other.

"There is the bigger problem to worry about, though," Olivia pointed out. "We're not safe. And I don't know if there's even anyone who can help us."

"You're right," I said, gathering my strength. "We still have all those books at home, and who knows what else. There's gotta be something in there to help us take them down, and we'll find it."

Claire took a step away from me. "Whoa. I don't think you understand. We have to walk away from this. From everything." She said that last part almost like an order.

"What are you talking about?" I asked her. "You know what I do, right?"

"Yeah, I do actually," she said. "Bres told me everything about what you've been doing. You're trying to help people."

"Not trying! I *am* helping people!" I shot back.

"Yes, I believe you," she said impatiently. "But some very scary people are going to murder us if you don't stop. Do you think I'm afraid to die?"

I didn't know how to answer, and I sat there fuming, looking for words.

"The answer you were looking for is yes, by the way. I'm terrified of it, is that something you want for me?"

"Obviously not!" I practically yelled. "But what about all the people I've saved? They probably felt the exact same way you did, and now they're alive."

"And that's a good thing, but for them, it was their time," Claire tried to reason. "Any death is a tragedy, but you were erasing something that had already happened. How are you going to keep us alive?"

I had to take a moment to let the anger pass out of me before I continued. "You're right, I can't expect you to help me, but you can't ask me just to stop."

"Then let's vote on it," Claire said, arms crossed. "Three of us are involved, three lives which are directly in harm's way. Majority rules, sound fair?"

"Yeah, fine," I snapped. "Vote then!"

"All in favor?" Claire asked. I raised my hand and looked around. I was the only one.

"Olivia?" I asked in disbelief.

"All opposed?" Claire asked, raising her hand. Olivia followed her example.

"Bres just wants us to stop," Olivia said meekly. "We can't fight him."

"Yes we can!" I said defiantly. "You made him bleed! He's not a god!"

"Elana, the vote has been cast," Claire countered. "Do you see? We don't want any of this."

"I got lucky," Olivia muttered, folding her arms.

I started to reply to that when Claire took a step forward and confronted me. "Elana! *Look at me.* You were right, okay? When he held me up like that, it wasn't strength. It was power! He did it by sheer tyranny of will! I don't know what he did to me, but it was the scariest thing I've ever experienced. When he grabbed me, it was like... it was like I stopped being a person. I was weightless. I could see and hear, but I had no control over my body. Everything was gray and cloudy, and it was all just fading away. I couldn't shake the feeling that my body was already dead and that the rest of me would just slip away into nothing. When he let me go, all of the color and feelings rushed back, like I was just aware of my body again for the first time."

She looked with pleading eyes now. "Please listen to me! Call it supernatural or mystical or just plain weird, but I never want to experience that again. I don't know that I'll ever forget ... That... It's is too much for any of us or even all of us. We love you and appreciate your intent, but you're going to *die*. And you're going to kill *us* too!"

We stared at each other for several moments. Finally, I threw my bag on and started to walk out. Olivia grabbed my arm. "Where are you going?"

"I understand your fear," I said, gently freeing my arm as I looked at her. "I really do. I'm so afraid and angry that it's all I can do to keep from shaking. But you're wrong if you think you can just ask me to stop. I've saved lives, and I can save more, that's not something you just walk away from. Whoever has the most has to give the most, great power and the responsibility that comes with it, not escaping the responsibility of tomorrow by avoiding it today. I'm butchering them all, but one of those makes a complete quote and a complete point, so choose which-ever one you like, but it all means the same thing."

I went to the door, opened it, and looked back to them again. "I'm going to figure this out because I'm not here on ac-cident and no one is going to do this for me. I'm going to stop Bres on my own, and then I'm going to save anyone I can because they deserve it just as much as we deserve to know that we're safe."

"Elana!" Claire yelled, but I'd already turned to face the day. The doorbell gave a little jingle as the door shut behind me.

18

I wasn't certain exactly where I was when I finally pulled over. I must have driven a for at least twenty minutes trying to find someplace private to stop before I allowed myself to cry. I'd meant what I said to them, still meant it in fact, but it felt like something important had just broken apart in my hands. I'm already someone who isn't terribly close with a whole lot of people, and I'd just told two of my best friends that I didn't need them.

The difference was, I didn't have any choice in whether they helped me or not, and both Claire and Olivia were solidly out of this fight. They were afraid, and that was something I could relate to. I've been afraid of something most of my life, which might have been the difference between us at this moment. I'd never known Olivia to be afraid of anything, and Claire's fears were always manageable. She was scared of losing her business, so she worked harder. She was afraid of not having people who cared about her, and in time she made friends.

My fears, by comparison, had always been irrational. The fear that someone will think my nose is weird. The fear that I'd hid in the bathroom too long or too many times and everyone at the party will notice. The fear that even my closest friends would one day leave or decide I wasn't cool enough anymore. The fear that a group of strangers won't like me, but then will only pretend to be nice to me, and I'll never know it. They'd say something awful behind my back, and one of them would tell a lie about me, which would make someone else believe that lie, so they'd repeat it. Then two people would tell the same story, and the third and fourth people would also repeat it and then it would become something different, and soon entire groups of people I'd never met would be poisoned against me before we ever even had the chance to meet, before anyone knew I wasn't some huge jerk, and—

My heart was pounding just thinking about that scenario. My breaths were hard and shallow, my fingers hurt from where I'd been clutching the steering wheel. At least I'd stopped crying.

My point is, that for as terrifying as my fears were to me, I'd always found a way to get past them and function. Even when I was so afraid that I almost couldn't move, I could fake bravado. In a bit of irony, the fear of being seen as afraid made me move on as if I wasn't. To do otherwise would mean to just stop, and I've lived that life before. Sometimes days, sometimes weeks, sometimes months at a time... and you don't get that time back. So ultimately, you were afraid for nothing. If I could impart a piece of advice onto the world, it is that more than the crowds, more than fake smiles and unheard whispers, even more than our own base, loathsome selves, what we should really fear is stasis. Life will always move forward, whether we move forward or not. Even stumbling and flailing about, unable to find your balance and rolling down a hill head over heels is still moving forward. It might not be graceful, but at least you're not stuck with whatever you were trying to move past.

My hands finally relaxed off the steering wheel, my breaths normalized, and I told myself that this was no big deal for long enough to start the car again so I could do what it was that I needed to do. It took me a few minutes to get my bearings and find the general direction I was trying to move in.

That was one of the amazing things about Los Angeles. I've lived here my entire life and it was still entirely possible to find new places and things to see completely by accident. That's because Los Angeles isn't a city, it's a collection of cities all fused together, masquerading as a city, each with their own topography and planning. Some adhere strictly to a grid system; some decide the streets should only go one way or that they should abandon the north and south convention the last city adhered to and move crossways. Sometimes a city will just be in a place where a city should never have been, and we all just accept that fact. Fifteen minutes in LA could mean that you've traveled to the other side of the map or the other side of the street, depending on traffic.

I didn't live much more than fifteen minutes from The Book's End, but I wasn't going home. I was going to Olivia's place in Highland Park, which would take me twice that amount of time in the best of conditions. She lived far enough away from me that in this town, it wouldn't be unreasonable to a lot of people just to abandon the friendship. That's one of the jokes around here. *I'd take the 405 to the 10 for you.* As if friendships are so fragile and expendable that you deserve special praise if you have to spend more than ten minutes traveling to see someone, when others would have given up on you entirely. Because our primary criteria for companionship is proximity.

Hilarious.

As I thought about this, I also recognized that cynical observations like this were just my usual way of distracting myself from something really bothering me. In this case, that I'd just abandoned my friends.

Did I abandon them, though? Did they abandon me? Am I saving them or just running?

I didn't want to think about what I was doing until I was already doing it, and yet, here we were. Smart enough to come up with a plan to trick myself, also smart enough to realize what I'm doing. And I had almost made it, too. It made sense to get off the freeway and pick up snacks for the study session I had ahead of me. Something else to think about, and besides, I was ravenous at this point.

A short trip through the Hi Ho market to load up on snacks, complete with a friendly and life choice reaffirming greeting from the staff, and I was back at Olivia's place. I had the key in the door before I was gripped with the possibility that the house might not be empty. There wasn't really anything to stop Jason from coming back, was there? Would a locked door stop him? That seemed unlikely, but I also didn't know what he had on his plate. On the one hand, we *did* beat him up and take his stuff. There wasn't really a good way of phrasing that. We woke him doing it; it wasn't even sporting. So, he had plenty of reason to return if he absolutely wanted to. On the other hand, he didn't do a thing to me when I was utterly helpless. That was odd.

Just to be on the safe side, I pulled out a bottle of cream soda from the six-pack I'd just purchased and gripped the handle like a club as I turned the key as slowly and quietly as possible. The door was open now, and I wasn't dead, so I felt like I was off to a good start.

The house wasn't large, just a small two bedroom with a modest backyard and a shed, but that didn't stop me from taking almost half an hour to scour every inch of the place. Even the shed, which I doubt would ever see use by anyone who'd ever reside here. Most importantly, Jason's room, well, the room formerly belonging to Jason was a better way of putting it, was undisturbed. Confident I no longer needed a blunt head smashing weapon I applied a little pressure and twisted off the cap, taking in a congratulatory sip. It was time to get to work.

After bringing everything inside, I looked at the stacks of books, all of which seemed entirely unorganized. "Whoever you are, Jason, you're a crap dude and a worse student," I muttered to myself, taking a stack of books out of his closet.

The first seemed to be interesting, if not a bit worthless concerning helping me figure anything out. It was a textbook of some kind and explained something by way of otherworldly theory. Half of this I'd already heard from Paolo, so it really just acted as confirmation. One of the schools of thought was that fiction wasn't fiction the way people generally understand it. When we read books or watched a movie, it might be a small peek through a window into another universe. There was further debate as to whether the people writing these fictional worlds were divining information or if they were actually creating the worlds and playing God.

Another school of thought seemed to believe that in other worlds, everything was merely a construct. A character, as an example, perhaps thought it was alive, but where we had free will, they were subject to predestination. Their worlds were more two-dimensional and weren't subject to the same rights or even boundaries that we were in our world. In this school of thought, they were all akin to something like an artificial intelligence, where they all looked and sounded real, but it was important to remember that they were all at best a half-life. Not truly alive, but also still something to be respected in the sense that they'd still been created.

What I really learned from that textbook is that no one had any idea of anything at all, but if they used enough words they might feel better about that fact and convince themselves otherwise.

The next book seemed to be a little more helpful at least. It described the different abilities possible by people like me. That was a sudden, and chill-inducing thought. People like me. I'm not alone, which is great, but I'm also not alone which is ominous. The more I thought about it, the more improbable it seemed that I'd never really met anyone besides Lucia who could travel or toss around fire and wind or just view a person's entire life story. I had to wonder what else I didn't know, but judging from the stack of books as tall I was, I had to figure the answer was almost everything.

It went on to describe that while everyone had at least some level of talent in the natural gifts that went along with being a traveler, every so often something called an Adept would just show up. Someone would be immediately masterful at being able to Know someone, for example. Others would be able to tap into something called the Vigor. Supposedly, travelers were supposed to be inherently stronger and faster than the average Joe. Not exactly comic book levels, more "Usain Bolt" than "Powered by the radiation of Earth's yellow sun," but it was still something. Modest shards of power that gave everyone an extra boost. "Fairly certain I'm not a Vigor Adept," I said taking a swig of cream soda.

Something happened suddenly that I had tried to put out of my head this whole time. I thought I'd been hearing conversations somewhere just out of sight, but they felt like distant memories. I thought perhaps I might have been remembering something I'd heard somewhere else, stray thoughts just floating around. But I heard one so distinctly in my head that I could no longer ignore it.

"What you're talking about is war! All-out war! A devastation none of us will walk away from! A complete breakdown of magic itself!"

They weren't all this dire or jarring. Some were completely innocuous. But they were there, and the longer I spent reading any of these books, the stronger the thoughts became. Not that I was spending the time to sit down and read any of them cover to cover, I was committing the sin of skimming the books to find something useful. I made a promise to myself to read everything at some point and give all of these books my undivided attention, but for now, the clock was ticking.

A lot of what I was finding made absolutely no sense to me without context, so I began sorting the books as I went. One pile for lore, another pile for what seemed to be instruction or training manuals, and another I affectionately referred to as *AP Discombobulation taught by Professor Abner Broccoli.*

I decided to get specific with what I didn't understand. If the contents of those books refused to make any sense, then I wouldn't make any sense in categorizing them. I did manage to find two pieces of information that were invaluable. The first referred to that weird bubble of energy that was popping up around me, and it was called a Blister. It's one of the simpler, and more instinctual skills we can learn, so I didn't get too excited. The better part though explained why I had so little juice with it. Like anything, it required practice to create and maintain. In time, I'd be able to call and dismiss it on command. I also had to develop my ability to hold onto that power. It wasn't a well that could just be drained, it was that the power might have been there, but my well wasn't deep enough. I had one, though, which was the prerequisite to everything else. So if I worked on it, I'd be able to make a deeper hole. The text also indicated that sleep, or at least rest and meditation, were really the only things that allowed you to recharge. Right now I was at the point where I could block maybe one thing, then I was done until I took a nap. That didn't make me very formidable. In theory I'd be able to toss around a little water or fire, but it would be crude at best and again, I'd need a nap before I tried again.

More of the books described other abilities that could be learned, but I was worried about trying any of them at the moment. If I did have enough just for an emergency trick, I didn't want it to waste in in practice while danger loomed. The ideas seemed simple enough and appeared to rely on will and imagination more than anything, with a few mental gymnastics thrown in just because life is complicated. I couldn't just yell "I want that thing on fire!" and have a thing be on fire. But I could imagine something igniting, the fire welling up inside of me, and if I wanted to make the fire more than imagination, I could will it into existence. There was more to it than that of course, I was simplifying a process I didn't understand yet, but that was close enough for someone who'd spent a few minutes with a textbook titled *From Tinkering to Torqueing: A Beginner's Guide to Tractors and Tools* by Roger Welsch. I didn't know who this Roger fellow was, but I doubt he had flamethrower hands. Probably just regular hands, intimately familiar with tractor guts.

I had to put that one down when I started to hear an extended declaration of undying affection. I had no time for romance; I was trying to get stuff done. I decided to give one more a try, and this one lied about being a book on discourse analysis. I was assuming it was lying; it would be strange to find a book with the correct cover at this point. Sure enough, this was a good one. It was a field manual for finding Vagrants. According to the manual, Vagrants were travelers who left the protections of the Order and tried to live outside of the laws and structure provided to all who were talented. It went to great lengths to describe how dangerous these people were, even if their motivations were banal. While not everyone who ran left with the intention of causing mayhem or grievous harm, having that kind of power made them too dangerous to exist. Of course, there were also those who did have ill intent, and that was everyone's worst fear. It read equally as a how-to and as propaganda, but I supposed they were preaching to the choir. I don't think I counted as a Vagrant given that I was never invited to the party in the first place.

There were locations known as Dearths, areas where access to the energy all travelers needed to draw upon seemed to be at their weakest, meaning less of it to be thrown around. These places were a double-edged sword for the Vagrants. While it leveled the playing field, it also made them easier to find. So if you found one Vagrant in one of these Dearths, you probably found ten or a hundred more. This seemed like exactly the lead that I needed. If anyone could help me stave off the assault of these people, these Gardeners, it would be people who spent most of their time actively fending them off. It didn't hurt that they would understand my position. It was like finding someone wearing the same T-shirt as you, except with you know, reality altering powers.

I finished off my cream soda and packed for the trip. Snacks, reading material; that kind of thing. There weren't any locations listed, they would be worthless anyway even if they were, but the guide was pretty clear on how to find one. The telltale signs included electronics becoming unreliable, rot in the nearby plants, an unmistakable miasma seemingly emanating from everything, and perhaps the biggest giveaway, a changing landscape. If you had the talent and you were looking, doors would appear on walls, stairwells where you wouldn't expect one; it all sounded a bit M. C. Escher, but whatever.

I tried to think of places that matched this description that I've seen, and if I was right, I might have had a place to start.

19

The idea of cell service going out or of plants dying wasn't exactly an uncommon occurrence in Los Angeles, there were four million people in the city alone, all competing for the same cell towers and against general interference, so usually that just meant that your provider couldn't cover everything equally. It's reasonable, and no one complains too much. If you can't connect to the internet for some reason, you're likely to be asked what provider you have. Then, almost regardless of your answer, you're going to be told in an understanding tone that the source of your problem has been discovered. And as far as plants being dead or dying, that's just what happens when you live in a place where you're not allowed to water the lawn half the time. Most of the time we're in a drought until we get hit by biblical flooding.

There was a place, not terribly far from my apartment in Palms, which fit the criteria perfectly. An urban housing development in Mar Vista. My phone not only never worked when I was in that area, but it also sometimes just died entirely and wouldn't turn back on for hours. Along with that, cars would inexplicably break down in the area. Anyone turning off the 90 has seen at least a couple of cars stopped outside of the security gates, which were, of course, empty shells. Even the tire flattening spikes seemed to have rusted out of the ground at a rate that shouldn't seem possible given the age of the place. And as far as the local plant life was concerned, well, what could be said? You had brittle dead grass and a few urine stained, perpetually dying bushes and that was about it.

But the real kicker—and this is something I'd never actually told anyone because I was certain I had to have just imagined it —was that on more than one occasion, I would pass by on the street and could have sworn to you I saw a subway entrance leading below ground, right in the center of the development.

Try to imagine how maddening that is. Right in the center of a big, low rent housing area filled with apartments, a place directly next door to an elementary school no less; you see a subway entrance. And you don't even see it every time, maybe every other time. Then you start to think about it, and you couldn't have seen it. Could you? Why would it make sense for there to be a subway in the area? Besides the fact that while, yes, we do have a subway system in LA, it's barely a subway. Two of our lines are underground, and one of them is nowhere near here. And even if it were, a rail system stop would be packed with commuters, especially this close to the airport and one of the busiest freeways in the country. Not to mention, it's sitting in the middle of a bunch of homes, which would surely be some kind of zoning violation. And across the street from a school? Even worse! But again, the worst part of this would be that you know for a fact that it doesn't exist, and you can't tell anyone what you're seeing any more than you could ask if anyone had tried that new soup made entirely of tobacco and cough syrup. It doesn't exist, and everyone is going to think less of you for suggesting such a thing might be possible.

So I guess a part of me was really looking forward to finally going down those steps and being vindicated, to myself if no one else, that I really did see an utterly stupid thing and it definitely exists and that I'm not experiencing localized hallucinations of a very specific set of stairs in a very specific location.

I made sure to park a full block away since my car was a miracle on its own most days anyway, and I really wasn't ready for her to be a casualty if the rumors turned out to be true. My book bag slung over my chest, and it hit my side with a little extra oomph given its weight. I locked the car door and took a deep breath.

"Okay," I said to myself, trying to inspire confidence in myself for what I was about to do. "Let's go down the worst possible rabbit hole."

I made the walk over quickly enough, passing the guard station which now and likely always stood empty. The asphalt beneath my feet had warped and buckled over time, perhaps damaged by the rain. Periodically a pothole could be found, and the stench in the air of urine and uncollected trash, loosely dropped into bins made it hard to concentrate. It was thankfully a short and painless walk to where I'd spotted the old subway entrance in the past, but this time? Nothing. Just an island of dead grass, a few beat-up cars parked in front of it.

I walked around on the island, thinking for some reason that it was just invisible and I might bump into it. Hopefully I wouldn't fall down into it. No luck either way, but at least I probably looked like an idiot to anyone watching me slowly grope my way through the grass, afraid to tumble down a set of stairs that weren't there.

Eventually, I took a step back and gave it one last chance by gazing at where I thought it was supposed to be, satisfied that nothing else would show up. Except, of course, the possibility of concerned residents.

I checked my phone, hoping it wasn't too late to drive around and try another location or maybe to get a little more studying in. It was then that a mysterious event took place. My phone, I'd made sure had been charged up to full on the way over drained from one hundred percent to zero in about three seconds flat. While I tried to make sense of my inoperative phone, I noticed the immediate area had been lit by a new source of light. In front of me was the subway entrance, just like I remembered it, complete with two streetlights on each side, showcasing it.

Well, I found the thing. Now what? In a way, this wasn't exactly supposed to happen. With all of the insanity in my life as of late, it might have been easy to forget that magic murder men and sentient dreamscapes were a pretty recent development. A couple of months ago, my biggest problem would have been having to suddenly pee while stuck on the 405. Now look at me! I was about to investigate a hidden portal into a lair of dangerous rogues. Maybe I was growing up to be something I was always meant to be: a perfectly unhinged human being with a tenuous grasp on reality.

"Hello?" I called down, as I cautiously approached the stairs. "I'm going to come down there now. Please don't magic me to death!"

I'm not sure why I took each step so slowly, they were just stairs, after all. I kept yelling out warnings of my arrival, just to be safe. Perhaps I was just nervous about not being able to see into the dark. Then I thought, what if the stairs ceased to exist? I might be corporeally absorbed into the earth below them! Weird, I know, but that thought was the one that sent me running down to the bottom as quickly as my feet would move, nearly throwing me head first into the darkness.

Stars shot before my eyes as strong, thick hands grabbed me, pinning me to a wall. The sudden light flooding the room combining with the assault made it impossible to see anything, and I wasn't prepared for whatever tried to bury itself in my stomach. I couldn't breathe and wanted to retch. As I started to double over, the same rough hands picked me back up with ease, and two more blows landed on my torso. I was moderately expecting those, but only enough to clench up first. Not that it helped much.

Still disoriented, I briefly found myself in the air before crashing shoulder first into concrete. I rolled onto my back, my coat offering little protection, the weight of my bag digging into my ribs.

"Get her up." The voice above me was hard and indifferent.

I could see now who decided to ambush and beat on me for a bit. Five people, very different with two exceptions: all of them were noticeably filthy, and had physiques that seemed angrily sculpted from rough clay. A rough hand pulled me to my feet too easily to be human, and the man I'd heard a moment ago stepped forward, regarding me.

"Why?" I asked, still wanting to vomit. Every place I'd been struck was screaming in agony, and forming a sentence seemed like more than I was capable until I caught my breath.

"My name is Zhu Huang," he said calmly. "And you've come into my home without permission."

"Tried to ask." I wheezed.

"Yes, we all heard," he agreed. "The whole neighborhood did. Did you think we were all just waiting in this one room when you got here?"

After pausing to take a breath, I shot back, "I didn't have time to consider it before all of you decided to tenderize me."

Zhu raised an eyebrow at me. "You think now is a good time to be flippant?"

"As of late, I don't think I know why I do anything," I answered.

Zhu gave a nod, and I got a look at the woman who I guessed was the one hitting me in the stomach earlier. She was taller than me by about a head. Her hair was mostly shaved off and her arms were leaner and more muscular than perhaps anyone I knew. Before I could protest, she delivered another blow to my stomach, causing an unfamiliar sound to escape my throat. I didn't know anything could feel this bad. The only thing keeping me from total collapse was the enormous man holding me up.

"How many others are coming?" Zhu asked.

I couldn't get the words out. The throbbing in my stomach was unbearable. The woman moved to hit me again, but I pleaded with Zhu using my eyes, and he held up a hand, causing her to stop.

"No one... Just me...," I finally managed.

Thankfully, Zhu seemed to believe me. "And who sent you? Pacifiers? Gardeners?"

"Came for help...," I gasped. "With Gardeners. You... you're Vagrants, right?"

The mood of the entire room seemed to darken when I said that. "You don't like the name," I said, starting to recover my breath. "Okay, then. Sorry."

Zhu was across the room before I saw him move, his hand at my throat. "You know who calls us that? Gardeners. So where did you hear it, if you're not with them?"

"Read it in a book," I coughed out.

"This place is burned," the woman said, and the others in the room seemed to agree. "Either she was sent undercover and they're here already, or she led them here and they're only probably also here already. Do you really buy that she just found this place all by herself?"

Zhu nodded. "Agreed, we have to go. Get everyone ready, we leave in thirty, no excuses."

I watched the woman leave down the hall, sprinting faster than I would have thought possible. "So, you're not going to help?" I asked, immediately regretting my choice of words.

"Who are you?" he demanded.

"Oh, now you want to know who I am?" I asked with sarcastic laughter.

What is wrong with me?

"Your name!" he barked.

I nearly peed myself at that and, before I realized it, shouted, "Elana!"

The answer made him take a step back and soften his posture. Nervous glances were exchanged and Zhu seemed to be contemplating something.

One of the men, a squat, bald man with a handlebar mustache was the first to speak. "She's gotta be lying," he said. He started to say something else, but Zhu gave him a look.

"Take her someplace until I can know for certain," Zhu said, his brow creased. I opened my mouth to protest, and he shot me a look too. "Nothing else from you. If she talks, remove her tongue."

I made it an immediate point not to say a word. The man behind me let go of my arms, while Handlebars—I didn't know what else to call him—took my bag. He marched me down a hallway and when we finally came to the door he had in mind, we just stood there for a few moments. The door looked like one you might see in an old submarine, hatch wheel and all. I stared dumbly at it, not sure what was next.

"After you," he finally said, motioning to the door.

"You've got to be kidding me," I started. "I can't turn—" His look cut me off, and I remembered Zhu's instructions from earlier. "Fine," I said, gripping the wheel with both hands.

I strained as I put my weight behind it, but the man didn't seem to care that I wasn't making any progress. It took considerable effort, and I thought for a moment I was going to blow out my shoulder. But the wheel eventually gave way with a loud moan of metal against metal, and the subsequent turns went a little easier until the door opened.

I wanted a second to catch my breath, but I was shoved hard in the back, sending me into the room. I got up from the cold concrete floor and took a look around as Handlebars casually walked in behind me, shutting the door behind him. It was a simple room; bare walls, a bed with a flat, well used pillow, and a faded blanket. A TV sat in the corner of the room hooked up to a DVD player. There were no windows and, despite being a decent size, the room already felt claustrophobic.

"So, what?" I asked. "We just wait here until your boss figures out what he wants to do?"

Handlebars grimaced. "First, Zhu ain't my boss."

"He sure seemed like he was in charge," I countered. "He told you what to do, didn't he?"

He ignored my comments and continued, "And second, no, we're not going to just wait around on his say so."

He tossed my book bag to my feet and it hit the ground with a thump. "What are you doing?" I asked.

My eyes widened in disbelief as he produced a gun from behind his back and leveled it at me. "Pick up the bag," he ordered.

"Don't shoot me," I whispered, bending down to pick up the bag. "We'll talk this out, okay?"

"Turn on the TV," he said, and I sat confused for a moment. "Do it!"

I turned around, finding the remote next to the TV and switched it on. "Now hit play," he commanded.

I did. A zombie movie was on, something cheesy with survivors running in circles, the dead shambling after them. It was by no means well produced or even scary, but then again, I have never been a horror fan, so I'm not the right person to ask.

"You want to watch TV?" I asked, trying to understand.

"You know, I saw it on his face," he began. "Zhu really thinks you might be her. *Elana Black*. I'm not so sure. I don't think it really matters, to tell you the truth. So you see, this is what happened. You got the better of me with your superior skills and quick thinking."

Suddenly, he smashed the gun across his face, leaving a welt across his cheek that began to grow as I watched it, a thin stream of blood running down to his chin before it commenced a slow and steady drip to the ground. A chill ran through me as I put the pieces together. Calmly, he continued, "And that's how you got your bag and got away. Or that's when I shot you. Your call. The way I see it, I either just shoot you now, which solves our problem, or you stupidly traveled into a world of zombies and then, well, you're no longer our problem. If you're Elana like you say, you make it there just fine. If not, the Knowing probably kills you on the way. All roads lead to home, right?"

I was completely stuck, I couldn't process this. If these worlds are real, there's nothing good that I could do in a zombie flick. The whole point of those things is inevitability. I didn't want to die, but I really didn't want to be undead either. I started to see a way in, and it was like looking over a jagged, rocky cliff. I pleaded with him, "Please, I swear to you, my name is—!"

An alarm blared, loud enough to hurt, and a red light flashed overhead. A loudspeaker announced frantically that they'd been found, that everyone needed to leave immediately. It distracted my captor for just a moment, and that's when instinct kicked in. My mind immediately thought of water. Perhaps it was the oddly placed submarine door underground, but that was all I could think about. A torrent of water, a hard stream! With a cry, I stretched my hand out in his direction.

He barely had time enough to register his surprise as a waterjet which could have been mistaken for the stream from a fire hose hit him square in the chest, pinning him to the wall and flooding the room up to my ankles within seconds. The gun fired, striking the pillow and sending pieces of fluff into the air, but the sound of that tiny explosion in this confined space was deafening, even over the alarm. And then just as suddenly as it began, I felt the power deep inside of me, somewhere not physical, drain out like the last drops of milk into a bowl of cereal, and the water stopped.

I realized I had maybe a few seconds before he got to his feet and worse, the water might short out the power on the television, leaving me with absolutely no option. I turned to stare at the screen, focusing on the way in when with a crash, the door swung open. I turned to face the doorway and saw the smug face of Bres smiling at me, quite satisfied.

"Got somewhere to be?" he asked, his grin widening.

20

"Gonna... kill you, you—"

"No, you're not," Bres said, nonchalantly raking his scythe across Handlebar's throat, releasing a spray of blood that immediately mixed horribly with the water at our feet. Something in the air changed as the life left his eyes, it was like all at once there was a surge of emotions in the air that lasted for but an instant, shards of every emotion that I could imagine filled every inch of me. Ecstasy, contempt, trust, awe, fear, anger, contentment, surprise, disgust, joy; all hit me in a flash, and I felt strangely rejuvenated, but I also felt a profound sense of loss.

Bres shivered as if he felt it too, but he reacted like someone who'd just gotten a pleasant head scratch. "Sorry about that, where were we?"

Even with all of the danger in front of me, even seeing Bres disconnected from the murder he just committed, and even with an escape right in front of me, I was hesitating. I was not a fan of horror, and if it were up to me, I'd never jump into this kind of show or movie. The only worse thing I can think to leap into would be a disaster film. Not only would I be helpless in there, there's nothing I can really do to actually help anyone in that entire world. A zombie outbreak is just a complete breakdown of civilization, everyone inside is doomed to die, sooner rather than later. It's a problem without a solution.

Of course, I wasn't going to get to contemplate the decision much longer. Stay and die now, jump in and maybe I don't die right away. It wasn't much of a choice.

"No you don't!" Bres shouted as I allowed myself to be enveloped by the show, haphazardly tumbling into it. An invisible, hot bolt of energy seared the air behind me as I fell in. One moment I was standing ankle deep in cold water, feeling claustrophobic with not one, but two people threatening to kill me. The next I felt sunshine, and my nostrils burned with an acidic scent in the air. I also took a header into a table full of gardening supplies, crashing hard and knocking over several ceramic pots.

It took me a second for the dread of what I'd just done to wash over me as I heard a grunt and a moan. Two people—well, former people—turned to look at me as I got a full view of my surroundings. It was a small farm, complete with a field and a barn; everything you'd want in the country minus the undead. These people were likely the former owners. Both appeared elderly, but that could have just been the gangrene and ruined flesh.

"Help us!" a voice shrieked. "He's stuck!"

I peered past the couple in front of me to see two children in the field, a little girl with one arm trying desperately to free a messy haired little boy on the ground in blue jeans whose pant leg was caught on a tractor.

The zombies (I couldn't believe that was really happening) moaned, mouths gaping open. I was simultaneously filled with dread and sympathy at the sight of them. Even past the dead eyes and jaundiced skin, they looked like they might have been pleasant people at one point. Between the kids and me, they seemed confused about which way they wanted to turn. I knew which way I wanted to turn, and that was around and to get the hell out of there, but I couldn't just leave children to die. I picked up one of the few potted plants to survive my entry and hurled it, scoring a direct hit on the side of one of their heads.

"That seems to have made everyone's decision for them," I muttered to myself, trying to remain calm. Then I screamed to the little girl, "Get him out of here!"

The girl nodded as I hurled another plant, and it seemed to harmlessly crash against the old woman. The undead started in my direction and I looked for something else to use against these monsters since they didn't seem terribly bothered by pots and flora. I spied a pitchfork between us and got over my abject horror enough to make a dash for it. Ripping the large implement out of the ground, I hoisted it over my head and then fell backwards from the surprising weight of it, just in time to avoid the old man as he fell in my direction, his arms outstretched towards me. He was going to bite me!

Minor setback! I can do this!

I scrambled to my feet and backed up, too quickly, and my back slammed into the wall of the barn. I winced hard; I was still feeling the effects of the beatdown from earlier and things could not have been going worse. Lifting my arms overhead made my ribs scream in agony.

Must have pulled something when I lifted the pitchfork. Can't dwell on that right now.

I swung it at the old woman, trying to use my hips as much possible to avoid straining my ribs. Whatever I experienced earlier did nothing for my injuries. The blunt side of the pitchfork caught the woman, sending her to the ground.

Something grabbed my ankle, and a rasping noise from just out of my view caused me to nearly jump out of my skin. I slammed the gardening tool into the earth and heard a sickening sound, like chewing bananas with your mouth open, but much louder. The shock of striking something reverberated up my arm, and I looked down to see that I had pinned the old man to the earth through his neck. Putrid fluids pooled around him, seeping into the dirt as his grip on my shoe loosened.

The old woman got to her feet. Beyond her, I could hear the tearing of pants and the children stood up in a panic

"Go!" I yelled, and they ran off, apparently not needing any extra convincing. I took off as fast as my feet would take me and rounded the corner, with the hopes of maybe taking shelter in the barn. I couldn't go back, the way I came, given what was waiting for me, but maybe—

I stopped suddenly, looking at the front of the barn. It was barred shut, bales of hay and heavy equipment stacked in front of the doors and the word "NO" painted on it in large letters. A loud *thump* jostled me back to reality then, as did the moaning of the old woman stumbling towards me.

Another *thump*. Two more.

The noise must have gotten the attention of whatever was inside. More *thumps*, like an uneven drumbeat. The wood creaked. Terrified, I ran away from the barn and towards the road leading to the world outside of this farm. I couldn't see the children anymore. I could only hope they were safely away at this point. For now, I had to get away before something really, really bad happened. I pumped my legs as hard and fast I could. Everything hurt and I felt sick. *Keep moving.* My lungs were on fire. *Keep moving.* I was cramping up all over. *Keep moving!*

A terrible crash sounded behind me. I couldn't help but look, and immediately regretted it. The ruined wood of the barn had given way, a mass of flesh poured out into the sunlight, bodies tripping over each other and they'd seen me, thoughtlessly shambling in my direction. I couldn't stay here, but there wasn't anything to escape to. The road ahead of me bent to the north, but outside of the trees and the house and barn behind me, we were alone out here.

I forced myself to keep moving, the road feeling like the only option. I could get to the forest, but if I got lost there, or if a zombie managed to sneak up on me, I was dead or worse. I'd seen my fair share of zombie media, and I hated all of it. The unseen zombie behind the tree or car or whatever was familiar enough that I was innately cognizant of that possibility and refused to chance it. So I kept out in the open, at least for now. I'd put maybe sixty or seventy yards between them and me, and being able to clearly see what was in front of me was the safest possible thing at the moment.

The sound of them behind me was unnerving all on its own, even without the threat of being mauled by a ravenous crowd of the undead, but that danger kept me moving. Even as my sprint was reduced to a jog, then to a pained walk, I refused to stop. Because they wouldn't stop. And at that moment, everything else that had mattered up to this point suddenly went away and was replaced by the knowledge that if I stopped moving, if my legs stopped working, that could be it.

As I rounded the corner, I saw hope in the distance. Past the dense woods on either side of the street, maybe a hundred yards down the road or so, were a couple of houses with plenty of space between them. Given everything else I could have just very well been marching to my death, but for me it was the nearest house or nothing. If I were lucky I could hide somewhere, wait this out, maybe get home somehow. Each step brought a stab of pain to my side, and I really started to think something was seriously wrong, but I had to keep moving. Left foot, right foot. Left foot, right foot. Thank the stars these weren't fast zombies.

My body slumped into the door when I reached the house, threatening to shut down completely from pain and exhaustion. The horde wasn't far behind and showed no signs of stopping. I managed to catch the door handle with one arm, bracing myself in the doorway, which kept me up as I tried the door. It opened without incident, and it was then that I really did collapse, falling face forward into the house.

Summoning all the strength that I could, I pushed the door closed with my leg. Looking up from the floor I could see there was one of those little chains to prevent the door from being opened more than a crack, but there was absolutely no chance I was going to be able to latch it, at least not right away.

My body was pushed as far as it could go without a rest. The way I was lying on the ground, I may as well have been pinned to it. I wanted to cry, or sleep, or do anything but run, but even now with the relative safety of the door, I knew that wasn't a viable option. I couldn't get enough oxygen. Blood rushed to bruised areas and then pooled under my skin, cramped muscles tightened and fought for my attention. Ribs tensed under the strain of lying on my back and shifted, trying to align themselves in new and painful ways. It was hard to think, but I had to.

The air in the room was stale. The only light came from thin streams of sunlight shining through the imperfect boarding on the windows. The boards were on the inside. A job done to keep things out. Traces of rotten food waste remained on the living room floor along with an uneven collection of assorted items from the house.

There was a stairway up to a second floor, also littered with refuse. It looked as if maybe a group of people had made shelter here, and then one day having exhausted the usefulness of this place, just walked right out the front door.

I could hear them coming now. Going back might have been a death sentence, but I couldn't stay here anymore. I closed my eyes and gripped my bag, and thought of home. I also thought about the shooting pain in the center of my back that felt like my spine was being severed. I adjusted slightly, finding the right combination of tensed muscles and relaxed, and thought about home. And then I also thought about Handlebars getting his throat slit and Bres waiting for me.

My ribs throbbed. My mind and body were both fighting with me; I couldn't focus. Trying to calm my five senses here would be impossible. I had to keep telling myself that I was in peril, I was harmed, but I was not dying. If I could get to safety, if I could hide, I would be all right.

The first heavy *thump* against the doorway made me dart my eyes to the door. The silhouette of a man's head bobbed unevenly in the window of the front door, but I knew it was not a man. Two more *thumps*, another head shadow, and I was on my feet. I made my way through a kitchen to find a backdoor, also boarded shut. Someone had decided the only way in and out of this house was through a front door that soon would be swarmed with zombies. I could have maybe kicked through the boards if not for my ribs.

My heart raced. I just needed a moment. If I could focus, then I could get out of here! The door wouldn't hold forever, so I was officially out of any option except going upstairs. And that always seems like such a bad idea in these things, but I was starting to see the appeal. Face whatever was upstairs or just wait for the undead to break in. The glass shattered on the front door. The stairs seemed like an excellent choice given the circumstances.

I heard and felt pops in my back and hips as I gripped the banister, pulling myself up the stairs. I stopped for a moment when I heard the groan of wood weakening around the doorframe. I glanced back to see the door bending in on hinges as a mass of inhumanity pressed into it, giving the wood the appearance of breathing. As I reached the top of the stairs, I could hear the door finally collapse inwards, along with the sound of corpses falling over each other.

There would be maybe thirty seconds before one of them figured out where I was, and hiding was a much smarter plan than fighting. There were a couple of options, but I made my way into the first door I saw, a bedroom with windows that faced out towards the street. I closed the door, locked it, and hid behind the bed. Enough was enough. Going back was probably a death sentence, but I absolutely could not wait here any longer. I just had to block out the noise around me, put aside the pain and breathe through it. When I felt ready, I took a couple of breaths and...

Nothing.

Okay. Okay... I was thinking about home. Maybe *that* was the problem. Think about the room. The water, the old submarine door, the feathers littering the room...

Nothing. Still nothing!

I started to panic. This had never happened before, and I didn't exactly have the time to figure it out. I wouldn't know where to begin, even if I knew where to start!

A *thud* in the hallway. They'd found me. I didn't know if it was scent or just dumb luck, but they were coming upstairs now. Something heavy slammed into the door. Then, another something joined it. This was a bedroom door, nowhere near as sturdy as something like the front door to a home. I was running out of options in a hurry, so I looked out the window. There was a ledge, but there were maybe twenty or thirty of those things milling outside, coming not only from down the road, but milling out of the woods as well. I was out of time, no choice.

I opened the window as the wooden door developed its first splinter crack. I wasn't sticking around to see them come in. Maybe I could climb onto the roof. Or something! I had to get out of this room and I had to do it right now.

I was outside and away from the window, but it only took one of those things spotting me before the rest of them did as well. They were single-minded, arms grasping for me, unable to reach, but I was far from safe, and there was nowhere to go. There was nothing to climb either; the roof might as well have been on the moon for all the safety it could have provided me. That's when I heard it. Something past the moans and growls, the flapping of bodies spilling over each other. It was an engine, loud and roaring. And around the corner I'd come from, a vehicle like I'd never seen before came barreling towards the house. It had eight wheels and some kind of protective guard railing around it. It also didn't slow down as it sped towards the house. I let out a yell and averted my eyes as it plowed through the front yard and into the roiling masses. It was going to strike the house. It was going to hit the porch and take me down with it.

21

Brakes squealed, and there was a cacophonous series of thuds as metal collided with flesh and wood. I wasn't watching, but the noise was descriptive enough. The crash I was expecting, however, never came. I wasn't knocked from my perch. Instead, I was just yelled at.

"Get in! What are you doing? Come on!"

I peered down to see an older man in stained fatigues behind the wheel, halfway into the porch, but that still meant that six wheels were visible instead of eight. That was still a lot of wheels. The opening of the vehicle was a strange mix of open air and homemade cover.

Now didn't seem like the appropriate time to admire the aesthetics of this vehicular monstrosity, so I carefully made the jump down into the cab, which was a straight drop thankfully. It was honestly more of a two-foot fall into the machine than a leap, and it did no favors to my existing bruises, but I was grateful for his arrival.

"Hold on!" he yelled with fierce determination, slamming the car into reverse, a couple of stray zombies falling off the side.

The vehicle made a sharp one-eighty-degree turn as he sped back towards the road. The growl behind me nearly made me leap out of my seat, and I turned in time to see one last zombie, hulking in size, had managed to climb or fall onto the vehicle with us.

"Straggler!" the man yelled as the engine screamed. "You need to take care of it!"

I wanted to ask how or with what, but I didn't have time as the former man began to stand and climb into the cab, mouth agape. He must have been six-and-a-half feet tall at least, maybe three hundred pounds. Fresh terror gripped me; there was nothing I had at my disposal that would have done anything anyway, this guy must have carried live horses on his back while he was alive.

As he began to fall towards me, as I smelled the rot from his mouth and saw the hunger in his eyes, my mind flashed with images of getting away and of pushing him away. My hands stretched out in front of my body defensively, more to guard my face than anything, when a gale force wind seemed to emanate from them for just a moment, but it was more than enough for the zombie to sail about thirty feet into the air. I looked at my rescuer, and he looked at me, both of us surprised, and that was when I lost consciousness. I never even saw the zombie hit the ground.

There may have been a light poking in my general shoulder area, but I was so absurdly comfortable that I was willing to just let it happen. And so I did. Small fingers prodded me, and an equally small voice asked me, "Are you still alive?"

"Maybe," I answered, refusing to move anything other than my lips.

I heard a tiny gasp at hearing my answer, and the poking stopped. I couldn't remember when I'd slept as heavily as that and I would have given just about anything for another hour or so of it, but it didn't feel right to leave my host waiting. I opened my eyes and sat up, stretching my arms hard above my head as I did.

"Hi," I said.

"Hi!" the little girl replied happily. She had short, curly black hair and intensely blue eyes that seemed out of place with her crooked but impossibly wide grin. She might have been nine, maybe, and even then seemed small for her age. It all distracted me for just a moment from another defining characteristic. She was missing her right arm from the elbow down.

"What's your name?" I asked, trying to recover.

"Lainey!" she said, still smiling. "Or Elaine. Most people call me Lainey, though. What's your name?"

"Elana," I answered, matching her smile. "Some people call me."

"What do they call you?" Lainey asked.

"They usually just call me," I answered. "They call out like, 'Hey Elana, you should come look at this cool thing!'"

Lainey laughed at that. "You're funny!" she said.

"I know," I said, making a face at her.

While my eyes were moving crossways for effect, Lainey took me off guard, falling into me, her cheek pressing against mine as she wrapped her arm under my arm and squeezed my back.

"Thank you," she said, and I returned the hug, unsure of what was happening.

"Ha, it's okay, it was just a face," I said nervously.

"No, not that," Lainey said, letting go. "For saving Jayden before."

"Oh!" I said, trying not to let my surprise show. I had nearly forgotten that happened. "No big deal, right? High five!"

Lainey gave me a high five with everything she had, and it made an adorable little smack against my palm. It gave me a moment to look around the room. On a rack were my coat and book bag, while my shoes sat at the edge of the bed. The floor and walls were all concrete. If I wasn't mistaken, this was either a prison or a military barracks. There were lockers, so probably not prison. I knew what both things looked like from movies, so I was making what could only barely pass for an educated guess.

"Are there other people here?" I asked Lainey, standing up. I tested my back and legs, and especially my torso. I wasn't 100%, but I was definitely much better.

Lainey remained at the edge of the bed with her legs crossed in front of her. "Yeah, but they all got up for breakfast and chores. You looked like you need to sleep."

I reached down for my shoes and sat on the bed across from her to put them on. "That was sweet of you," I said.

"You can ask about it," Lainey said casually. "I don't mind. Everyone does."

"About what?" I asked.

"My arm," she said turning that side of her body towards me. "It doesn't hurt or nothing."

"Oh, I wasn't going to—"

"I was born like this," she continued. She raised her arm towards me to show what I had initially thought might have been a scar, was actually a hand which had never fully formed. "Mom says the rest of it just didn't keep growing. See, I have little fingers and everything! They don't work, though. I have a cool arm, though, wanna see?"

I nodded and she beamed as she ran out of the room, almost knocking over the man I'd seen earlier, the one who drove me away from that house.

"Whoa, no running!" he chuckled. He smiled towards Lainey then shifted to a look of concern for me. "Hey, feeling rested?"

"Much better, thank you very much," I said, slipping on my coat. "I don't know what I would have done if you hadn't shown up when you did."

"Leaving already?" he asked.

"I'm really sorry, but yeah," I said, slinging my book bag over my shoulder. "I don't belong here."

"I saw what you did back there," he said with a touch of pity in his voice. "Don't bother denying it; I know what I saw. We should have been dead. I want you to know that it's all right, I'm not going to tell anyone."

I paused a moment, unsure of how to react to that. I don't know what he thought he saw, but I wasn't sure of it myself, so I just accepted it. "Thank you."

"No, thank you," he replied. "For saving my daughter."

"Lainey is—?"

"The reason I keep going," he said with a sigh. The smile returned, and he offered me his hand. "My name is Roger. It's a pleasure to meet you, ma'am."

I took the hand and gave it the briefest shake possible, trying not to trigger anything. I wasn't sure I'd survive the trauma of Knowing what these people must have gone through. "I'm Elana," I said, withdrawing my hand quickly. "Lainey is really cool."

He shook his head. "Her and that other one, they stay so positive. It's probably why they ran off to explore the way they did. Or do. I try to keep an eye on them, but they just—"

"They're kids," I finished for him, and he nodded.

"Lainey told me what you did, and we appreciate it. All of us," Roger said, regaining his composure. "We're not usually keen on adding to our group, but we would welcome you to join us when we shove off from here. And from me, personally, I cannot ever thank you enough. With everything else going on, I can't lose her. She's all I have."

I thought about that. "You're leaving? This seems like a military base, more than secure enough, why would you leave?"

He openly sighed at that. "Walk with me to breakfast, and I'll tell you all about it."

He took me through the halls towards a common area. "Safe enough from the outside, sure, but we're just about out of everything. That stunt with the ICV might have been one of our last hurrahs here."

"ICV?"

"Big armored car with extra wheels," he clarified. "Runs on diesel, and a lot of it, which we're just about out of. We're also just about out of food and medicine. Clean water we're good on due to the river, but that's about it. We're headed to the base in Volk with whatever we can. Vehicle won't make it the whole way, but with any luck, we won't need to."

"What's in Volk?" I asked as we entered in what looked like a mess hall.

"One moment," Roger said before addressing the room. "Everyone listen up. This here's Elana, and she's the one who —"

Lainey bounced past us, into the room. "Here I am, Dad!" She beamed, lifting her arm to show off her prosthetic. "Found my arm!"

"That's good, sweetie," Roger said, lifting her up. "Right here. This woman saved Lainey and Jayden, and as far as I'm concerned, she's with us. Everyone agree?"

There was brief applause and I saw the other child from before, still wearing those ripped jeans, stand up and walk over to me, head down in shame. "Thanks, ma'am," he said sullenly. "Sorry for any trouble."

"Jeez, you don't have to, I mean." I was suddenly very embarrassed by all of this. "Anyone would have done the same thing."

"No," Jayden said sadly. "They wouldn't."

Roger cleared his throat and gave Lainey a little bounce in his arm. "Right then, let me get you introduced to the rest of the crew." He first walked me to a slight man, maybe in his early thirties, who was sitting with Jayden. His hair was prematurely thinning and he had a gaunt, unhealthy look. "This here is Kenny. I believe you know his son."

Kenny stood up and greeted me with a hug before I could protest. He didn't say anything, but after a moment I could feel his sobbing through my coat as his grip tightened. I let him hold it for a moment, comforting him with a steady stream of rubs on his back to wordlessly let him know that it was okay. Roger didn't rush him and, eventually, Kenny let go on his own, his eyes thoroughly red and puffy.

"Thank you," he said quietly, looking a little ashamed as he turned from me and sat, rubbing at his face.

"Right, then," Roger said taking me a table over to where a couple sat, holding hands. "I'd like you to meet the newlyweds. This is Asha and Than."

The pair stood. Asha was surprisingly tall, maybe a full foot taller than I was and at least as tall as Roger. Her hair had been chopped down to a very short length. Not cut, chopped. It was uneven, without the hint of style or intent. Her face was the opposite by comparison with eyes that welcomed me and a smile that almost made me forget about everything else and join her.

"We're all glad to have you," Asha said warmly. "Thank you for saving the young ones."

"Yeah, we've had enough, uh," Than stammered, before glancing over to Roger and Lainey. "Never mind. We're all real glad you were there is all. Real glad."

I recognized that look from Than. He was tired in a way that sleep wouldn't fix. Whatever had been going on, and given our circumstance I was hesitant to think about the possibilities, it weighed on him. He needed something to go right, and I felt humble at the moment because I might have just been it. The way he looked at Lainey and Jayden, I don't know that he would have survived if something happened to them. There was something more gentle about him than the rest and I had the feeling that by all rights he wasn't meant for this world. Not that anyone should be, but I was suddenly very glad that he and Asha had each other.

"It's nice to meet you both," I said with a smile to them both, the mixture of emotions making me uncomfortable. I understood them both, but I didn't know how to react to them as a couple. Asha saw the bright side, Than was just relieved that tragedy had been averted. Neither were okay; I had the sense for a moment that Asha was just better at hiding her pain.

"Don't be sad, Than," Lainey said quietly, and it seemed like she did the impossible and the tension evaporated.

Than's unshaven face, which seemed so hopeless a moment ago, came alive as it stretched into a smile, a tear reaching his eye. He teased, "Hey, who do you think is sad, huh?"

Roger set Lainey down and turned his attention back towards a food prep table in the corner. "And last but not least, our savior, Grace," he said, waving a hand in her direction.

Grace was an older woman, maybe in her late fifties, who stood about my height, with a frame that suggested she'd spent a lot of time doing manual labor. Rugged might have been the best word to describe her. At the moment she was slicing carrots, and had a pile of sliced potatoes and another of apples already prepared at the end of her table.

"How do you do, Elana?" she asked, glancing up. "You're up in time for breakfast, I see. Hope you're hungry!"

"Grace grew up farming, she's responsible for our daily feast," Roger said proudly. "Though she refuses to let anyone help."

"You'd only get in the way," Grace said matter-of-factly. "Besides, you all have your jobs and I have mine."

"Fair enough, but we haven't found much in the way of dry or canned goods in weeks, the least we could do is cook for you for a change," Roger replied.

"I don't need help steaming potatoes; you can help by clearing your plate," Grace chided him.

I almost fell over when I suddenly realized what I'd had in my bag. Besides the books, I had made a stop at the store and loaded up on snacks. "Uh, I'm sorry I didn't bring this up earlier, but please," I said opening my book bag and digging into it, "I'd really like you to have this."

From my bag, I produced my bounty: two bags of Peanut Butter M&M's, a huge pack of beef jerky which was supposed to last me a week, two bottles of cream soda which somehow hadn't broken throughout all of this, and a liter bottle of water. From the looks I got from the people around me you'd have thought I just opened the briefcase from *Pulp Fiction*. Everyone looked shocked except Roger, which I'd made a mental note of.

"Where'd you find this?" Grace asked.

"Is there more?" Kenny interrupted.

"I thought we'd just about cleaned out everything in a five-mile radius, what else could we have missed?" Than mused.

"Yay, candy!" Lainey shouted.

"Awesome!" Jayden whooped, offering Lainey a high five.

The questions and comments came faster than I could handle. "Everyone just calm down," Roger said, shushing everyone as they had gathered around to see the food.

"It was a little corner store, maybe 10 miles south," I lied, not ready to reveal the fact that I had just recently bought all this and more on a whim. "There was nothing else. I found this in the back, it was hidden. No one else came the whole day, so I figured no one was coming back and I took it. I didn't see anything else around, sorry."

Roger nodded then asked, "Are you sure?"

"About the store? Yeah, of course," I said, suddenly nervous that he didn't believe me.

"Not that," he said. "That you want to share all this. I know there are some groups that would just take this from you, but I don't want you to feel obligated. Your belongings are your own; we don't operate like that."

"You knew what I had in my bag," I said, understanding.

"Of course I did, I heard the glasses clinking together," Roger said plainly. "But I meant what I said. This belongs to you and, if anything, I owe you for saving my daughter. I'm not about to repay your kindness by robbing you."

That struck a nerve with me. They had so little right now, and they didn't take anything even when I was helpless. Genuinely, I said, "Please, I want you to have it. I mean, you saved my life and offered me breakfast, it seems like a fair trade to me."

Roger grinned at that and announced, "Well, sounds like we have ourselves a celebration! Grace, I'll get us some cups. I think it's been too long since any of us have had anything carbonated. You just make sure my little girl doesn't get cavities before I get back. Candy and soda for breakfast, everyone!"

There was applause at that, and I felt my face grow hot, feeling unworthy of the praise. Roger turned to me and asked, "Elana, give me a hand? I think I saw some whiskey glasses back in one of the offices."

I followed Roger out of the mess hall, and once we were out of earshot, the smile seemed to fade as he spoke. "You know, I'm not an idiot."

"Excuse me?" I asked.

"It was a good lie, but there was no store," he said. "I think everyone else might just be too excited to notice or even want to notice, but that food is too new. Besides the fact those expiration dates on the food shouldn't even exist, beef jerky molds after a while, and no one has produced it in years."

I didn't say anything as we walked, so he continued, "Then there's the fact that you're even here. No one would have survived out there alone without a weapon for very long, and we've been canvassing the area for weeks. We would have noticed you, so I have no idea where you came from. Lainey says you appeared out of thin air. Then you launched that big sucker into the sky like a rocket! You're not who you say you are."

"Well, like I said, I don't belong here." I adjusted my book bag, not looking him in the eye as we rounded a corner into an office. "I'll leave after breakfast."

Roger stopped and placed a hand on my shoulder. "If you feel you absolutely have to, we won't stop you. But I meant what I said before. You saved my girl. I don't need to know where you've been. You can stay as long as you like, and I won't tell the others. And if I'm being real honest, whatever it is you're hiding is something I think we could really use on our side. It might just make the difference between us surviving and not."

I considered it for a moment. "What's in Polk?"

"Volk," Roger corrected me, giving me a curious look. "You're not from Wisconsin, are you?"

"First time visiting actually," I said.

He nodded and stepped behind the desk to retrieve the glasses and he explained, "Volk is a base, air base, outside of Camp Douglas. That's not the interesting part, though, there's not much use for planes these days and no way to get them into the air. No, what makes Volk so interesting is that a few years before all this started, a good chunk of the base was converted into farmland as part of a training initiative to export farming methods to the Middle East. Found the glasses."

Roger handed me a small stack of the whiskey glasses, and we headed back down the hall. He went on, "I'm afraid they're on their own now as far as crops are concerned, but the land is ideal now. I'm positive others will already be there, but it's not a small area. There should be no trouble taking us in."

We rounded the hallway back into the common area and, as I looked to each of the faces there, I knew I couldn't stay, but I couldn't just go either. Lainey smiled at me, eating an M&M with pure bliss on her face.

"All right, Roger, I'll go with you," I said looking at him finally. "I'll get you to Volk."

O ur breakfast was far more pleasant than I'd expect a meal of root vegetables and candy in the middle of a zombie apocalypse would be. We took our time eating and just enjoying the morning. It felt incredibly awkward being around so many people who were just genuinely kind to me, but I felt that leaving them now would have been something I'd judge myself for later.

I did what I would do in any other situation like this, and that was to get everyone to talk about themselves and take the focus off of me. Roger, for example, was an officer in the Marines, a Lieutenant Colonel in fact. At this point he says he was, now he's just a guy who is trying his best to make sure others survive until this is all settled. He holds out faith that it will be. Lainey is nine and a half and can do a cartwheel; it's incredibly impressive. Jayden loves to climb trees. Well, he loves to climb anything, but trees are the most abundant thing to climb. Grace has been to all fifty states but otherwise has never left the country. Her favorite place is Mount Nebo in Utah during the winter. Asha and Than met oddly enough on the day of the outbreak while trying to fly out of the state. Asha was heading home to Nigeria and Than was heading to Boston on vacation, because he's a self-described U.S. history nerd. She saved his life, he saved hers, and she saved him again. At some point, they just accepted that they were each other's lucky charms, and eventually that blossomed into love. Kenny managed a diner in his former life and was an amateur locksmith, a hobby he picked up in high school. A skill that has proven useful on occasion. He spoke at length of all the supplies they've found that were simply left behind because people couldn't get past a decent lock. His wife, Harriet, always thought it was a waste of time, but she put up with it. He hasn't heard from her since the day it began. She was in Canada visiting her mother when this all started. It was Canada though, so maybe she was okay. The mood dipped a little bit after that, and people began to excuse themselves to their chores.

There wasn't much to take to Volk, especially since everyone had to be able to carry their supplies on their back. Roger figured they could maybe get twenty miles before they ran out of gas, and at that point, they'd either need to get lucky or start hiking. Everyone had a pack with some basic first aid gear found at the base, a gallon of clean water, and whatever potatoes or apples they could carry. Whatever we had would have to last, so we planned carefully, resigning ourselves to leaving behind a fair amount of perfectly good food.

One thing the group was in no danger of running out of anytime soon, was guns and bullets. Not that there was anything to hunt in the area, the zombies had either killed or scared off anything they could find. And firing a shot was no different than sending out a signal flare for every undead thing to come and swarm you, so bullets really were the last resort. There was always the possibility of needing them against other survivors, but that was far less common than you'd think, according to Roger.

For most people, the idea of trying to rob each other was a losing effort these days. You either stayed to yourself, or you decided to join another group. Very few people wanted to risk stealing from someone else. There was just too much that could go wrong, and not a lot to really gain. Roger tried to insist I take a firearm, but having a gun held to my head recently was enough to assure me that I wasn't interested in guns anytime soon.

That night I dreamt again, this time I was flying. Floating might have been a more accurate statement, but I knew I could fly at any moment. It was a thing I'd suddenly remembered how to do; a thing anyone could remember how to do, and we'd all just forgotten. I also knew instinctively that I would also forget when this dream was over, so I decided to make the most of it while I could. I looked up at the dense layer of clouds and willed myself towards the stars, feeling the moisture gently cover every inch of me as I passed up and through it. Before me, there was an infinite sea of planet-sized spheres made of a dark energy, tethered to something beneath the clouds and floating like naval mines in the deepest ocean. The more I stared at them, the more I saw. Swirling energies and voices I could not place nor ever forget.

"That's not for you," a familiar voice said from a location I couldn't place. "Not yet."

I was no longer flying, which was terrifying for a split second until I realized I was standing at the top of a stairway leading into a cloud. Someone or something must have sensed my apprehension because a handrail helpfully appeared, and I took it and walked down to the bottom of the steps to a gazebo, suspended from a rocky cliff, which itself was suspended from nothing. Two reclining beach chairs sat in the middle, one empty and one occupied by someone I'd met before.

"Aos Sí," I greeted the man as he lounged in the chair.

He blinked and gave me a greeting in return. With a nod, he said, "Human. Please, sit, and we can make more observations about the apparent nature of who we are."

"Okay," I said trying to sound confident. "You're a Celtic fairy or deity or monster or something. You might not even be Celtic. I think I nailed it. Not vague at all."

The Aos Si laughed and the sound of it seemed to echo off of the sky itself. "Well, you're quite funny. But you're also someone who doesn't understand."

"I still don't understand what I'm supposed to understand," the mild frustration was starting to make itself known in my voice. "I don't understand why I'm here or why you're talking to me, or you know what? Anything at all. I don't understand anything that has happened to me at any point in my life."

"Wow, you really are human," he said, raising his eyebrows. He stood up and glided over next to me, his movement graceful enough that it was easy to overlook the fact that he had to take steps. "I'm not in the habit of giving away anything for free. So I won't. I could be convinced to take it easy on you, however. What do you say? Can we find some common ground with which we can trade?"

"No offense, but isn't the lesson in any of the stories involving Fae never to make deals with them?" My arms crossed my chest as I said it. I felt like he was ready to take advantage of me, and that was something I had little tolerance for.

"And who said I was Fae?" he asked, feigning ignorance.

"Come on dude," I said rolling my eyes. "A shape-shifter who won't give me their name? Oh, and you already told me you're Aos Si. It took me about five minutes to look that up."

The Aos Si mocked me with his praise. "Why, look at you, with your little library card!"

"Well, yes," I agreed. "But in this case, it was the internet."

"The most reliable source of information," he concurred. I was mostly pretty sure that it was probably sarcasm. "I'm sure you can trust everything you read on it, especially regarding nigh immortal beings who exist outside of what mortals would perceive as reality."

His point was interesting enough to make me blink in surprise. He was right, my knowledge of what he might have been was limited to whatever I'd read in old fairy tales and websites about mythology run by people who were just trying to make decent fodder for their D&D campaign. It would have been nice if one of the books in Jason's room was marked as *Fae Do's and Don'ts* but no such luck.

"Like I said, I'm not in the habit of giving away anything for free, Elana, but I'm also not in the habit of begging," he said dismissively. "So I will make you my offer, and that will be that. You will accept it or you will not. What I propose: I will not directly answer your questions, but I will ask you questions and confirm when you are correct. I will do this until you leave this place. In exchange, you will share a meal with me. Do we have an agreement?"

"Before I answer, a question of my own," I replied. "Why not just tell me what you know? Wouldn't that be easier?"

"Easier, yes," the fairy replied with a tightness in his voice. "But I am not here to make things easier for you. If you are not intelligent enough to solve your own issues from time to time, then I'm wasting my time, and that is not something I will abide."

I thought about it a moment. "Alright, this sounds easy enough. We have a deal," I told him, extending a hand to him. "So, what are we having?"

The Aos Si took my hand, and I felt electricity in the air as he spoke. "A deal has been made. And don't worry about the food, I'll let you know when I'm ready to eat."

Nothing happened as he took my hand. Was it the place or was it him? I thought I could cheat my way through this by just Knowing him, but he would have seen that coming if he was who I thought he was. The sly grin he gave me chilled my blood. It was a shark's smile. For no more than a flash, he bared his teeth. He knew what I tried, and that look said he was letting me get away with it just this once.

"Let's get started, shall we? Since you have no idea how long you actually have here, allow me to start things off. First, what do you know of us?"

He sat at the edge of one of the chairs, crossing his legs. I was unsure if he meant Aos Si or Fae in general, but asking questions wasn't part of my bargain. I sat across from him and began.

"Well, if we're talking about Fae, that seems like a huge question. One we're not going to have time for, so I'm going to assume you mean Aos Si. You're traditionally seen as guardians in the folklore, but that doesn't imply good or evil, given that your methods on how you handle your business can range from the whimsical to pants filling horror. You seem to guard places. So lakes, woods, or even a specific tree."

"We can be guardians, yes," he replied. "Good and Evil is a human concept, we just... are. Next question. Where are we?"

I wanted to protest that I wanted clarification from his answer and that I wasn't finished, but I had the feeling that I wasn't making the rules at this point. Honestly, I answered, "I don't know."

"Yes, you do," he said locking eyes with me. "Think back, it's been revealed to you. Like all things, this place has a name, and names hold power. Remember its name."

I shut my eyes and tried to concentrate. Revealed to me? Had I read it? Seen it?

Wait.

"The Knowing?" I asked, opening my eyes. "But that's a thing that I can do, not a place."

"It is both," the Aos Si confirmed. "You are in The Knowing. And you can Know someone. Why do you think those facts are connected?"

I began to think hard about this one. It didn't seem like the Aos Si wanted to give me questions that I didn't know the answers to, but I was coming up blank. "I really have no way to respond that. I don't even know what this place is."

The Aos Si took on a stern impression. "You can answer, you just have to think. Quit giving up so quickly and think."

I shut my eyes again, thinking it would help, but I felt like I was concentrating on this for hours when I did that. There wasn't anything to grab onto here when it came to centering myself, it was all too dreamlike. And then suddenly, it came to me. I opened my eyes and looked into his, confident in my answer.

"Pass," I told him. He blinked hard at that.

"What do you mean, 'Pass'?" he asked incredulously.

"I mean exactly that. I'm taking a pass on this question and moving onto the next," I explained. "We already agreed that I don't know how much time I have here, so I don't want to waste my time trying to figure out one issue when I could be looking at the next ten with what time I have left. So, pass. Let's see what else you got."

The Aos Si looked incensed for a split second before regaining his composure. "As you wish. Follow me."

He stood up and walked to a ledge, overlooking the landscape, pointing to the middle distance. "There. What do you see?"

I scanned the landscape, trying not to get sick in the process, and found what he was pointing at. "People. Are they marching? It's too far away for me to see."

"They are nearing a destination that they move towards with purpose, yes," he replied evenly. "But distance is not a problem for you in this place, look closer. But not too close, lest they see you as well."

The thought of that happening made me pause for a moment, I'd already seen something here as it saw me, and it wasn't pleasant. Still, I focused on the point, and my vision began to tunnel until the sight of them magnified. No, not that. We were physically closer. "It's a group of Gardeners, in red and black suits. None of them are in white. There are eight of them that I can see. They have weapons, and they've been used. Recently. There's something on them, blood maybe? I don't know what's leading them."

"Describe it to me," he said.

Can't he see it? It's right there!

"Seriously?" I asked him. "It's, I don't know, a demon? Do demons even exist?"

"Many things exist, like demons," he said, not looking away from the approaching Gardeners. "Look at it again." As he said this, there was a sound of a fluttering of tiny wings, like maybe a giant moth. I tried not to get distracted by it.

The monstrosity at the head of them flickered and shifted, and if any of the Gardeners noticed, they didn't show it, or they didn't care. I audibly gasped with understanding. "Wait! That's—"

"Yes, but I'm afraid we're out of time," the Aos Si said, gripping my shoulders and turning me to face him. "Remember when you stated that you didn't know how much time you had left here? Well, I'm afraid that I do. Your time is coming to a close here, and I have one last bargain for you, but you'll need to decide quickly."

Anger flushed in my face and I protested. "You intentionally waited until the last minute to make—"

"Yes, yes, you're right, but that's my nature. Though this was much tighter of a window than I would have liked. The bargain is this. Your shield. It's fading too quickly because you're not strong enough yet to hold it. But you don't have to hold it; you can ground it and let the earth hold it for you. I can show you, but I will require a favor from you. One day I will ask you to tell me a story, and you will tell me everything you know about that tale, holding back nothing. Do we have a deal?"

"And I will regret this deal," I told him. His eyes lit up as I said it. "Per the terms of our original deal, as long as I am here if you ask me a question you have to confirm when I am correct on an answer. So you will tell me, now, if I will regret this deal."

"Oh, that is too clever," his smile was laced with anger. "And your answer is yes; it is very possible that you will regret this. But to not take this deal can also very likely lead to your destruction. Just because you'll regret this deal doesn't mean you have an attractive alternative. Life has handed you two proverbial lemons; one is just less destructive than the other."

He was telling the truth. He was bound to if what I knew of him was correct. "Fine, we have an agreement."

"We'll skip the handshake for the sake of time, now watch carefully." As he said that, we were suddenly no longer in the sky, but were standing in a clearing in the woods. I could hear the march of someone or something coming this way. "In time, you won't need sigils or glyphs or any of this nonsense for the more elementary spells, but for now you are still learning to walk, and everyone has to start somewhere."

With a long stick in his hand, he began to draw symbols in the dirt and spoke hurriedly as he did. "What I am showing you will work for your purposes, but it is also something of a cheat sheet. You can use this for gathering energy, making contact with things that you definitely don't want to be making contact with, or divining the location of your car keys."

I kept quiet trying to carefully detail in my head the locations of the drawings in the dirt. The Aos Si continued his lesson. "These represent the elements. Spirit at the top, followed by Water, Fire, Earth, and lastly Air. In this order."

"Yeah, I know what this is!" I exclaimed, happy to be ahead of the curve. "I mean, I've seen TV shows with this, and I think every Instagram Wiccan has at least a dozen pictures of this posted somewhere."

"The symbol to one without access to power is about as effective as a crayon drawing of a car is to a child who wishes to go home from school early," he said impatiently. "Now focus, we're almost done."

He abandoned the stick and planted the heel of his shoe into the dirt above the spirit symbol at the top of his collection of drawings. "Now, the more perfect the circle, the harder it will be to disrupt. Your first outings won't be anything to brag about, but you're not going to have much time to practice I'm afraid." He turned like a dancer on the heel of his boot at the center and turned, dragging a perfect circle into the earth. "With the circle complete, simply will your shield into it. You've already had practice with that, you have merely to know why you want it to be, and it will be."

A soft pink glow filled the shallow trench he had just made, and the air slowly solidified up into a dome around him. "That's incredible!"

"No, this is necessary," he corrected. "And my part of the bargain has been fulfilled. Well, both parts I'm afraid. You are out of time."

As he said this, he vanished from sight, an instant before Bres and his small army of Gardeners came through the trees; confusion and shock in their eyes. "How?" Bres growled at me. "How are you here?"

23

My eyes snapped open to the scene of people getting ready for the day. Asha wished me a good morning as she left the room, and elsewhere I could hear the sounds of movement as people packed to say their goodbye to this base. I was dazed for a moment before I threw myself out of bed, almost losing my balance in my haste. I jammed my feet into my boots, stubbing my toes in the process. I wanted to believe that it was just a dream, and that danger wasn't at our doorstep, but I knew that was wishful thinking. I was desperate for time.

Lainey skipped into the room, smiling eagerly as she greeted me. "Hi, Elana!"

"Lainey!" I shouted at her, making her jump a little. "I need you to get your Dad right away, okay?"

"O-oh, okay," she stammered, taken aback. "I'll find him."

Roger walked around the corner with a look of concern. "No need darling, I'm right here," he said eyeing me. "What seems to be the trouble?"

"We have to talk. Now. It might already be too late; I'm so sorry!" I was trying to focus, trying to get my bag and jacket.

The concern on Roger's face was evident now, his brow furrowed. "Lainey, why don't you go help Jayden while I speak with Elana?"

His daughter nodded in agreement and headed out of the room. "Now what's all this about?"

"You won't believe me if I tell you how I know, but there's no time anyway." I was speaking too fast, but I couldn't slow down. "There are some very dangerous people after me, and they're here. We have to leave before they find me."

"Easy," Roger said, trying to calm me down. "We can take care of it. We've been through some pretty bad situations; we'll take care of you."

"No, you won't," I urged him. "If they find me, the best I can do is run. I don't have anything to take them on, and I won't rely on your guns either."

Roger looked like he was taking it all in. "These people, they can do what you do? With the wind and that sort of thing?"

"What I did with the wind was mostly a mistake on my part and not even close to what they're capable of," I said, doing my best to keep my voice even, slowing down my words.

"Okay, we go now then," he said with a nod. "Not your fault. You're being chased. It will be fine."

Deep down I think we both had the feeling that was a lie, but we could debate it later if there was a later. Something changed in Roger almost immediately. He changed from the understanding, caring man who welcomed me into a regimented commander, barking orders and expecting them to be followed. For their part, everyone understood and moved quickly, and in what seemed like a matter of minutes the entire base was packed into the armored vehicle, and we were ready to go.

I was checking my bag and making sure I had everything I'd need when I felt a tug on my jacket.

"What's happening?" Lainey asked me, the same fear in her eyes the day I met her at that farm.

"We just have to leave, that's all," I told her. "It's not safe here; you understand that, right?"

"Yeah. It seems like it's never safe," she replied sadly.

I wanted to tell her that one day it would be, that this was just temporary, but the reality of this world told me otherwise, and my heart sank. How do you tell a child that their fate is inevitable? That they were created just to be destroyed. I couldn't look her in the eye at that moment, and she shifted uncomfortably. Before I could say anything, Jayden leaned into the room, wide-eyed and nervous. "Something's happening outside," he whispered.

We were too late. I knew it. I hated that I was right. I hated even more that I was helpless at this moment. I told him, "Okay. Stay here with Lainey. I'll go help."

I gave Lainey a little squeeze on the arm as I left. The series of shots fired made me quicken my approach. As I rounded the corner to the outside, I could hear that horrible voice that made me freeze in my tracks and cling to the wall to avoid being seen.

"Listen, you lot, it's real simple," Bres shouted with a hint of scorn in his voice. "We don't care about you, just bring us your smallest, most annoying ginger, and we'll leave you to being eaten alive by undead or whatever it is you were planning on doing."

"Not gonna happen!" I heard Roger shout back. "Elana's with us. She saved two of ours, as far as I'm concerned a threat to her is a threat on all of us!"

"Yeah, of course, it is," Bres impatiently replied with disdain. "Was that not obvious?"

I didn't give myself a chance to back out of this and forced myself to move out into the open, instantly regretting that decision. Everyone in the group had guns drawn and trained on Bres and his Gardeners. The base was surrounded by two fences. One very thick, sturdy security fence meant to stop everything but a tank from getting through. It formed an outer rim all along the perimeter of the base with a second fence meant to be used as a final checkpoint before someone would be able to fully enter. Bres, for his part, was standing in between the reinforced fence, which kept out anyone from the outside world, and the secondary chain link fence, which, to be honest, was probably pretty useless given the current situation. On the other side of the security barrier was a milling throng of zombies, growing by the second.

Roger yelled at me to get back inside, or something along those lines, but I couldn't take my eyes off of what was happening just outside of those gates. It was like someone doubled the size of the group that attacked me in that house, and then doubled it again. And more seemed to be coming from nowhere in particular.

How was Bres so calm? How was anyone here not in an absolute panic?

"Hey!" Bres screamed at me, waking me up to the more immediate situation. "I'd really appreciate it if you'd engage in this conversation. Because I! Am! Talking!"

"What are you even doing here?" I demanded. "I was probably going to die here eventually anyway, why chase me down like this?"

"First things first, we both know that's not true," he said, walking up to the chain link fence separating us. "I'm not even going to ask how you got back into the Knowing and then back here again. Or why, for that matter. Yeah, you didn't think I saw you, did you?"

"I'm tired of this, Bres," I pleaded. "What do you *want?*"

"To do my bloody job!" he yelled, his face contorting in anger as he did. "You, Elana Black, are an infant with a hand grenade! Why do you think I've spent so much of my time trying to deal with you? You and these people, you're heading to Volk, yes?"

"That's right!" Than shouted from behind me. "And we're going to get there, too!"

Bres made a pained expression of frustration before shaking his head and opened a gripped fist to point in his direction. "One more word out of you, boyo, and I will see to it that you jump to the top of my to-do list!"

Than seemed to visibly blanch at being addressed like that. Bres turned his attention back to me. "Do you know what was supposed to happen to these people on the way to Volk?"

"How would I know that?" I asked.

"They die," he replied coldly. "All of them. Horribly. And the little ones? They were supposed to die at the barn. And no one was ever going to care. No one would never know their names. They are set dressing. And now you're getting ready to march them head on into the main plot."

It was an idea that I'd always feared, just the thought of coming into contact with a character and changing the story had always seemed like a remarkably bad idea, not that I could explain why.

He continued, "That's what we do! We are tasked with keeping the stories on track because there is a natural order to things. People live, but most of the time they die. Countless lives are affected by the smallest alteration, and you are making a mess of biblical proportions. Every time you take it upon yourself to rescue one of these unfortunate souls, you risk destroying entire worlds. You cause ripples across time and space, across multiple universes, and have you ever once thought to consider the horrible possibilities? The damage you could do, the consequences that you'll have to face?"

"Then what's the point of having these powers?" I asked him. "We can help people. Whatever else, they're not dead yet. You can't ask me to let them die."

"That is precisely what I'm telling you to do," Bres snarled. "At this point, they'll make it or they won't. But you are going home. Right now."

"What's waiting for me when I get back?" I asked him.

"My men are standing by," he confirmed. "You'll get a trial. Maybe. You'll get put into a training program. Possibly. Or you'll just die resisting."

I resigned myself to that fact, but it didn't mean I couldn't do a little good first. "Bres, hear me out. I'll go back, peacefully even. I'll even smile the whole way if you like, but listen." I swallowed hard, looking back at the worried faces of everyone, their arms visibly growing weak from holding up their guns. "There are children here. So I'll make you a deal. I'll go back, but only if you promise me the safety of everyone here. You said it yourself, they were supposed to die, but if they just go somewhere besides Volk it shouldn't matter. Keep them safe and I'll do whatever you want. Do we have a deal? Please."

Bres looked back to his Gardeners and the growing horde outside of the gates, nodding his head in agreement. "Okay then, I'll tell you what," he said thoughtfully. "No."

I took a step back. "No? What do you mean no?"

"I mean, you haven't been listening," he sneered at me, gripping the fence with both hands. "Our job is bigger than you, and these people are already dead. And I really think it's time you learned that lesson the hard way."

His words made me afraid, and that fear made me angry. He gave a nod to his group who then formed a tight circle around each other as a familiar looking dome covered them all. Bres then sauntered away from the fence, licking his lips as he did, a mirthless smile crossing his face. Pointing at either fence, he quietly said, "You did this, Elana, you did. You killed them all."

An invisible cone of heat spread from his hands, and the barriers on either side of him began to burst into flames and rapidly melt. Bres walked backward, easily stepping through the protective dome.

"Just go home, Elana!" he shouted. As he did hundreds, maybe thousands of zombies descended upon us, falling over themselves in a frenzy. Shots rang out, and each one seemed to drop a zombie, but it was too much.

"Get inside!" Roger screamed at me, genuine terror crossing his face in a way I didn't think was possible. "Save the kids! Keep Lainey safe!"

The situation was too hideous for my brain to process it as reality and I didn't even think as I turned to dash into the building. Kenny was the first scream I heard. Then Grace. And then Than and Asha almost simultaneously. And lastly, I heard Roger die.

It couldn't have taken more than fifteen seconds, and they didn't even have the dignity of their deaths being witnessed by anyone other than Bres and his crew. Anger flooded me at that thought, and I was determined more than ever to fight fate. I was going to save the kids. I had one desperate, monumentally stupid idea, but I was going to try anyway. And when I did, I was going to make Bres pay for what he'd done.

I made it back into the barracks without being pursued, but it was maybe a matter of seconds before the zombies found their way inside. There was just too many of them; it was more of a space issue than anything else. This place would be flooded any second. "Where's my Dad?" Jayden yelled at me as I rounded the doorway into their room.

"I need you both to come with me!" I yelled at them both; there was no time to coddle them. "Now, let's go!"

Lainey gripped Jayden's wrist, pulling him to his feet and the three of us headed back down the hall towards the office. Behind us, I heard the zombies pouring into every available space, getting closer. "In you go, get behind the desk!" I told the children, locking the door behind me, shoving a bookcase over in front of it as a precaution.

"I'm scared." Jayden was in shock, his words barely audible. Lainey was something else. She had a calmed demeanor that could only have come from her father.

I huddled behind the desk with them, lowering my voice as I opened my bookbag. "Hey, I'll tell you what we'll do while we wait this out. I will tell you a story."

They were scared. They must have known I was scared too, but I pulled out a book anyway. Trying to sound excited, I said, "Oh, this is a good one! *The Wonderful Wizard of Oz!* Do you two know it? No? Wow, you're in for a treat, come cuddle with me, and I'll read it to you. It's a story about a child, much like the both of you, who was carried away on a cyclone into a magical world where she makes friends, and she is given a quest to kill an evil witch."

The relevance to our current situation was not lost on me. The children obediently crawled under my arms and looked at the pages as I read.

"Dorothy lived in the midst of the great Kansas prairies, with Uncle Henry, who was a farmer, and Aunt Em, who was the farmer's wife. Their house was—"

A loud bang on the door made the children jump.

"It's all right, ignore that, trust me, focus on the story," I said, calmly trying to continue. "Their house was small, for the lumber to build it had to be carried by wagon many miles. There were four walls, a floor and a roof—"

The office began to fade. A mist. Azure and emerald, began to swirl from the book as I read. It felt as if the book itself was straining under the weight of my words, the clamoring at the door started to fade from my awareness.

"What is that?" Lainey asked, her voice shaking. Jayden gripped my jacket tightly.

"—which made one room; and this room contained a rusty looking cookstove, a cupboard for the dishes, a table—" I refused to stop reading, I blocked out every sound, every sensation. I thought I heard Lainey scream and the sound of the door giving way. I kept going. Soon saying the words felt less like speaking; more of an experience.

We were suddenly falling. Then sliding, all three of us. Jayden must have been surprised by all of it because I lost him just about as soon as we began to shift directions in this impossible tunnel. I looked just in time to see him swallowed by the swirling mists, a look of pure shock. No time to make a sound.

"Jayden!" Lainey cried out, reaching for him. Her sudden movement put me off balance, and I instinctively reached to grab anything. My hand caught her prosthetic, which dislodged from the rest of her arm, and she too was swallowed by the mists.

Before I could react to even that, I was dropped into a lawn, maybe greener than I'd ever seen in grass. I looked up to see a mansion, improbable in design, it looked like a mad artist's idea of a house. "Oh! Where did you come from?" a shrill voice said behind me.

I turned on my heels and had to look down to see a small man, bald but with a long and well-groomed white beard, maybe three feet tall if that, and wearing a tuxedo only from the waist up with a black skirt and old swashbuckler boots from his waist down.

"Yeah, no time for that," I said impatiently. "Two children, did you see them? They might have gotten here just before me."

"Here? As in my home?" he asked in a voice that I could tell would be grating any second now.

"Here as in this world," I said, my eyes darting around. "Yellow Brick Road, Munchkin Town, whatever. Have you seen two kids? One was a little girl, had one arm, wiry black hair? Another was a boy, he had a big tear in his pants, really messy hair?"

"Are you a sorceress?" he asked, tilting his neck to examine me.

"You know what? Maybe. I can't really answer that right now; I'm kind of in a hurry. Wait a second, are you Boq?" I asked him.

"Indeed I am!" he said, puffing out his chest, gripping the lapels of his coat proudly.

"That's great Boq, listen, some great and powerful wizards are probably going to be here in a moment, and they're going to massacre anything they see, so you need to get inside and hide under your bed or something. Cool?"

Boq's face went pale at the matter-of-fact way I said that to him, or maybe it was just the mention of wizards. Either way, he wasn't moving. "Move!" I yelled at him. That did it.

There was something I'd been considering for a while, and now was the time to test it. The kids were either alive or they weren't, and if they were, they weren't being eaten alive by zombies, which I had to take as a victory right now. My theory involved an excellent reason why Bres hadn't instantly caught up to me, and I think the Aos Si unwittingly showed me a little something extra. Or he meant to show it to me but didn't want to say anything.

For now, my thoughts had to be on the safety of the kids. I would stay on the top of this hill, visible in every direction. When the Gardeners arrived, if the kids were with me, great. If not, I'd have to keep their attention and force them to give chase.

I opened my bag and looked through the remaining titles. The first book I saw was quite important to me; I didn't want to use it unless I absolutely had to. The second book I saw was *Unleavened Bread* by Robert Grant. My face twisted in disgust, I wasn't sure why I grabbed this one, but whatever. It would work.

I patiently waited on the hill, legs crossed, the book opened, and I slowly read about horrible people in 19th century English high society. Each way in I paid careful attention to, calming the book as I did, resisting its hungry pull. Eventually, maybe an hour in the unnaturally comfortable sun, Bres and six Gardeners appeared out of the air. Bres looked at me with murder in his eyes and a scythe in his hands. I gave him a gentle wave and a smile, trading the sunny hill for the gloomy overcast of England.

Still, the square at the center of town was humdrum enough that I was able to relax at a fountain and read *To Venus in Five Seconds* by Fred T. Jane, a delightfully weird science fiction novel. It was like Douglas Adams decades before he was born. By the time Bres arrived, it had been maybe an hour-and-a-half this time, and now he only had five of his Gardeners with him, all looking worse for wear. One of them was visibly pained from a gash in his arm, held tight with a tourniquet.

"Are you missing one?" I asked him smugly.

"Stop! Please!" he shouted at me.

I was now in a lush, jungle environment with a blinding sun. It took me a moment to find a quiet spot to sit and read under the shade of a canopy, but the day was bright and fine. I waved pleasantly at a pair of passing Thotheen. They waved back, presumably. It was difficult to tell with their anatomy. Still, it was nice to have a full two-and-a-half hours on another planet, relaxing in the shade, lying on my back with my feet up, reading *Captains Courageous* by Rudyard Kipling.

Bres finally emerged, down to just three Gardeners with a look of hysteria on his face. He cried out to me, "You don't know what you're—"

I was on a beach in San Diego on a beautiful mid-morning, a time before industry or ports had come in and tainted the landscape or muddied the crystal blue waters. Nothing around as far as the eye could see. I opened my bag, just one book left. A first edition of *Jane Eyre*, all covered in burgundy leather.

"I guess this is it," I said to myself, as I got to work smoothing out the sand until it was shallow enough to draw on without being in danger of washing away with the tide. I marked the symbols the way I was shown, carefully and deliberately, and did my best to create a circle as perfect as possible. I knew it wasn't quite right, but it didn't need to be for this, it just needed to be good enough. With the extra time, I carefully brushed away any imperfections in the symbols, dug the trenches just a little bit deeper, and when I felt I couldn't do any better, I sat cross-legged in the sand and opened the book. The note from George felt like a punch to my heart. Safe travels indeed, my friend.

When Bres arrived, he was down to two Gardeners, both women in red suits, stained with blood in various other shades of red, presumably their own and... others. He fell flat on his face into the sand, and as he did, I took in a calming breath, inhaling through my nose and raising the protective dome as I did. I willed it as easily as I did the breath. "You really, really need to stop!" Bres screamed as he struggled to find his footing.

"Weapons down," I told him victoriously, enjoying the warmth and weight and life pulsing through the book in my hands. "Then we'll all have a nice little chat about how it's going to be."

24

res and the others disarmed, they were spent. One of the women looked like she could barely stand under her own power. "We've put down our weapons, but you have to go back now, this isn't a negotiation," Bres said, trying to find his breath. "You do not know the danger we're all in because of you."

My anger rose at that. "Well, then why don't you just do what you should have done from the beginning and just tell me?"

"You're a Wildling, okay?" Bres spat. "You're not supposed to have access to your power. You are a child living in a house made of glass, with no windows and no doors, who has been given a bag of stones. Traditionally we just put you down before you can do too much damage, but sometimes we try to give you another way out."

"Yeah, I get it, you don't want me changing the story," I said cutting him off. "That part isn't going to stop. If I can save people, I will."

"I'm not talking about that!" he yelled. "What you're doing now, the way you travel, you're—"

"An Adept," I said, finishing for him.

He seethed at that. His companions also looked like they had a bad taste in their mouths. "If you are," he said through gritted teeth. "And that's a big if, you don't deserve that gift. The way you're traveling is an anathema."

"You're just saying that because you can't keep up," I declared with a grin. "I suspected as much, but seeing you in the Knowing confirmed it."

"You arrogant little—!" Bres looked as if he were ready to throttle me on the spot. "What you're doing, it hurts everything! It damages the Knowing directly, and the worst part? The part that really turns my stomach? It forgives you!"

"What do you mean I'm hurting it?" I asked. He spoke as if it were a person.

"You are punching holes in reality every time some fool story catches your fancy," he explained. "You haven't even made an attempt to use the ways. Even if we could do what you're able to, we wouldn't unless we absolutely needed to because of the mess it makes. And what you've done today, you... For Christ's sakes, you're about to detonate a bomb that will consume countless worlds! It will take those people years to recover from all of the damage, and you and I won't even be memories when they do!"

"So why don't you stop me?" I asked suspiciously.

"What do you think we've been doing this whole time? Good men and women have died today trying to catch up with you through the Knowing! When you leap from one world to another, you stretch the fabric of time and space like a rubber band. But when you jump into another world from within another world, particularly the way you've done it, the rubber—"

"Dude, shut up!" I shouted, all patience gone. "Not what I meant! I meant, why haven't you just killed me? Well?"

When he didn't answer, I went on. "You can't, can you? At least not directly, right? Someone is pulling your strings, because you obviously want me dead, you're not allowed, are you?"

Bres looked away, a mixture of shame and anger on his face. "Oh, you've had so many chances too! The hospital, the day you met me at the bookstore, even with Claire at the bookstore. It was all theater! You know where I live. You know where I work! You could have killed me in my sleep if you'd really wanted to. You thought you could scare me off, but it didn't work, did it?"

Bres was red in the face now. "You don't have the—"

"No Bres, now *I* am talking! And you will give me your attention because this next part is of paramount importance to you. This is the part where you learn a lesson from me. Lesson one? Leave well enough alone!"

"We can just tear down your pathetic little Blister, you insignificant, stupid brat!" Bres raged.

"No question," I said, jumping to my feet. "But not before I jump again, so let's not even pretend like that's an option for you. You could have let those people live and taken me back, but you didn't and look what it got you. So here's the new deal. My friends are off limits. That includes the children, wherever they are. Everyone and anyone I care about, you are to bring no harm to. You or your people. I will bind you to this. And you will allow me safe passage home. After that, I'll deal with whatever you can bring. I will bind you to this as well."

"Why would I agree to this?" he asked. "You're right, I can't kill you, but there has been nothing said for them. I will slaughter them all, just to spite you."

"Because I will play by your rules," I told him plainly. "For the sake of the Knowing and those lives unseen on the worlds I may harm, I will stick to the ways and I won't, as you put it, go around punching holes in reality. I will never stop trying to save people, but I will use the ways and avoid the more direct routes. Unless, of course, I absolutely need to. If your words are good enough for you, they're good enough for me, right?"

Bres slammed a fist against my dome repeatedly as any illusion of calm from him faded away. "If you do not come out of that circle right now I will skin everyone you've ever met! I will deliver a fresh set of bones to your doorstep every morning! I will lay waste to every place you have ever called home, and when I'm done I will walk the streets at night with a flashlight looking for survivors!"

"No. You won't," I said flatly. He screamed at this, and even his remaining companions looked nervous. I snapped back, "Calm down, you're making a scene! You're only mad because you know you've lost. Admit it and quit wasting everyone's time. You and your sad bunch of psycho wildebeests can yell at each other in your pitiful little poo circle all you want, but the people I love are left out of it. Now do we have a deal or not? This book is getting a bit heavy."

Bres looked like a wounded animal, more dangerous than anything I'd ever imagined, but neutered for the moment. I'd pay for this eventually, no question, but for now, he had no choice. "Fine, we have an accord," he finally agreed.

"Swear it," I told him. "Like this is actually official and matters."

I waited another moment. Then, finally, he started, with a hint of sarcasm in his voice.

"I, Bres Mordred, swear to abide by the terms of your deal."

"I'm sorry," I sweetly replied, holding a hand to my ear. "Do it again, please. I'm not sure we all heard you."

Every inch of Bres stiffened in indignation. Louder this time, he began, "I, Bres Mordred, swear to abide by the terms of your deal!"

"That's twice you've sworn to me, Bres," I said with a grin. "Once more should do it."

"What good will *that* do?" he complained, exasperated and fed up. "I've agreed to your deal, what more could you ask for?"

"I could ask for one more thing," I replied. "And that's for you to swear it three times. Oh, right, that was the other thing I figured out. My favorite thing, really. You, Bres Mordred, are Fae. When I said that I would bind you to the deal, I meant it. Fae who swear to an agreement three times are bound by their very souls, isn't that right?"

"You don't know what you ask," he seethed. "I won't do it. I'll burn first!"

"If that's what you want." I shrugged. As I opened my copy of *Jane Eyre,* I muttered a quiet goodbye. "Safe travels, George."

The book swirled as Bres and his remaining Gardeners froze in terror, mouths agape, eyes wide. He shouted, "You'll kill us all!"

"Yeah, I will!" I yelled back, making sure to be louder than him. "And my friends will live because you won't be there to threaten them! Now I will not ask again! Will you swear to me three times?"

"I will!" he cried out. "I, Bres Mordred, swear to abide by the terms of your deal!"

A surge of power and a sonic boom spread across the beach, centered where Bres had been standing. The way he was standing, a gentle breeze could have knocked him over. He was right, maybe I didn't know what I was asking of him, but I knew what I was asking for. I willed the dome away and stepped towards him from the circle.

"I may not be allowed to kill you," Bres said through labored breaths, "but you'd be surprised what you can live through."

"Yeah, but that's the trick, isn't it? I'll live."

I stopped walking for a moment as a thought dawned on me. "Oh, my God, that's the stupidest thing ever!" I said, chuckling to myself. I'll live. Olive. It was a metaphor. It wasn't a pear or a plum, or anything else. On the tree, it was an Olive. As in Olivia. I was certain of it.

Why couldn't the Aos Si just say that? Why does everything have to be a puzzle?

Bres eyed me as I continued my walk towards him, feeling lighter than ever. "Oh, and one more thing," I said standing toe to toe with him, head held high to meet his gaze. "Where I'm from, we seal deals with a handshake."

The expression on his face morphed from exhaustion to confused laughter. "You're out of your head." He laughed. "Piss off."

"I thought you'd say that," I said thoughtfully. "Okay then, I'll tell you what... Yes."

"What are you on about?" he asked.

"For Lucia, who you took from me. For George, whose path was changed. For Lainey and Jayden, who are now orphaned. For Kenny and Roger and Grace and Asha and Than, who you murdered. For my friends who you traumatized and harmed. And for me, who you have terrorized, you are going to learn this lesson the hard way. You are bound. And if I break our agreement, none of us will be around to regret it," I said extending my hand sharply in his direction. "So, yes. You will take my hand right now, or the next thing you experience will be the sound of the universe tearing itself apart."

Bres gave me a dispirited look, and for a moment the only sound to be heard was the waves crashing on the beach. No one dared even to breathe. With a sense of finality, Bres gripped my hand with all the strength he had left. I could feel him trying to take my story from me, but keeping him out took less effort than shoving one of the cats off the counter at work. But in that same moment, I took it from him. All of it.

He was Bres, but had another name. His True name. I knew it, though I could not form it without hearing it from him. Bres was a half-breed, and though he never knew his father's name, he knew that everyone despised him, and by extension, they despised the half of him that was Fae. His mother, for her part, was incapable of being alone and raising a child that she never wanted; she was an imperfect woman, and by extension, Bres hated the half of him that was imperfect. He particularly hated being given another name and being asked to hide his face from the world. But he was special, and he knew it as much as everyone else. He was the half-breed with gifts from both sides. He was, however, disappointed to learn that this was not a story about him. He had a role to play, but he was not mentioned in the ancient texts as a great hero, there was no prophecy surrounding his role in the events to come. He was merely unique. Or in his mind, a less kind word was abnormal.

He would never have the bliss of being fully Human and thus absolved of the responsibility that came with being Fae. But he would also never be truly accepted among the Fae, for his blood had been tainted. He excelled then in his studies. Magic and combat came naturally to him, but he still struggled to fit in. Death came easy for him as well, but he lacked the compassion needed when taking a life, and worse from the perspective of his employers, he lacked the professionalism that came from being a killer. He had a habit of toying with his prey. He enjoyed their fear.

And why shouldn't he? If he was no hero, he had none of the duty and responsibility of being a hero. Those in power thought he didn't hear their whispers, they believed they could control him, but he knew what he was and what his purpose was. Still, he wasn't without a sense of duty. He wasn't without the ability to love. There were those out there in his world who would never know the wars that were fought, the blood that was spilled, the ever encroaching darkness of an infinite number of universes all trying to take their rightful spot as the one true world. His duty was to them, whatever the cost. It wasn't his fault that he just happened to enjoy doing the work no one else wanted to.

And all of that would be acceptable if not for the constant chain holding. The fail safes. The lack of trust! It made him sick. First keeping that damned brat Lucia alive because of the prophecy. To think that a human could save everyone! Meaningless! Madness! Overriding his wisdom that she was too dangerous to be kept alive. And now, they're actively moving her through the Knowing, how stupid could they be? How many times did they have to make these particular mistakes before they did the smart thing and wiped out the wildlings on sight? Keeping them alive was one thing, taking them on a tour behind the current was unconscionable! And with this assignment, sending in a White to keep an eye on the situation! Like he needed supervision from their kind, at least they had the decency to order everyone killed, should he—

My hand retracted from his; it burned. Everything felt wrong. Bres slumped back and sat in the sand, laughing weakly, but incessantly. "Well, you wanted it, you got it! It looks like you have a decision: Lucia, the would-be savior of us all, or whoever those other two are." He continued to laugh at his own joke. "Tick Tock, Elana! Tick Tock!"

The other two Gardeners parted and cleared a path for me, opening a way back into the Knowing. If I took it, I'd get to Lucia in time. Past his story, I felt the weight of the prophecy behind his emotions. If they were right, Lucia had a purpose, a destiny, one with the potential to be all that stood between peace and oblivion. Bres didn't believe it, but he knew those who did. I wasn't sure he was the best source of advice at the moment any-way. More than all of that, she's been enduring god knows what for a decade. Each day that passed from this point on was my responsibility as far as I was concerned, if they didn't just kill her outright.

I knew what I was doing, though, looking at that portal. I was trying to make myself feel better about the fact that I was leaving Lucia to her fate with the Gardeners or whoever else she ended up with. I had a vague idea about where she was, and even if I did find her, what then? I wanted to go into the unknown and save my friend so desperately that it hurt, but I knew that I couldn't abandon Claire and Olivia. I was responsible for their current situation even more than anything that was happening with Lucia, and their lives were every bit as important as any Fae, or fated hero, or myself. They might not have meant any-thing to Bres or whatever organization he belonged to, but their lives mattered to me, and I was going to do anything to get them back. Going into the Knowing ensured that I'd never make it back in time.

"I'm going to save my friends, Bres," I said looking back at him, removing my copy of Jane Eyre and clutching it with both hands. "I'd say that particular quest qualifies me for an 'abso-lutely need to' pass, wouldn't you?"

I willed myself back, and the rush was like nothing I'd ever experienced in traveling. I was falling horizontally is the best way I can put it. The sensation you get when you fall, regardless of how brief a moment in time that is, you know that your speed is growing exponentially. With nothing to break your fall, the landing has the potential for disaster. Instead of happening in-stantaneously, it took a couple of seconds, and I was filled with the knowledge that was I going to hit something though I could not tell what.

Dumbfounded eyes looked into mine far too late to react in any meaningful way. I was already swinging my thick, leather-bound copy of *Jane Eyre* at the burly red-suited man, hurled at him by the Knowing with the velocity of an express train. The sound of the book against his skull reverberated around the room as he went limp, the shock of the impact vibrating up into my shoulder. A second man, also in red, wasn't fortunate enough to have been looking in the direction I shot into the room, and my collision with him as I went through his partner sent him head first into the steel submarine door. I recovered faster than he could have hoped to, given the Grade 9000 concussion he just suffered. To be safe, I raised the heavy book over my head and brought it down once more like a mallet, rendering him useless.

There was no one else there, no one living at least. Blood spray coated the walls and there were a couple of bodies on either side left in the halls, unmoved or untouched from where they were dropped. I held my breath and did my best not to get blood on my shoes, trying to avoid looking at the faces of the dead as I navigated my way out of the ruined shelter. Only when I was at the top of the stairs and on the street did I allow myself to breathe again. My phone was in my hand as I broke into a run back to my car, still dead. I plugged it into my charger, anxiously counting the seconds until I could begin to dial everyone. Calls went straight to voicemail when I tried Olivia and Claire, and they could have been anywhere, but on a hunch, I dialed the Book's End and got a busy signal. That's not supposed to happen.

Jason was there, I could feel it.

Big Sister pulled away from her spot at speeds that threatened to shake her apart. I needed a miracle not to get pulled over on my way up there, but the way I was driving made that scenario likely. The freeways were mostly clear this time of day, but that didn't stop me from weaving around the other cars. One thought kept repeating, one truth haunted me the whole way there. This was my fault. I knew there were dangerous people, I knew they'd come for us, and I left the people I loved alone. I walked out on them, and I hated myself for it. I just had to make it there; I had to believe that I wasn't too late. I had bound Bres and his people from harming my friends, but Jason didn't answer to Bres. He was free to act as he saw fit, and he was the contingency plan. I saw it from Bres when I took his story. I thought I was so damned clever at the time, and now I wasn't sure I'd ever forgive myself.

My car bounced up the curb and skidded to a stop in front of the door; the shocks threatened to shake the axles loose from the rest of the vehicle. I practically fell out of the car as I ran inside, slamming the door open to see a gaping tear in the skin of the universe in the center of the shop, hideous tendrils of purple and black reaching out from nothing towards nothing. And in front of it, a sharp dressed man in a white suit, propping up a table at an odd angle with Olivia and Claire tightly chained to it.

"Jason!" I yelled, challenging him with death soaking his name.

He turned and grinned, giving me a small nod as he acknowledged me. Casually he pushed the table forward into the Knowing, drawing screams from my friends. "Too late."

25

My feet were moving towards the portal without a second to lose. I crossed the length of the Book's End, ignoring the goosebumps forming all over my body, the unmistakable impulse to stop, the sense of dread that comes from your sense of self-preservation peeking its panicked eyes out its hiding place so it can plead with me to stop, or at the very least consider what I was doing. Just a moment of hesitation might have stopped me, and of course, I wasn't going to hesitate. Though in hindsight maybe I should have.

I didn't know what I was rushing towards, a foe who had every advantage over me into a battlefield of his choosing. More than that, I very much had something to lose here, he did not. I barely knew what this place was; he presumably had traversed it more times than I'd driven outside of Los Angeles proper. And yet, here I was, leaping into the unknown with no plan, no weapons, no backup. Which is why it shouldn't have surprised me when a ten-foot Tiki Head dropped from the sky and nearly crushed me to death.

Okay, so that's not right, that should have been a surprise to anyone, because honestly, who the hell expects that? I didn't have a whole lot of time to think about that or really anything with how fast it happened. It felt like the blink of an eye, a split-second reaction that saved my life. As soon as I jumped through I had to scramble out of the way, nearly twisting my ankle as I did. It wasn't until then that I managed to get a look around, and I really wish I hadn't. The world around me seemed corrupted somehow, more dangerous. In pain. Caged. There was the stale odor of meat that had been left to rot in the sun, and the overgrown and brittle grass swaying in the wind was a sickly yellow. Like the world itself, it was jaundiced.

I wanted to charge ahead, but a thought occurred to me that this was not just any other place, things didn't seem to work right here, or they worked at such a hyper degree as to be ludicrous. I closed my eyes and rather than trying to focus my senses on the world around me, for once I decided to let the world in before I extended my senses out. I allowed it to breathe into me before I breathed out into it.

Something happened, something almost symbiotic. I was aware of the world for miles around, and of things, and then the things around me; air spilled over me like water, water rustled like paper, the earth was as temporary as clouds. It was absurd, meaningless, but I understood it intimately in that moment. I opened my eyes and saw a maze of traps and triggers ahead of me. It felt like it must have taken Jason months to do something so elaborate, but he entered into the Knowing with maybe a head start of seconds. I don't know why that didn't click with me right away, time of all things doesn't seem to work here.

An effort of will was all it took for the traps to become disarmed, and as I did so the odor on the wind became less overpowering, the grass became less brittle, turning green. The more immediate concern was my friends and as if in response, I knew intrinsically that Olivia and Claire were alive. More than that, I couldn't tell how I knew that, but it was enough for me to move forward. I considered asking the Aos Si for help, in fact, I was surprised he wasn't here already, but I remembered what happened the last time I cried out for him and how the world around me seemed to react. On top of that, nothing came for free from him, and I've learned the hard way that asking for help out of desperation from people who are willing to take advantage of you is something you nearly always regret.

I was really starting to kick myself given how avoidable my current situation was. Sure, there was some blame on the part of the Gardeners. They could have just been less murder happy and taken the time to explain to everyone what these powers were. I guess the argument was that the more people there are who have access to potentially destructive forces, the more likely someone was going to be destructive, but there had to be a better option than just leaving innocent people to die in a shadow dimension. I'm not excusing them or their actions at all, but I should have been better prepared. I should have been a better friend. I wasn't there for Lucia as much as I could have been when she was in the hospital. I didn't bother to do anything useful with my powers until I was forced to. And worst of all, I left two of the closest people in my life by themselves and tried to do everything on my own. Be the hero. Save the day. Beat all the bad guys.

What a bunch of crap.

You're not the hero if you're trying to rescue people who are in peril because of what you did. You aren't really saving the day if you're stomping out your own fires. And bad guys or no you accept help when it is offered, and you listen to the wisdom of those you love, specifically when your decisions affect their lives. And I know what this sounds like, but this is not self-pity. This is responsibility and self-reflection. I was starting to own my mistakes, and I was prepared to do right by the people whose lives I've endangered.

Perhaps one of the dumbest mistakes I'd made recently was overlooking Jason. In hindsight, it was evident he Knew me back at the party. I didn't go after him when I had him on the ropes. I stupidly thought he wasn't going to be a problem when he stopped Bres from killing Claire and Olivia. I wasn't in any real danger, of course, I can see that now. If I were to die, it would have to be indirectly and not by his hand. For all his talk, he couldn't just smack me down. But to treat Jason like he was out of sight and out of mind was just asinine and shortsighted. And now, here he was, holding two people hostage when he could have just killed them. If I had to guess, he was keeping them alive as a bargaining chip until I'm out of the way. His orders were to take out everyone who knew about me, and I assumed that included, well, me.

I'm a lucky duck.

There wasn't anywhere else to go. I mean, it looked like there were miles of land stretched out before me, but it felt empty ahead as far as I could tell. I extended my senses again, and a cave leading below ground, lit by an unknown source appeared to my right. Maybe I was getting good at this, or maybe Jason was just leaving me breadcrumbs. There was still a lot I didn't know. Still, I felt remnants of energy expended in that direction, and I took it. The sensation that something was off returned, but there weren't traps or tripwires or anything of the sort ahead of me, and yet, there was something.

Pebbles dropped from above me as I walked down the spiraling slopes of the cave, which was lit from some invisible source seemingly neither above nor below. It wasn't until I was sure that I heard breathing that was not my own that I became convinced that I was being stalked by something, and my senses were only telling me that it was huge. I wasn't sure how my magic, if I was calling it that now, I guess I was; was going to work here or if this was the right time to use what little I had, but I readied it in my mind, focusing on stopping whatever was above me. The thought crystallized in my mind, and I spun on my heel, ready to let loose with an elemental blast of wind or ice or—

My eyes went wide with an emotion I could best describe as "Holy Crap!" and whatever ideas I had about offense went out the window as I raised an arm defensively, summoning my shield of competing red and blue swirls just in time for talons nearly as large as I was bounced off it, pushing me down to a knee. The creature shrieked in surprise and flew up and away for a moment allowing me to get a good look at it. It was crow, perhaps, but twisted and enormous. Its wings were spread for just a moment before it clutched at the walls of the cave with its talons and claws. It had both because it held the body of a person if that person had weighed half a ton and were over eight feet tall. The hideous thing had a glaze on its skin that looked like it had been dipped in crude oil and then polished to reflect shining shades of black, blue, and green. The face though was what would give me nightmares later on. The beak on it looked like it had been carved hastily from limestone, and the eyes narrowed at me with a look of pure evil. Even its breathing now was a hiss, and its breath filled the cavern with the same decaying scent I'd been assaulted with when I arrived here.

One small detail in the middle of all of this, however, gave me hope. I noticed that the shield on my arm was no longer swirling with competing splotches of red and blue, but that they melded together to form a brilliant violet and more importantly, the shield took shape and solidified on my arm. I could feel the well in the pit of my being refilling with power from the walls, the air, even the colors around me. I didn't have long to celebrate this news, however, as the bird creature above me shrieked cruelly and a cloud of spores fell towards me. With my free hand, I sent a gust of wind in their direction, sending them into the wall where the stone seemed to bubble and steam upon contact.

I gulped, knowing what that could have done to my decidedly not stone-like flesh that I possessed, but I felt the power refill almost as quickly as it left, and I got an idea. "Okay ugly," I challenged the beast. "I got magic powers, this sweet shield, and a jerk to punch in the nose! Let's see if you can keep up!"

I took off into a run down the winding rocks, sliding under where rocks jutted out from the wall. The creature dove after me, but the relatively close quarters of the cave didn't give it the most maneuverability, and I was going to use that to my advantage. I made the mistake of glancing down when I stopped and saw that at ground level was a body of water, glowing faintly blue, and the open mouth of the cave. They say, "Don't look down," for a reason. My plan further took shape and instantly qualified as one of the stupidest things I'd ever come up with, but I tried to remind myself that not everything worked correctly here, and if I didn't come up with a better plan soon, I'd be eviscerated by the reason I may never trust birds again.

When the beast seemed to be at its least mobile, I stopped and faced it, daring it with my eyes to make a move. It angrily sent another cloud of spores, but I was anticipating that this time, and focused my wind gust, pushed them into the stone walkway directly above it. Only this time I breathed out, extending my senses, feeling for the weak spot in the stone. The slab bubbled and sizzled louder than before now that the spores were concentrated, but the creature did something I hadn't counted on and lunged for me.

I raised my shield, trying to maintain my hold on the corroding stone, but the slashing of its free claw as it dug into the wall less than three feet away from me made keeping my concentration something akin to gripping thawing ice. I needed to gamble, it was one thing or the other, and if I tried to do both I was as good as dead. I let down my guard for less than a second, extending my palm and all of my senses towards the rock, dislodging it and pulling it directly into the skull of the abomination.

The blow dazed it, long enough to not realize the rest of the cave was coming down around it. We had descended quite a way and passed a whole of lot of rocks as we did, and I just knocked out the support beam. Like the worst game of Jenga, this tower was collapsing. Not wanting to be caught up in it, I took a leap of faith, down towards the pool, bird and rocks alike fractions of a second behind me. I felt the power return, filling me up, and praying that I was timing this right I let loose into the side of the cave wall with every fiber of my being, focusing on the largest gusts of wind I'd ever experienced and held onto it all with everything I had. I propelled myself out of the cave as tons of stone and debris, and yes, even a bird man creature somewhere filled the pool, then the mouth of the cave, nearly erasing any evidence that an entrance might have existed.

I landed first on the shield as I exited before bouncing and rolling a good twenty feet or so from the entrance, the ensuing cloud of dust causing me to cough heavily as I slowly got to my feet. Not because I was hurt, I just couldn't believe that worked! I am Elana Black, Monster Slayer! Well, I didn't know if it was dead. Okay, revision. I am Elana Black, Monster Burier! Better.

I had no idea what that thing was, but I really hoped one of them wasn't hanging around outside because I really didn't know to fight one in the open. The entirety of my strategy in all of my monster fights to date is "Bury it." It has worked one hundred percent of the time. To be safe, I took a look out into the deep amber sky for additional bird things, and then turned around to look into a valley below the cave as the dust billowed around me, the natural wind blowing my hair and jacket around me.

Below me I saw Olivia and Claire chained to an altar, unconscious, with Jason looking up at me in his perfect white suit, pompously offering a greeting. "Hey, look who decided to make it," he said, spreading his arms out before him. "It really is a shame though, after my traps and the locals who I poisoned against your scent, you must be—"

With thanks, not apologies, to a particular Star Spangled hero, there was something I'd really been wanting to try almost as much as I wanted Jason to shut his stupid mouth. Without a word, I flung my shield down into the valley, catching him off guard as it slammed into the bridge of his nose, causing him to recoil in shock and pain. His yelp sounded like an injured kitten, something in stark contrast to his tone only a second before. I willed the shield back to me, and it gave the illusion of ricocheting back to my wrist. Okay, as potentially deadly as this situation was, that was really cool.

Jason stumbled to his feet, his perfect suit now stained with a tiny spray of blood. "You have got to be kidding me!" he wailed, tears involuntarily welling up as he clutched the flesh between his eyes. "That is twice now with my nose!"

I thought that I had something really witty to say about the having the high ground or something along those lines, but I didn't have the chance as the ground shook around me, beginning to break apart and threatening to swallow me whole. It was then that I did something that Jason didn't expect. I charged at him. I was half his size and in no way trained to fight, but trained or no, whether I wanted it or not, I was in a fight. And as it turned out, for once I really, really wanted one.

Jason whipped his jacket open, revealing a sword in a scabbard that he began to reach for, but I was already airborne having taken a running leap off the hill, and my entire frame collided with him, knocking the sword free and sending it spinning out of control and out of reach. He couldn't keep his footing, some of that was my dive, some of that was his summoned earthquake, and the two of us went tumbling over each other. The commotion must have woken up my friends; I could hear them yelling, but I was a little busy at the moment.

When we stopped rolling, I found myself on top of his chest, which I took as the perfect opportunity to ball up a fist and punch Jason square in the face. I immediately regretted it. It turns out faces have bones in them and bones are very hard, and I wasn't entirely uncertain I hadn't just broken every bone in my hand. If anything, the blow only made Jason furious, and he sent a wave of fire, a momentary burst of flame from his hand inches away from my face. If not for the shield I would have been burned alive. As it was I felt the intense heat radiate through my protective shield and into my wrist, causing me to cry out and fall away. Jason was on his feet in an instant, his suit now scorched and stained, ruined. Ire and shock painted his face as he eyed me like an insect who had given him too much trouble to let live, and he was going to get satisfaction from squashing me.

Okay. So maybe sometimes the bad guys actually do win.

26

Jason fumed as his palms opened at his side, balls of fire appearing in either one. My body screamed in exertion as I willed it to scramble behind a tombstone, fire erupting behind me as I did.

"You know, I'm not typically a killer, things don't often come to that on my side," he yelled to me over the howling of the wind. "But with you? I'm definitely going to enjoy this."

The gravestone I was behind started to pulse with a sickly green light and I sprinted a few headstones down as it burst in a corrosive spray. Jason was toying with me.

"For someone who doesn't read a lot, you sure sound like every gloating super villain since, like, ever," I yelled back. I had an idea, but I needed to keep him talking. "Why did you even go through all this effort? Why bring us here?"

"It's cleaner," he replied. I could hear soft footsteps; he was trying to sneak up on me. "Disposing of people in the Knowing doesn't leave anything behind for the authorities to find. Sometimes people just go missing, who knows what happened to them? We do. We know what happened."

A light flashed above my head, and it gave me just enough time to move again before dozens of stakes made of what looked to be hard light stabbed the ground and vanished. I caught a glimpse of Jason, arrogant and casual as he tracked me. He was directly between me and where I needed to get to, the stone slab my friends were chained to. Using a minuscule amount of will I felt out in the direction of the sword he'd lost earlier in our tussle. I didn't know if I could do this with the sword, but I managed it well enough in the cave so I might as well give it a shot. I saw something like this in a movie once, after all.

"If you're just going to hide all day, I can start with your friends," Jason called out. "Who should I start with?"

I tried to ignore him, gripping one hand into the dry ground and getting a handful of dirt as I felt out with my senses towards the sword, focusing on its specific matter. I concentrated on blocking out anything else around it from what I could perceive. Then, careful not to use all of my power on one spell, I slowly unsheathed it and sent it through the air at Jason's chest. He was ready for it of course, but that was the distraction.

He caught the hilt in mid-air with a laugh and turned in my direction to gloat. I threw the dirt in his direction and channeled the rest of my energy into a directed gust of wind aimed directly at his eyes. It all happened too fast for him. An inelegant sound left his mouth as the dirt stung his eyes and filled his nostrils. He dropped the sword and began to cough and furiously rub at his face. I stood up and sprinted towards him, shield up in front of me, and with a gut full of terror I let out a battle cry as I smashed it into the side of his head. The shield flickered and popped, a small crackle of energy dissipated into the air as it did.

"Let us help you."

I thought I heard a whisper on the winds as I made my assault, like a thousand people saying the same sentence at the same time, but I couldn't stop to figure out what it meant. I'd probably bought myself maybe a minute until Jason was back on his feet. I paused my run just long enough to pick up the sword and get to the altar.

"Quick! We need something for these chains!" Claire shouted, struggling with the restraints. "Will that sword cut through metal?"

"Can you, like, magic them off or something?" Olivia asked.

"Sorry, no time," I said, carefully dragging the sword in a circle around the altar. This was going to be far from perfect, but it would have to do. "I don't have time for the symbols, so I'm really kind of gambling here. Oh, and I'm sorry."

"For what?" Claire asked, confused about what I was doing.

Jason got to his feet and swore a curse. With the circle complete I tossed the sword into it, next to the altar and focused on the meaning of protection and slammed my palm into the ground, releasing the thought into the circle. A pink dome sprung out of the ground, struggling to complete at its peak, but it got there. I fell back, collapsing in a breathless heap.

"Wow, that really is harder without the cheat sheet," I muttered.

"Let us help you."

I heard it again, identical to what I'd heard earlier. And again, I still had more pressing issues. Jason seemed to notice it as well, as he craned his neck, taking his eyes off of me for a moment. I just needed a couple more seconds to draw in a little more power. I tried something a little too strenuous, it would seem, and I was slower to replenish what I just spent.

"Well Jerkface, that's that," I said, getting to my feet. "They're off the table now. It's just you and me."

He gave his attention back to me. "What... *that?* That's one of the worst protection circles I've ever seen. You think that will stop me?"

"Maybe not," I replied. "But you're going to have to go through me first."

"Happily," he said with a grin, extending his palm sharply in my direction. An invisible force like a major league fastball struck me in the stomach sending me toppling over a headstone.

"No fair wasn't ready," I coughed hard, trying to shake my shield out. Jason extended his hand again, and I instinctively raised my arm to shield my face, turning a little as I did. The blow caught me in the shoulder, sending me to one knee. My entire back flared with white-hot pain, but I couldn't show it. "Still wasn't ready."

"Let us help you!"

Jason stopped, visibly concerned, and looked around. "Who's there?" he shouted, and then turned back to me. "Is this you? Are you doing this?"

"You're not worried about something, are you?" I taunted.

He looked uneasy. "What are you planning?"

My well was full and I wasted no time sending a cone of ice from my hands in his direction. Jason waved a hand dismissively in front of him, leaving a trail of flame for a brief moment. My ice became steam, and the two things canceled each other out.

"Give it up," he said, now more annoyed than ever. "I gave you a sporting chance, but you didn't have it in you. I don't know how you're pulling out so much magic, but nothing you're casting is all that special. It's almost like you're—"

I stumbled back and cast a ball of fire in his direction. It was no larger than a baseball, but it was still something. On reflex Jason held out his other hand, a sphere of water appeared in front of it, engulfing my fireball.

"Oh, that's it! Clever," he said knowingly. "You have the magical depth of a puppy, but you've found a way to replenish on the fly! Now that is useful."

I was growing frustrated. One of these had to be a weak spot for him!

"Show me what else you have, then. What haven't you tried yet?" he asked, motioning for me to bring it. I didn't have a sphere of water as he had, but I managed a jet stream that would have been enough to knock over the average person. Assuming it hit them. Jason casually summoned a whirlwind, sending my water skyward and harmlessly creating a few seconds of light rain.

"No one likes a smug winner," I said, my mind racing with new ideas. "If you have some big finale, why don't you just get on with it?" Attacking Jason head on wasn't working. I had nothing to counter.

Come on, Elana, think!

"Sure, I have something kind of cool I can show you," Jason replied, resting his hand on a statue. "This is called stone shaping. It happens to be my specialty, at least as far as combat arts are concerned." As he spoke the grand reminder of a life once lived, an eight-foot tall marble statue of two angels around a cross, suddenly seemed less rigid. Before my eyes, it became malleable, like clay on a potter's wheel, and was turned into an amorphous blob.

I watched transfixed as Jason moved his hands around it without touching it; the mass spinning and then thinning until it kept the solid shape of a club. He gripped the handle, and the other end struck the ground hard enough to startle me.

"The genius part about this, however, is that I get to swing around seven tons of marble like it's seven pounds." His expression was giddy. "I really don't get to play around like this too often, so indulge me here. Have you ever been crushed under seven tons of marble? Would you like it to be the last thing that ever happens to you?"

Jason raised the club overhead and swiftly brought it down on top of me. This time I did get the shield up, only for it to shatter upon impact. The deflection sent his blow into a headstone which broke it in a spray of pebbles. I tried to recover and get away from his second swing, but lost my balance and landed on my back.

I sat up, and Jason stood over me, swinging it again. I think he was exaggerating about the ease with which he was able to swing the reformed stone, but it was still easy enough for him to be deadly. I ducked awkwardly out of the way, and the club buried itself nearly two feet into the ground next to me. The last move may have saved my life, but as I tried to stand I slipped on a piece of rock, and I looked up to see Jason winding up to deliver the coup de grâce only to be interrupted by the whispers forcefully making their presence known.

"LET. US. HELP. YOU!"

The hissing was insistent, and the way the voices came from everything, the soil, the wind, the headstones; Jason's eyes shot open as wide as they could. I could see what was behind those eyes. It was dread. Jason was afraid of the unknown, and if he made a mistake here, it was a doozy. He brought me to a place made entirely of the unknown. He thought this place was his, but I knew something from my first visit onwards that he clearly struggled to understand.

This place, every inch of it, was alive. Not all of it was in harmony, but if you have an endless number of voices in a crowd that tries to remain neutral, beautiful things can happen when enough of them agree on something. Sometimes the most important thing is getting on the same page with the people who matter to you.

It was then that I smiled and dusted myself off as I stood. Jason's eyes were darting around looking for the source of the cacophonous sound, his mind even now trying to deny what he knew in his soul; there was no single source.

"Hey, eyes on me," I said, his head spun back to me. "You asked me a question, and I have your answer. Do you really want to know what I haven't done? Accept help when it has been freely given to me and trusted in the outcome."

I looked at the ground with love in my heart and spoke warmly to it. "I will accept your help, and I trust you."

As if caged, dozens of hands sprung out of the ground, soil soaked and blackened by being underground. "Oh, I've certainly taken help on the small stuff, when it didn't matter, to what I thought were the bigger issues. A meal here and there, a place to sleep, a shoulder to cry on... Small, but crucial."

I continued as Jason swiped furiously at the hands grasping for him, trying to back away. For each one he struck down, it seemed half a dozen sprung up in their place.

"But I was walling myself off. And yes, I did take help on the big stuff, but only when there were strings attached. I could understand the idea of a bargain; the concept that nothing was free. This whole time, though, I kept acting like the unlikely hero of some story. And you know what I learned? I'm not Spider-Man, someone to take all the responsibility and drown in it. I'm Buffy Summers, someone who needs a family, and I'm lucky enough to be surrounded by people who care about me. And I care about them. And together, we can survive anything!"

Behind the dome, I watched as hands grabbed the chains and snapped them like licorice vines, freeing Olivia and Claire. Jason meanwhile was struggling and looked soon to be overwhelmed.

"You're looking a little surrounded yourself!" I called to him.

Jason howled as he threw down his weapon, focusing an intense flame around him in his own protective circle. "This is place is supposed to be neutral!" he spat. "It doesn't take sides."

"Apparently it does, and you're on the wrong one," I replied as a familiar looking beetle landed on my hand, looking at me. I greeted it. "I will accept your help, and I trust you."

The little bug burrowed beneath my skin, and in an instant, my skin was on fire and I felt a burrowing in my chest. No, something deeper than that, something not physical. The pain was indescribable, even if it lasted only a moment. Not the effect, though, that was unmistakable. That well within me, the shallow pool where I'd been drawing my power from, the beetle furiously tunneled into me until it felt like my bones would snap under the strain of my insides expanding.

And when I thought I couldn't take it anymore, the beetle came up my throat and left through my mouth, flying away. And in its place: Life! My well, now truly a well, filled with the stuff of creation and everything felt new.

Jason rose into the air under his own power, away from the now overwhelming number of hands grasping for him. He was hovering maybe twenty feet or so above me, chanting to himself with his eyes closed as he stood suspended in the air. His eyes opened, and they glowed with the same dark, disconcerting green of a reptile you didn't expect to see. "I don't know how, and I don't know why, but I will not accept this result!" he yelled to me. "I will wipe you, and your friends, and even this landscape away from memory itself!"

Something bad was in the air, but I wasn't afraid, and I wasn't worried. Not for myself and not for my friends, because I knew that we were not alone. I lifted my neck to look past him through the clear night sky to see the milk-white moon, and I shouted one more greeting. "I will accept your help! And I trust you!"

Clouds converged from every angle, profound and brilliant blues, bright and terrible purples, and they blocked out everything else in the night as they did, bringing with them an electricity in the air. Jason was gathering power, the air around him began to pulse. Suddenly one of the writhing hands shot out of the ground, an untangling rope falling upwards with the consistency of an eel, and it wrapped around his ankles before its colors shifted, and impossibly before my eyes, it became a tree, trapping Jason in midair.

There were no specific words spoken, but I could feel it. I knew what to do now. All of the other elements prepared me for this moment. I reached out to the storm clouds themselves, treating it as an equal, and felt it, asking it silently for permission. The energy rushed through me and out of me, and with both hands raised, a downpour began and I cried out, allowing the clouds to hurtle towards each other and collide, becoming denser until—

Jason saw it maybe half a second too late, I ripped lightning from the sky, straight into him. He screamed as a barrier of energy formed above him, which blasted apart and provided little to no protection. And then, just as suddenly, the sky was clear again. No downpour, no clouds. Jason hung limply from the now ruined tree, and it began to crumble at its base, dropping him unceremoniously to the ground with an anticlimactic thud.

"Thank you," I said to everything. I could feel the appreciation.

I walked over to Jason, depleted of power. It was coming back, but at a trickle now, not a flood. He looked at me, scorched and in pain, but alive.

"This… isn't possible…" he said weakly.

"Everything's possible, idiot," I corrected him. "Even magic."

The sound of tunneling made us both look at the ground, dread and panic filled his face as hands shot up, grabbing at every inch of him.

"Help me!" he screamed, extending a hand to me.

I don't know why I reached out to him. I didn't owe him anything and he'd tried to kill us. All the same, I dove to the ground and reached out my hand to his, and felt the power as we grasped at each other. It only lasted for a second; he was ripped away from me and dragged into unknown depths. His story started to play in my mind.

His name was Jason Harris and now he doesn't exist.

I sat for a second, disquieted. It was so short. So final. The hands were all gone, as were the whispers. I didn't know how to feel about what just happened. I couldn't explain it, but it seemed worse than death somehow. Jason was an awful person, but he was still a person, and now he wasn't even that.

Oh, crap! My friends!

I stood and ran to them, willing away the dome and they were free. We all gripped each other in tight hugs, needing the moment. Claire was the first to speak.

"Elana, that... that was—"

"A soul-shatteringly hideous nightmare event?" I interrupted.

"Awesome!" Olivia shouted.

"No, I'm voting with Elana on this one," Claire finished.

I picked up the sword I tossed in earlier and turned to face my friends. "Listen, I still don't know a ton about this place, but I'm just about out of juice and with Jason gone I'm not sure if his portal home is closed or will stay open for another hundred years or something in between."

"Well, don't you know how to open another one?" Olivia asked.

"Not really," I admitted.

"Okay, so we have to move now, in that case, good tip," Claire said, looking around. "Which way?"

I pointed at the mountain range in the distance. "Well I came through a cave which descended about two hundred feet down a spiraling path which—"

"Great, let's move." Claire interrupted.

"—which I caved in completely on some eldritch horror on my way to rescue you."

"Who *are* you?" Olivia breathed in disbelief.

"We can find out later," I replied. "Come on; we have to figure something out."

The three of us ran up the slope as best we could, and when we reached a point where we could see the ruined mouth of the cave, we also saw something else, something new. Thousands of those hands from the graveyard, now made of petrified wood, had formed a spiraling staircase hundreds of feet into the air through a localized, low hanging cloud cover. The three of us stared at it dumbfounded for a moment.

"Well, that was considerate of them," I said finally. "Think that will work?"

"Yeah," Claire said.

I lead the way up the stairs, running on the pure excitement and anxiety of nearly being home free. As I passed through the cloud cover, I was suddenly on the now green and verdant plains where I entered, free of traps and yes, even one conspicuous Tiki head. The portal was still open, still flickering, and behind me, Olivia and Claire popped out of the air as well.

"We're almost home, come on!" I shouted, taking off in a run towards the tear between worlds. I was breathing deeply, my lungs sucking in as much air as possible when suddenly the grass began to become brittle and yellow, and the taste in my mouth from the atmosphere took on a taste of stale, decaying meat.

The flapping of wings was the first heralding sound of the crow-like creatures followed by that horrific screeching.

"Oh, God, no. Not now," I mumbled under my breath. Maybe a dozen of them were approaching and coming directly for us.

Olivia screamed. Claire's mouth went slack. "What is—?"

"Move!" I shouted, smacking them both. "Do not stop until you're through!"

Olivia made it through first, and Claire was nearly through when a heavy talon gripped my leg, tripping me. I yelped in surprise, turning the sword as I fell and striking the creature's leg. It made a sound of discomfort and temporarily retreated into the air to wait for its friends to catch up with it.

"Elana!" Claire screamed.

"Get through!" I reiterated. "If I am trapped here, I at least have a chance to get home. Don't let this all be for nothing, go home!"

She hesitated for a second before nodding in understanding and jumping through the portal. It flickered and vanished as she did, leaving no trace it had ever existed. My heart sank. "That, uh, that really sucks," I said in disbelief.

I got to my feet, trying to shake the circulation back into my leg as I did. Nothing around me but grass as far as I could see. Monstrosities began to land and circle me, hatred in their eyes. The Knowing was silent, my power was a fraction of the way full, just enough for me summon a shield before I was utterly empty again. I didn't even bother to try and calm myself. I knew how bad this was.

"Okay then," I said, hoping my voice wasn't shaking too much. "Which one of you is coming down with me?"

The beasts took a moment, circling me, occasionally offering a threatening screech as they closed the gap between us. But then, there was another sound. Familiar soft tones, repeating in the distance, but getting closer and louder. The beasts seemed equally confused and began to sniff the air. I took the distraction to thrust my sword into the gut of one of them. It wailed madly and lashed with a claw, catching my shield and knocking me down. Before it could follow up, the sounds grew louder, clearer, and closer. And it became impossible to keep my eyes open. "No!" I tried to yell, and it came out as a yawn. My eyelids flickered. And then blinked. And then shut. And there was nothing. Everything let go.

27

My invitation read:

**LOGAN KOBAYASHI HUMBLY REQUESTS
YOUR ASSISTANCE IN UNVEILING HIS
MOST PROVACTIVE PERFORMANCE ART
TO DATE, "26 YEARS OF LIFE"
(MY BIRTHDAY. BRING PRESENTS OR HUGS.)**

**DATE: MY BIRTHDAY
LOCATION: THE BOOK'S END
TIME: SOMETIME AFTER THEY CLOSE
ATTIRE: KEEP IT VAGUE**

Logan's birthday was held at the Book's End rather than at a home or a bar. It had been a week since the showdown with Jason, but I could tell that Olivia and Claire had already grown closer. Not that they were on bad terms before, but this was a unique situation, and sometimes tighter relationships form from traumatic experiences.

Claire hadn't fired me, which gave me hope that our relationship could be repaired. She was strong in a way that didn't require her to puff out her chest and prove it; her strength came in her ability to weather anything and adapt, to push through and keep on going. Still, she'd been put through the fire on this. She'd been kidnapped and taken into another world, nearly killed, and someone she'd cared for was, at least in part, responsible for her suffering. That was going to take time to process.

Olivia was the surprising one. That relationship felt exceptionally strained, but again, not beyond repair. I'd been making excuses about why I didn't want to take the books home with me from her place, but she also didn't seem as if she wanted to be too involved either. She wasn't warm, not upset, just indifferent. I was trying to give her space, none of that was easy for any of us, it was just that Olivia has always been there for me. When I couldn't deal, when I was overwhelmed, she was my safe place. I didn't know what it was like to have her like this, and I couldn't shake the feeling that I'd taken her for granted. I'd give her space. That was all I had left to give at the moment.

I never figured out how I got back. One moment I was certain that I was dead, the next I was taking a nap. According to Olivia and Claire, a second portal opened into the store just after the first one closed and I came rolling through it, unconscious. I had a guess about what happened, but until I could confirm, it was just a guess. I haven't tried to travel since any of this happened, it just felt like the stakes had been raised and I needed to learn more about all of it before I got back in there. That was going to happen, eventually, when I was ready and not a moment before.

In the meantime, this was a party, and there's only one thing to do at a party! Spend a moderate amount of time with my friends before hiding in the bathroom until I find an excuse to sneak out! I've learned that some things can, in fact, magically change. There are even alchemical potions that can alleviate my social anxiety, you just need to drink plenty of water with them, or you'll be hungover the next day. I liked the Scottish ones the best, preferably neat and not mixed with soda or anything. Look, magic powers and tremendous responsibility aside, I'm still not someone who likes parties, and this wasn't a problem that was going to be solved with a fireball. With great power comes the tacit promise with yourself that you won't spam fireballs in a polite society.

I use self-deprecating humor as a method to avoid the things about myself that I'm uncomfortable with. On an intellectual level, I understand this, and I'm even okay with it. But as I stood in the back of the room, looking at the forty or so people who I knew, or didn't know, to varying degrees I thought about my life growing up in Los Angeles. In life, you will meet people. In my case, I've met a lot of people, and I'm probably going to end up meeting more than most. And in a place like this, it's easy to speak with any of them and be struck with the knowledge that they are interesting and funny and intelligent and kind and gorgeous and passionate and stylish and on and on it goes; they are so many things! But then you get to know them a little better; you spend a little bit of time with them outside of a party.

Maybe one day you see them sick. Or you give them a ride home from the airport after long and uncomfortable flight. Or you see them on a Wednesday when they've decided they just don't want to try so damned hard to hide anymore, and it's at that moment that they reveal to you that they're just a big ball of nerves and anxieties. Just like everyone else. The eyebrows come off. They stop sucking in their stomach. They throw away a piece of imperfect art before anyone can see it. And you don't need to magically Know their story to understand this; you just need to spend time with them.

All too often these incredible, marvelous people will have the sense that they're not good enough. They will doubt themselves, and they'll worry that the right people won't like them. Rather than realizing just how rad they already are, they will never stop comparing themselves to the impossible standards they project onto others and be content to consider themselves part of someone else's social circle, letting their lives just sort of happen, not quite alone, but just not quite. The number one thing I've learned in these past couple of months, the thing I want everyone to understand is really simple. The idea that you're not cool enough? The idea that you're not important or that your story means less than anyone else's? That evil and insidious thought is horse trash. If I could tell everyone one thing, it would be this: You are important. No more, but no less than anyone else. And regardless of who tells you otherwise, your life belongs to you. Everyone has a story to tell, and you are the only one who can tell yours. Your story means as much to time and space as anyone's. Even if the spotlight isn't on you, even if you're not on camera, and even if great tales aren't written about you, your story matters. You see the spotlight whenever the sun rises. Every open eye is a camera. You write great tales on the skin of the universe every day.

At the moment I didn't have the energy for those stories, but I didn't feel that I needed to be a part of all of them at the moment either. I looked for an excuse to walk away, scooped up a cat, and headed to the bathroom. I sat on the toilet seat with Jameson on my lap, scratching behind his ears until his contented purr was loud enough that I thought it might be heard over the music outside. He was shedding, which was going to be hell getting out of my jacket later, but I didn't mind. I could have sat here all night if no one knocked on the door. "Thank you, therapy cat," I whispered to him, and his jaw stretched to cartoonish proportions as he answered with a satisfied yawn.

After an hour or so, Jameson eventually wanted to be somewhere else and politely, but decidedly, let me know he wanted to get off my lap and I let him. There was a copy of *Captain Courageous* in the bathroom, and I opened it to a random chapter in the middle and began to read. It took a couple of pages, but the way in began to appear. I smiled and closed the book. It was as I thought, if I didn't impact the story too much I could go back in. That would be good to know later on. Feeling better about the recharge time I stretched and snuck back into the party, confident that I wasn't missed. I quietly made that awkward farewell tour that one must make at every party, apologizing for leaving early, but instantly atoning for the sin with a warm and sincere hug, and I left to drive home.

The sense of imminent catastrophe that had followed me around until recently had seemed to subside for the most part, but each day some of the loose ends bothered me more and more. Car rides are perfect for letting stray thoughts become overwhelming. Lainey and Jayden were my chief concern, but I was certain for some reason that they were alive. It might have been in Oz, or the Knowing, or somewhere else completely but I didn't think they were dead. I just had no way to start looking for them, and that was the troubling part.

There was also the knowledge that Wildlings were being regularly killed by being thrown into an ever-changing dreamscape filled with monsters and wonders. And yet, they hadn't just outright killed Lucia or myself. I really needed answers there, and I wasn't sure when or how I'd get them. I felt pretty good that it wasn't a matter of "if" though.

Then there was the Aos Si. So, Celtic deities exist, that's a thing I get to carry out into the world now. And I am obligated to have lunch with one, that's also a thing. But he exists because the stories about him were written down, which meant that all the deities ever written about likely existed somewhere. And all the heroes, villains, and everything in between. I had the unsettling feeling that I was just handed a career that I wasn't allowed to leave.

That night I dreamt again, and I realized that by now I had completely stopped being surprised by ending up in the Knowing. I was standing outside of a mansion, and in the near distance, I could hear the sounds of an ocean. The sun felt incredible on my face. There was a garden, and the scent of the flowers was intoxicating in the literal sense, I was already feeling a little tipsy just standing there. Ahead of me was an Elven woman holding an open book with one hand, a fountain pen in the other. At least I was assuming she was an Elf based on the ears. I might have been presuming too much. She was stunning to look at, but that didn't surprise me either. She was wearing an elegant black dress over her long, athletic frame, and even the material seemed to breathe with her, matching her every move. I'd never seen anything like it, not even on red carpets or in fashion shows.

I started towards her and stopped after a step to look down. I was in something similar, though more regal. I was dressed in a silk dress, sage green, adorned with gold leaf and brilliant crystals. I felt around my neck to find that I was wearing a delicate collar and a green chiffon cape flowed down my back and arms, so light that I almost didn't feel them. An oversized gold buckle held a sash in place around my waist which flowed down to my knees. Unexpected as this was, it also didn't surprise me.

The Elf woman greeted me with a brilliant smile as I approached her.

"Name?" she asked, and even just that one syllable word gave me a touch of serenity.

"Elana Black," I answered, taking in the scenery.

Her eyes sparkled at that, and she snapped her book shut, offering me a deep bow. "Oh, how splendid! Our guest of honor!"

She beamed before composing herself, her face becoming a mask of stoicism and etiquette. "Elana Black, may I be allowed the honor of presenting you to the guests of your celebration?" Okay, that part was surprising.

I offered a quick bow as well. I didn't know there would be bowing. "That sounds suspiciously like a party," I remarked as I rose. The Elf woman regarded me while waiting for my answer. "Okay, yeah, sure. I would be delighted."

I had hoped that I wasn't too rude, but judging by her smile at my answer I wasn't worrying about it. I was a little weirded out that anyone was this excited to meet me, but whatever. This is a weird place, so I am going to have to live with getting weirded out from time to time.

She offered me her arm, and I awkwardly offered mine in return, not really sure what the proper way to accept this was. Without missing a beat, she wrapped her arm around mine in a way so flawless you would have thought that entire exchange was intentional. "I'm sorry, what was your name?" I asked her.

"You may call me Chalsarda," she said, still beaming. "Thank you for asking. Ooh, this is exciting!"

"May I ask why?" I asked uneasily.

"I'm afraid that's not my place," she replied but then grinning finished the sentence. "But there's no rule that says I can't enjoy the moment, is there?"

I didn't know the answer to that. Are there rules? Are they written down somewhere? Ugh, I wasn't even in the door yet, and I was already getting a headache.

Chalsarda opened the doors into the mansion, and produced a bell from... somewhere? I don't know where she could have been hiding it, honestly. She struck it once, and a clear, piercing, but pleasant tone rang out, and all at once everyone stopped talking and turned their attention towards us. The room was just, well, it was nuts. I'd just gotten used to Chalsarda, and now there was an entire room full of people who at least matched her in elegance and outward beauty, if not surpassed it. And not just elves either, I was getting dizzy trying to take in all the clothes, species, and... wait, are those fairy wings real?

"Honored guests and friends of the court," Chalsarda announced in a declamatory tone that filled every corner of the room, "it is my pleasure and privilege to announce to you our guest of honor this day: Elana Black."

The room began to applaud, and I figured out where I was. I was in hell. This was hell, and I was being punished for something terrible. Eating my roommate's cookies or yelling at people in traffic or getting lemonade at the Del Taco when I asked for a water cup and just because the liquid was clear I thought I could get away with it, but I knew what I was doing. I didn't know any of these people, and the longer this went on, the more uncomfortable I became, so I thought maybe if I smiled at waved, that would stop it. It did not stop anything.

"Everyone, please! This is a party," a familiar voice announced. "Act accordingly!"

Aos Si!

My discomfort transformed into irascibility. You shouldn't make me irascible. You wouldn't like me when I'm irascible.

"You!" I proclaimed.

"Me!" he replied full of mirth. "And more importantly, you! Correct me if I'm wrong about any of this, but you have humiliated and neutered a captain of the Gardeners and a Fomorian no less, slain your first monster, and even killed a Gardener, saving your friends in the process! It looks like someone is starting to learn how to take care of themselves."

I was about to ask what a Fomorian was, but I remained focused. "We need to have words."

"Of course," the Aos Si replied, turning to my escort. "Chalsarda, that will be all, I believe. Please, enjoy and partake for the duration to your liking."

"Very generous of you, thank you," she replied as she bowed to him. Looking to me, she offered a smile. "Perhaps I will see you later."

She glided away, and the Aos Si spoke again. "And perhaps we can have our conversation somewhere more private. I have a room for such things, shall we?"

I followed him upstairs and into a study. In any other house I would have described it as grand, but compared to everything else I'd seen so far, it was modest. Where the rest of the house seemed to be all about opulence and festivity, the study was respectable and mature. Lots of leather and high quality wood work. I'm pretty sure those things are respectable and mature. This was a place where business was conducted.

The instant the door shut I launched into him. "Where are the kids? You live here. If anyone would know it would be you?"

"Now, now," he said patiently, pouring me a drink. "You may be the guest of honor, but there is still a way things are done."

"Are you going to ask me to run errands for you every time I have a question?" I asked, then pausing, I added, "Not counting that one."

"No, of course not, and you're right in that you do deserve answers," he agreed. "So you may ask your questions, and I will answer where it suits me."

"Where are the kids?" I reiterated. "Are they alive?"

"That they are," he responded, sitting in a chair and facing me. "They are even doing well as far as I know, but they are beyond my reach at the moment."

Tension left my shoulders at the sound of that, stress I wasn't even completely aware I'd been carrying until he said that. "Oh good," I said looking at the chair as he made a motion of acknowledgment for me to sit. I took him up on the offer, plopping into the chair heavily, taking a sip of something truly delightful. "Alright, that was kind of my big one, I think I'm good with that. Thanks. And Lucia? Also alive?"

"Also alive," he confirmed, and I answered him with a nod, sinking into my seat.

The Aos Si sipped a drink as we sat in silence for an uncomfortable moment. "Was that it, were those your only questions?" he asked finally.

"Oh, not even close!" I practically shouted. "What is your name?"

"Not yet," he answered wryly.

"Ugh, fine," I said. "Why did you save me from those bird things?"

The Aos Si nearly choked on his drink; it was incredibly satisfying to elicit that response from him. "You put that one together, did you?"

I nodded. "It was the tones on the wind that gave you away. So just exactly how powerful are you? Or did you have help?"

"Better question," he replied, setting his drink down. "Why didn't you ask for my help with odds against you like that?"

"A couple of reasons," I granted him. "First, you were right. I do need to get better at handling things on my own. But I also need to balance that with knowing when to accept help from others. And this was my mess to clean up, no question. But honestly? Your help comes with strings, and I was more afraid of the price you'd extract than anything else. Though, to that point, I have a theory if you'd indulge me."

"Of course," he said bemusedly. "I would love to hear it."

"The scene you kept showing me, it's a metaphor for some-thing," I started. "Objects and things are somehow related to this prophecy that everyone keeps freaking out about, but you were showing me the symbols of things. Olivia is the Olive, Lucia represents the light. How am I doing so far?"

"All accurate," he confirmed.

I continued, "But the tree, that huge oak, I started to think about what that had to do with anything, and I thought about my own name. I had always heard that it translated to a Torch, but I looked it up. That's the Greek translation. And I'm not Greek. My name holds another meaning. It means Tree."

The Aos Si gave me a little golf clap. "Exquisite, and it only took you—"

"I'm not done," I said cutting him off. By the sour expres-sion on his face, I didn't think he was used to that. "See, you asked what I knew about Fae and Aos Si and everything else, and do you remember what I told you?"

His expression stiffened slightly. "I do."

"The Aos Si are guardians, yeah?" I asked, knowing the an-swer. "Usually places of great power, sacred places, that kind of thing. Lakes, Woods, Fairy Circles; but there was one more. Sometimes they are responsible for guarding a specific tree."

He was taking deep, controlled breaths through his nose now; his words came out harshly. "If you're going to say it, then say it."

"You're my guardian. In the cosmic sense, it's your job to protect me. So I guess to that I would ask, are you protecting me because of my name or was I named so you'd have to protect me?"

No one said anything for a moment, and in the blink of an eye, the Aos Si burst into laughter and applauded as he stood. "Outstanding! Truly! Bravo! And though you are correct about my duty, I hope you'll understand if I don't answer your larger question."

"No need," I said standing as well and meeting his eye. "I'll find out."

"I'm sure you will," he said crossing the room to look into an oval mirror, roughly his height in size. "I'd like you to see something first."

As I watched the mirror, our reflections faded and I saw the city, the tree, the beams of light and lastly the olive. The branch holding the olive grew rapidly towards the light until it reached the cross point in the beams. The light became more brilliant, bright enough to make me want to shield my eyes, and then the olive burst into flames, disintegrating before my eyes. I gasped, and as I did I watched the form of Lucia appear, no longer as a symbol, but as a person floating above the city. She lifted her hands, and everything was perfect. No shadows, no darkness, and everything was made new.

The image shifted away, and it was just the two of us again, but my expression came as a surprise. I wasn't afraid or sad. I looked defiant, and I knew that prophecy or no, I was going to find a way to save Olivia.

"Now, the people down there, they are uncertain. Of you, of the validity of the prophecy, but mainly of themselves. Some believe you will be a hero, others a villain. So before we get back to the party, there's one more thing I must ask of you."

He then spoke more carefully to me as he said, "I would ask you to address them. You need to know who you are, and so do they."

"I have something to say all right," I agreed. "Let's do it."

The Aos Si gave me a look of concern, opening the door for me. "Be ready and be brave," he said. As I started to walk past him, he stopped me for just a second to whisper in my ear. "And thank you for the sword. That will come in quite useful. Consider our debt for the rescue to be paid."

I approached the balcony and looked out on the room full of beautiful beings of elegance and power that could likely end me without a second thought, and I spoke with more authority and confidence than I ever had in my life.

"Hello everyone! And thank you all for coming out to this wonderful celebration! I'm not certain what we're celebrating. I'm not certain that it matters. The fact that you all came out is important enough, because you could have been anywhere, and you chose here, so thank you. And you know, when I say anywhere, I mean exactly that. Oh yes, somebody or something messed up very, very badly. They gave me the power to go anywhere, travel into any world, and then some silly little suits thought they could tell me that I wasn't allowed to use it. I plan to show everyone exactly how wrong they are. They've tried to stop me, and so far, that hasn't gone well for them, has it? I understand you need to know who I am, so allow me to make it as simple as possible for everyone here so that there's no ambiguity later on. My name is Elana Black! I am a story loving nerd, a fast food taco connoisseur, and now I know magic! And if you threaten the innocent, I will be the greatest enemy you'll ever know."

I raised my glass to the silent crowd and smiled as I asked. "Anyone want to drink to that?"

ABOUT THE AUTHOR

My name is Danny Bell. I want to tell stories and avoid writing author profiles. I read—when I should be interacting with people, I named my cat after a cat I liked in a book, I'm pretty sure I saw a ghost one time—though I'll never admit it publicly, I'm too tall for the earth, and I've never eaten a vegetable. *I lied about the vegetable part.* Wait… is someone going to read this?

This is where my Facebook page is:

https://www.facebook.com/ElanaRuthBlack/

If you write on it I promise to reply…
unless you're a racist jerk or something.

54611518R00164

Made in the USA
San Bernardino, CA
21 October 2017